THERE WAS TROUBLE BREWING....

"They're 'The Fifteen Masters.' These babies are famous. One of them cooks sausages that people fight duels over. They meet every five years on the home grounds of the oldest one of their number. Nero Wolfe is the guest of honor. They'll do a lot of cooking and eating and drinking, and tell each other a lot of lies, and elect three new members, and listen to Nero Wolfe make a speech—and oh yeah, one of 'em's going to get killed."

Bantam Crime Line Books offer the finest in classic and modern American mysteries. Ask your bookseller for the books you have missed.

Rex Stout
The Black Mountain
Broken Vase
Death of a Dude
Death Times Three
Fer-de-Lance
The Final Deduction
Gambit
Plot It Yourself
The Rubber Band
Some Buried Caesar
Three for the Chair
Too Many Cooks

Max Allan Collins
The Dark City
Bullet Proof

A. E. Maxwell
Just Another Day in Paradise
Gatsby's Vineyard
The Frog and the Scorpion
Just Enough Light to Kill

Loren Estleman
Peeper

Dick Lupoff
The Comic Book Killer

Randy Russell
Hot Wire

V. S. Anderson
Blood Lies
King of the Roses

William Murray
When the Fat Man Sings
The King of the Nightcap

Eugene Izzi
King of the Hustlers
The Prime Roll
coming soon: Invasions

Gloria Dank
Friends Till the End
Going Out in Style

Jeffery Deaver
Manhattan Is My Beat
coming soon: Death of a Blue
Movie Star

Robert Goldsborough
Murder in E Minor
Death on Deadline
The Bloodied Ivy
The Last Coincidence

Sue Grafton
"A" Is for Alibi
"B" Is for Burglar
"C" Is for Corpse
"D" Is for Deadbeat
"E" Is for Evidence
"F" Is for Fugitive

David Lindsey
In the Lake of the Moon

Carolyn G. Hart
Design for Murder
Death on Demand
Something Wicked
Honeymoon with Murder
A Little Class on Murder

Annette Meyers
The Big Killing

Rob Kantner
Dirty Work
The Back-Door Man
Hell's Only Half Full

Robert Crais
The Monkey's Raincoat
Stalking the Angel

Keith Peterson
The Trapdoor
There Fell a Shadow
The Rain
Rough Justice

David Handler
The Man Who Died Laughing
The Man Who Lived by Night

Jerry Oster
Club Dead
Internal Affairs

A NERO WOLFE MYSTERY

TOO MANY COOKS

Rex Stout

BANTAM BOOKS
NEW YORK · TORONTO · LONDON · SYDNEY · AUCKLAND

TOO MANY COOKS

*A Bantam Book / published by arrangement with
the author*

*Bantam edition / May 1983
3 printings through November 1989*

ISBN 0-553-27290-X

Published simultaneously in the United States and Canada

*Bantam Books are published by Bantam Books, a division of Bantam
Doubleday Dell Publishing Group, Inc. Its trademark, consisting of the
words "Bantam Books" and the portrayal of a rooster, is Registered in
U.S. Patent and Trademark Office and in other countries. Marca Regis-
trada. Bantam Books, 666 Fifth Avenue, New York, New York 10103.*

PRINTED IN THE UNITED STATES OF AMERICA

O   11 10 9 8 7 6 5 4 3

FOREWORD

I USED as few French and miscellaneous fancy words as possible in writing up this stunt of Nero Wolfe's but I couldn't keep them out altogether, on account of the kind of people involved. I am not responsible for the spelling, so don't write me about mistakes. Wolfe refused to help me out on it, and I had to go to the Heinemann School of Languages and pay a professor 30 bucks to go over it and fix it up. In most cases, during these events, when anyone said anything which for me was only a noise, I have either let it lay—when it wasn't vital—or managed somehow to get the rough idea in the American language.

ARCHIE GOODWIN

1

WALKING up and down the platform alongside the train in the Pennsylvania Station, having wiped the sweat from my brow, I lit a cigarette with the feeling that after it had calmed my nerves a little I would be prepared to submit bids for a contract to move the Pyramid of Cheops from Egypt to the top of the Empire State Building with my bare hands, in a swimming-suit; after what I had just gone through. But as I was drawing in the third puff I was stopped by a tapping on a window I was passing, and, leaning to peer through the glass, I was confronted by a desperate glare from Nero Wolfe, from his seat in the bedroom which we had engaged in one of the new-style pullmans, where I had at last got him deposited intact. He shouted at me through the closed window:

"Archie! Confound you! Get in here! They're going to start the train! You have the tickets!"

I yelled back at him, "You said it was too close to smoke in there! It's only 9:32! I've decided not to go! Pleasant dreams!"

I sauntered on. Tickets my eye. It wasn't tickets that bothered him; he was frantic with fear because he was alone on the train and it might begin to move. He hated things that moved, and was fond of arguing that nine times out of ten the places that people were on their way to were no improvement whatever on those they were coming from. But by gum I had got him to the station twenty minutes ahead of time, notwithstanding such items as three bags and two suitcases and two overcoats for a four days' absence in the month of April, Fritz Brenner standing on the stoop with tears in his eyes as we left the house, Theodore Horstmann running out, after we had got Wolfe packed in the sedan, to ask a few dozen more questions about the orchids, and even tough little Saul Panzer, after dumping us at the station, choking off a tremolo as he told Wolfe goodbye. You might have thought

1

we were bound for the stratosphere to shine up the moon and pick wild stars.

At that, just as I flipped my butt through the crack between the train and the platform, I could have picked a star right there—or at least touched one. She passed by close enough for me to get a faint whiff of something that might have come from a perfume bottle but seemed only natural under the circumstances, and while her facial effect might have been technicolor, it too gave you the impression that it was intended that way from the outset and needed no alterations. The one glance I got was enough to show that she was no factory job, but hand-made throughout. Attached to the arm of a tall bulky man in a brown cape and a brown floppy cloth hat, she unhooked herself to precede him and follow the porter into the car back of ours. I muttered to myself, "My heart was all I had and now that's gone, I should have put my bloody blinders on," shrugged with assumed indifference, and entered the vestibule as they began the all aboard.

In our room, Wolfe was on the wide seat by the window, holding himself braced with both hands; but in spite of that they fooled him on the timing, and when the jerk came he lurched forward and back again. From the corner of my eye I saw the fury all over him, decided it was better to ignore realities, got a magazine from my bag and perched on the undersized chair in the corner. Still holding on with both hands, he shouted at me:

"We are due at Kanawha Spa at 11:25 tomorrow morning! Fourteen hours! This car is shifted to another train at Pittsburgh! In case of delay we would have to wait for an afternoon train! Should anything happen to our engine—"

I put in coldly, "I am not deaf, sir. And while you can beef as much as you want to, because it's your own breath if you want to waste it, I do object to your implying either in word or tone that I am in any way responsible for your misery. I made this speech up last night, knowing I would need it. This is your idea, this trip. You wanted to come—at least, you wanted to be at Kanawha Spa. Six months ago you told Vukcic that you would go there on April 6th. Now you regret it. So do I. As far as our engine is concerned, they use only the newest and best on these crack trains, and not even a child—"

We had emerged from under the river and were gathering speed as we clattered through the Jersey yards. Wolfe shouted,

"An engine has two thousand three hundred and nine moving parts!"

I put down the magazine and grinned at him, thinking I might as well. He had enginephobia and there was no sense in letting him brood, because it would only make it worse for both of us. His mind had to be switched to something else. But before I could choose a pleasant subject to open up on, an interruption came which showed that while he may have been frantic with fear when I was smoking a cigarette on the platform, he had not been demoralized. There was a rap on the door and it opened to admit a porter with a glass and three bottles of beer on a tray. He pulled out a trick stand for the glass and one bottle, which he opened, put the other two bottles in a rack with an opener, accepted currency from me in payment, and departed. As the train lurched on a curve Wolfe scowled with rage; then, as it took the straightaway again, he hoisted the glass and swallowed once, twice, five times, and set it down empty. He licked his lips for the foam, then wiped them with his handkerchief, and observed with no sign at all of hysterics:

"Excellent. I must remember to tell Fritz my first was precisely at temperature."

"You could wire him from Philadelphia."

"Thank you. I am being tortured and you know it. Would you mind earning your salary, Mr. Goodwin, by getting a book from my bag? *Inside Europe*, by John Gunther."

I got the bag and fished it out.

By the time the second interruption came, half an hour later, we were rolling smooth and swift through the night in middle Jersey, the three beer bottles were empty, Wolfe was frowning at his book but actually reading, as I could tell by the pages he turned, and I had waded nearly to the end of an article on Collation of Evidence in the *Journal of Criminology*. I hadn't got much from it, because I was in no condition to worry about collating evidence, on account of my mind being taken up with the problem of getting Nero Wolfe undressed. At home, of course, he did it himself, and equally of course I wasn't under contract as a valet—being merely secretary, bodyguard, office manager, assistant detective, and goat—but the fact remained that in two hours it would be midnight, and there he was with his pants on, and someone was going to have to figure out a way of getting them off without upsetting the train. Not that he was clumsy, but he

3

had had practically no practice at balancing himself while on a moving vehicle, and to pull pants from under him as he lay was out of the question, since he weighed something between 250 and a ton. He had never, so far as I knew, been on a scale, so it was anybody's guess. I was guessing high that night, on account of the problem I was confronted with, and was just ready to settle on 310 as a basis for calculations, when there was a knock on the door and I yelled come in.

It was Marko Vukcic. I had known he would be on our train, through a telephone conversation between him and Wolfe a week before, but the last time I had seen him was when he had dined with us at Wolfe's house early in March—a monthly occurrence. He was one of the only two men whom Wolfe called by their first names, apart from employees. He closed the door behind him and stood there, not fat but huge, like a lion upright on its hind legs, with no hat covering his dense tangle of hair.

Wolfe shouted at him, "Marko! Haven't you got a seat or a bed somewhere? Why the devil are you galloping around in the bowels of this monster?"

Vukcic showed magnificent white teeth in a grin. "Nero, you damn old hermit! I am not a turtle in aspic, like you. Anyhow, you are really on the train—what a triumph! I have found you—and also a colleague, in the next car back, whom I had not seen for five years. I have been talking with him, and suggested he should meet you. He would be glad to have you come to his compartment."

Wolfe compressed his lips. "That, I presume, is funny. I am not an acrobat. I shall not stand up until this thing is stopped and the engine unhooked."

"Then how—" Vukcic laughed, and glanced at the pile of luggage. "But you seem to be provided with equipment. I did not really expect you to move. So instead, I'll bring him to you. If I may. That really is what I came to ask."

"Now?"

"This moment."

Wolfe shook his head. "I beg off, Marko. Look at me. I am in no condition for courtesy or conversation."

"Just briefly, then, for a greeting. I have suggested it."

"No. I think not. Do you realize that if this thing suddenly stopped, for some obstacle or some demoniac whim, we should all of us continue straight ahead at eighty miles an hour? Is that a situation for social niceties?" He compressed

4

his lips again, and then moved them to pronounce firmly, "To-morrow."

Vukcic, probably almost as accustomed as Wolfe to having his own way, tried to insist, but it didn't get him anywhere. He tried to kid him out of it, but that didn't work either. I yawned. Finally Vukcic gave it up with a shrug. "To-morrow, then. If we meet no obstacle and are still alive. I'll tell Berin you have gone to bed—"

"Berin?" Wolfe sat up, and even relaxed his grip on the arm of his seat. "Not Jerome Berin?"

"Certainly. He is one of the fifteen."

"Bring him." Wolfe half closed his eyes. "By all means. I want to see him. Why the devil didn't you say it was Berin?"

Vukcic waved a hand, and departed. In three minutes he was back, holding the door open for his colleague to enter; only it appeared to be two colleagues. The most important one, from my point of view, entered first. She had removed her wrap but her hat was still on, and the odor, faint and fascinating, was the same as when she had passed me on the station platform. I had a chance now to observe that she was as young as love's dream, and her eyes looked dark purple in that light, and her lips told you that she was a natural but reserved smiler. Wolfe gave her a swift astonished glance, then transferred his attention to the tall bulky man behind her, whom I recognized even without the brown cape and the floppy cloth hat.

Vukcic had edged around. "Mr. Nero Wolfe. Mr. Goodwin. Mr. Jerome Berin. His daughter, Miss Constanza Berin."

After a bow I let them amplify the acknowledgments while I steered the seating in the desired direction. It ended with the three big guys on the seats, and love's dream on the undersized chair with me on a suitcase beside it. Then I realized that was bad staging, and shifted across with my back to the wall so I could see it better. She had favored me with one friendly innocent smile and then let me be. From the corner of my eye I saw Wolfe wince as Vukcic got a cigar going and Jerome Berin filled up a big old black pipe and lit it behind clouds. Since I had learned this was her father, I had nothing but friendly feelings for him. He had black hair with a good deal of gray in it, a trimmed beard with even more gray, and deep eyes, bright and black.

He was telling Wolfe, "No, this is my first visit to America. Already I see the nature of her genius. No drafts on this train

5

at all! None! And a motion as smooth as the sail of a gull! Marvelous!"

Wolfe shuddered, but he didn't see it. He went on. But he had given me a scare, with his "first visit to America." I leaned forward and muttered at the dream-star. "Can you talk English?"

She smiled at me. "Oh yes. Very much. We lived in London three years. My father was at the Tarleton."

"Okay." I nodded and settled back for a better focus. I was reflecting, it only goes to show how wise I was not to go into harness with any of the temptations I have been confronted with previously. If I had, I would be gnashing my teeth now. So the thing to do is to hold everything until my teeth are too old to be gnashed. But there was no law against looking.

Her father was saying, "I understand from Vukcic that you are to be Servan's guest. Then the last evening will be yours. This is the first time an American has had that honor. In 1932, in Paris, when Armand Fleury was still alive and was our dean, it was the premier of France who addressed us. In 1927, it was Ferid Khaldah, who was not then a professional. Vukcic tells me you are an agent de sûreté. Really?" He surveyed Wolfe's area.

Wolfe nodded. "But not precisely. I am not a policeman; I am a private detective. I entrap criminals, and find evidence to imprison them or kill them, for hire."

"Marvelous! Such dirty work."

Wolfe lifted his shoulders half an inch for a shrug, but the train jiggled him out of it. He directed a frown, not at Berin, but at the train. "Perhaps. Each of us finds an activity he can tolerate. The manufacturer of baby carriages, caught himself in the system's web and with no monopoly of greed, entraps his workers in the toils of his necessity. Dolichocephalic patriots and brachycephalic patriots kill each other, and the brains of both rot before their statues can get erected. A garbageman collects table refuse, while a senator collects evidence of the corruption of highly placed men—might one not prefer the garbage as less unsavory? Only the table scavenger gets less pay; that is the real point. I do not soil myself cheaply; I charge high fees."

Berin passed it. He chuckled. "But you are not going to discuss table refuse for us. Are you?"

6

"No. Mr. Servan has invited me to speak on—as he stated the subject: *Contributions Américaines à la Haute Cuisine*."

"Bah!" Berin snorted. "There are none."

Wolfe raised his brows. "None, sir?"

"None. I am told there is good family cooking in America; I haven't sampled it. I have heard of the New England boiled dinner and corn pone and clam chowder and milk gravy. This is for the multitude and certainly not to be scorned if good. But it is not for masters." He snorted again. "Those things are to la haute cuisine what sentimental love songs are to Beethoven and Wagner."

"Indeed." Wolfe wiggled a finger at him. "Have you eaten terrapin stewed with butter and chicken broth and sherry?"

"No."

"Have you eaten a planked porterhouse steak, two inches thick, surrendering hot red juice under the knife, garnished with American parsley and slices of fresh limes, encompassed with mashed potatoes which melt on the tongue, and escorted by thick slices of fresh mushrooms faintly underdone?"

"No."

"Or the Creole Tripe of New Orleans? Or Missouri Boone County ham, baked with vinegar, molasses, Worcestershire, sweet cider and herbs? Or Chicken Marengo? Or chicken in curdled egg sauce, with raisins, onions, almonds, sherry and Mexican sausage? Or Tennessee Opossum? Or Lobster Newburgh? Or Philadelphia Snapper Soup? But I see you haven't." Wolfe pointed a finger at him. "The gastronome's heaven is France, granted. But he would do well, on his way there, to make a detour hereabouts. I have eaten Tripe à la mode de Caen at Pharamond's in Paris. It is superb, but no more so than Creole Tripe, which is less apt to stop the gullet without an excess of wine. I have eaten bouillabaisse at Marseilles, its cradle and its temple, in my youth, when I was easier to move, and it is mere belly-fodder, ballast for a stevedore, compared with its namesake at New Orleans! If no red snapper is available—"

I thought for a second Berin was spitting at him, but saw it was only a vocal traffic jam caused by indignation. I left it to them and leaned to Constanza again:

"I understand your father is a good cook."

The purple eyes came to me, the brows faintly up. She gurgled. "He is chef de cuisine at the Corridona at San Remo. Didn't you know that?"

7

I nodded. "Yeah, I've seen a list of the fifteen. Yesterday, in the magazine section of the *Times*. I was just opening up. Do you do any cooking yourself?"

"No. I hate it. Except I make good coffee." She looked down as far as my tie—I had on a dark brown polkadot four-in-hand with a pin-stripe tan shirt—and up again. "I didn't hear your name when Mr. Vukcic said it. Are you a detective too?"

"The name is Archie Goodwin. Archibald means sacred and good, but in spite of that my name is not Archibald. I've never heard a French girl say Archie. Try it once."

"I'm not French." She frowned. Her skin was so smooth that the frown was like a ripple on a new tennis ball. "I'm Catalana. I'm sure I could say Archie. Archiearchiearchie. Good?"

"Wonderful."

"Are you a detective?"

"Certainly." I got out my wallet and fingered in it and pulled out a fishing license I had got in Maine the summer before. "Look. See my name on that?"

She read at it. "Ang...ling?" She looked doubtful, and handed it back. "And that Maine? I suppose that is your arrondissement?"

"No. I haven't got any. We have two kinds of detectives in America, might and main. I'm the main kind. That means that I do very little of the hard work, like watering the horses and shooting prisoners and greasing the chutes. Mostly all I do is think, as for instance when they want someone to think what to do next. Mr. Wolfe there is the might kind. You see how big and strong he is. He can run like a deer."

"But... what are the horses for?"

I explained patiently. "There is a law in this country against killing a man unless you have a horse on him. When two or more men are throwing dice for the drinks, you will often hear one of them say, 'horse on you' or 'horse on me.' You can't kill a man unless you say that before he does. Another thing you'll hear a man say, if he finds out something is only a hoax, he'll call it a mare's nest, because it's full of mares and no horses. Still another trouble is a horse's feathers. In case it has feathers—"

"What is a mare?"

I cleared my throat. "The opposite of a horse. As you know, everything must have its opposite. There can't be a right without a left, or a top without a bottom, or a best without a worst. In the same way there can't be a mare without a horse or a horse without a mare. If you were to take, say, ten million horses—"

I was stopped, indirectly, by Wolfe. I had been too interested in my chat with the Catalana girl to hear the others' talk; what interrupted me was Vukcic rearing himself up and inviting Miss Berin to accompany him to the club car. It appeared that Wolfe had expressed a desire for a confidential session with her father, and I put the eye on him, wondering what kind of a charade he was arranging. One of his fingers was tapping gently on his knee, so I knew it was a serious project. When Constanza got up I did too.

I bowed. "If I may?" To Wolfe: "You can send the porter to the club car if you need me. I haven't finished explaining to Miss Berin about mares."

"Mares?" Wolfe looked at me suspiciously. "There is no information she can possibly need about mares which Marko can't supply. We shall—I am hoping—we shall need your notebook. Sit down."

So Vukcic carried her off. I took the undersized chair again, feeling like issuing an ultimatum for an eight-hour day, but knowing that a moving train was the last place in the world for it. Vukcic was sure to disillusion her about the horse lesson, and might even put a crimp in my style for good.

Berin had filled his pipe again. Wolfe was saying, in his casual tone that meant look out for an attack in force, "I wanted, for one thing, to tell you of an experience I had twenty-five years ago. I trust it won't bore you."

Berin grunted. Wolfe went on, "It was before the war, in Figueras."

Berin removed his pipe. "Ha! So?"

"Yes. I was only a youngster, but even so, I was in Spain on a confidential mission for the Austrian government. The track of a man led me to Figueras, and at ten o'clock one evening, having missed my dinner, I entered a little inn at a corner of the plaza and requested food. The woman said there was not much, and brought me wine of the house, bread, and a dish of sausages."

Wolfe leaned forward. "Sir, Lucullus never tasted sausage like that. Nor Brillat-Savarin. Nor did Vatel or Escoffier ever make any. I asked the woman where she got it. She said her son made it. I begged for the privilege of meeting him. She said he was not at home. I asked for the recipe. She said no one knew it but her son. I asked his name. She said Jerome Berin. I ate three more dishes of it, and made an appointment to meet the son at the inn the next morning. An hour later my quarry made a dash for Port-Vendres, where he took a boat for Algiers, and I had to follow him. The chase took me eventually to Cairo, and other duties prevented me from visiting Spain again before the war started." Wolfe leaned back and sighed. "I can still close my eyes and taste that sausage."

Berin nodded, but he was frowning. "A pretty story, Mr. Wolfe. A real tribute, and thank you. But of course saucisse minuit—"

"It was not called saucisse minuit then; it was merely sausage of the house in a little inn in a little Spanish town. That is my point, my effort to impress you: in my youth, without a veteran palate, under trying circumstances, in an obscure setting, I recognized that sausage as high art. I remember well: the first one I ate, I suspected, and feared that it was only an accidental blending of ingredients carelessly mixed; but the others were the same, and all those in the subsequent three dishes. It was genius. My palate hailed it in that place. I am not one of those who drive from Nice or Monte Carlo to the Corridona at San Remo for lunch because Jerome Berin is famous and saucisse minuit is his masterpiece; I did not have to wait for fame to perceive greatness; if I took that drive it would be not to smirk, but to eat."

Berin was still frowning. He grunted, "I cook other things besides sausages."

"Of course. You are a master." Wolfe wiggled a finger at him. "I seem to have somehow displeased you; I must have been clumsy, because this was supposed to be a preamble to a request. I won't discuss your consistent refusal, for twenty years, to disclose the recipe for that sausage; a chef de cuisine has himself to think of as well as humanity. I am acquainted of the efforts that have been made to imitate it—all failures. I can—"

"Failures?" Berin snorted. "Insults! Crimes!"

"To be sure. I agree. I can see that it is reasonable of you to wish to prevent the atrocities that would be perpetrated in ten thousand restaurant kitchens all over the world if you were to publish that recipe. There are a few great cooks, a sprinkling of good ones, and a pestiferous host of bad ones. I have in my home a good one. Mr. Fritz Brenner. He is not inspired, but he is competent and discriminating. He is discreet, and I am too. I beseech you—this is the request I have been leading up to—I beseech you, tell me the recipe for saucisse minuit."

"God above!" Berin nearly dropped his pipe. He gripped it, and stared. Then he laughed. He threw up his hands and waved them around, and shook all over, and laughed as if he never expected to hear a joke again and would use it all up on this one. Finally he stopped, and stared in scorn. "To *you*?" he wanted to know. It was a nasty tone. Especially was it nasty, coming from Constanza's father.

Wolfe said quietly, "Yes, sir. To me. I would not abuse the confidence. I would impart it to no one. It would be served to no one except Mr. Goodwin and myself. I do not want it for display, I want it to eat. I have—"

"God above! Astounding. You really think—"

"No, I don't think. I merely ask. You would, of course, want to investigate me; I would pay the expense of that. I have never violated my word. In addition to the expense, I would pay three thousand dollars. I recently collected a sizable fee."

"Ha! I have been offered five hundred thousand francs."

"For commercial purposes. This is for my guaranteed private use. It will be made under my own roof, and the ingredients bought by Mr. Goodwin, whom I warrant immune to corruption. I have a confession to make. Four times, from 1928 to 1930, when you were at the Tarleton, a man in London went there, ordered saucisse minuit, took away some in his pocket, and sent it to me. I tried analysis—my own, a food expert's, a chef's, a chemist's. The results were utterly unsatisfactory. Apparently it is a combination of ingredients and method. I have—"

Berin demanded with a snarl, "Was it Laszio?"

"Laszio?"

"Phillip Laszio." He said it as if it were a curse. "You said you had an analysis by a chef—"

"Oh. Not Laszio. I don't know him. I have confessed that attempt to show you that I was zealous enough to try to surprise your secret, but I shall keep inviolate an engagement not to betray it. I confess again: I agreed to this outrageous journey, not only because of the honor of the invitation. Chiefly my purpose was to meet you. I have only so long to

11

live—so many books to read, so many ironies to contemplate, so many meals to eat." He sighed, half closed his eyes, and opened them again. "Five thousand dollars. I detest haggling."

"No." Berin was rough. "Did Vukcic know of this? Was it for this he brought me—"

"Sir! If you please. I have spoken of confidence. This enterprise has been mentioned to no one. I began by beseeching you; I do so again. Will you oblige me?"

"No."

"Under no conditions?"

"No."

Wolfe sighed clear to his belly. He shook his head. "I am an ass. I should never have tried this on the train. I am not myself." He reached for the button on the casing. "Would you like some beer?"

"No." Berin snorted. "I am wrong, I mean yes. I would like beer."

"Good." Wolfe leaned back and closed his eyes. Berin got his pipe lit again. The train bumped over a switch and swayed on a curve, and Wolfe's hand groped for the arm of his seat and grasped it. The porter came and received the order, and soon afterward was back again with glasses and bottles, and served, and again I coughed up some jack. I sat and made pictures of sausages on a blank page of my expense book as the beer went down.

Wolfe said, "Thank you, sir, for accepting my beer. There is no reason why we should not be amicable. I seem to have put the wrong foot forward with you. Even before I made my request, while I was relating a tale which could have been only flattering to you, you had a hostile eye. You growled at me. What was my misstep?"

Berin smacked his lips as he put down his empty glass, and his hand descended in an involuntary movement for the corner of an apron that wasn't there. He reached for a handkerchief and used it, leaned forward and tapped a finger on Wolfe's knee, and told him with emphasis: "You live in the wrong country."

Wolfe lifted his brows. "Yes? Wait till you taste terrapin Maryland. Or even, if I may say so, oyster pie à la Nero Wolfe, prepared by Fritz Brenner. In comparison with American oysters, those of Europe are mere blobs of coppery protoplasm."

12

"I don't speak of oysters. You live in the country which permits the presence of Phillip Laszio."

"Indeed. I don't know him."

"But he makes slop at the Hotel Churchill in your own city of New York! You must know that."

"I know of him, certainly, since he is one of your number—"

"My number? Pah!" Berin's hands, in a wide swift sweep, tossed Phillip Laszio through the window. "Not of my number!"

"Your pardon." Wolfe inclined his head. "But he is one of Les Quinze Maîtres, and you are one. Do you suggest that he is unworthy?"

Berin tapped Wolfe's knee again. I grinned as I saw Wolfe, who didn't like being touched, concealing his squirm for the sake of sausages. Berin said slowly through his teeth, "Laszio is worthy of being cut into small pieces and fed to pigs!—But no, that would render the hams inedible. Merely cut into pieces." He pointed to a hole in the ground. "And buried. I tell you, I have known Laszio many years. He is maybe a Turk? No one knows. No one knows his name. He stole the secret of Rognons aux Montagnes in 1920 from my friend Zelota of Tarragona and claimed the creation. Zelota will kill him; he has said so. He has stolen many other things. He was elected one of Les Quinze Maîtres in 1927 in spite of my violent protest. His young wife—have you seen her? She is Dina, the daughter of Domenico Rossi of the Empire Café in London; I have had her many times on this knee!" He slapped the knee. "As you no doubt know, your friend Vukcic married her, and Laszio stole her from Vukcic. Vukcic will kill him, undoubtedly, only he waits too long!" Berin shook both fists. "He is a dog, a snake, he crawls in slime! You know Leon Blanc, our beloved Leon, once great? You know he is now stagnant in an affair of no reputation called the Willow Club in a town by the name of Boston? You know that for years your Hotel Churchill in New York was distinguished by his presence as chef de cuisine? You know that Laszio stole that position from him—by insinuation, by lies, by chicanery, stole it? Dear old Leon will kill him! Positively. Justice demands it."

Wolfe murmured, "Thrice dead, Laszio. Do other deaths await him?"

Berin sank back and quietly growled, "They do. I will kill him myself."

"Indeed. He stole from you too?"

13

"He has stolen from everyone. God apparently created him to steal, let God defend him." Berin sat up. "I arrived in New York Saturday, on the *Rex*. That evening I went with my daughter to dine at the Churchill, driven by an irresistible hatred. We went to a salon which Laszio calls the Resort Room; I don't know where he stole the idea. The waiters wear the liveries of the world-famous resorts, each one different: Shepheard's of Cairo, Les Figuiers of Juan-les-pins, the Continental of Biarritz, the Del Monte of your California, the Kanawha Spa where this train carries us—many of them, dozens—everything is big here. We sat at a table, and what did I see? A waiter—a waiter carrying Laszio slop—in the livery of my own Corridona! Imagine it! I would have rushed to him and demanded that he take it off—I would have torn it from him with these hands"—he shook them violently at Wolfe's face—"but my daughter held me. She said I must not disgrace her; but my own disgrace? No matter, that?"

Wolfe shook his head, visibly, in sympathy, and reached to pour beer. Berin went on: "Luckily his table was far from us, and I turned my back on it. But wait. Hear this. I looked at the menu. Fourth of the entrées, what did I see? What?"

"Not, I hope, saucisse minuit."

"Yes! I did! Printed fourth of the entrées! Of course I had been informed of it before. I knew that Laszio had for years been serving minced leather spiced with God knows what and calling it saucisse minuit—but to see it printed there, as on my own menu! The whole room, the tables and chairs, all those liveries, danced before my eyes. Had Laszio appeared at that moment I would have killed him with these hands. But he did not. I ordered two portions of it from the waiter—my voice trembled as I pronounced it. It was served on porcelain—bah!—and looked like—I shall not say what. This time I gave my daughter no chance to protest. I took the services, one in each hand, arose from my chair, and with calm deliberation turned my wrists and deposited the vile mess in the middle of the carpet! Naturally, there was comment. My waiter came running. I took my daughter's arm and departed. We were intercepted by a chef des garçons. I silenced him! I told him in a sufficient tone: 'I am Jerome Berin of the Corridona at San Remo! Bring Phillip Laszio here and show him what I have done, but keep me from his throat!' I said little more; it was not necessary. I took my daughter to Rusterman's, and met Vukcic, and he soothed me

14

with a plate of his goulash and a bottle of Chateau Latour. The '29."

Wolfe nodded. "It would soothe a tiger."

"It did. I slept well. But the next morning—yesterday—do you know what happened? A man came to me at my hotel with a message from Phillip Laszio inviting me to lunch! Can you credit such effrontery? But wait, that was not all. The man who brought the message was Alberto Malfi!"

"Indeed. Should I know him?"

"Not now. Now he is not Alberto, but Albert—Albert Malfi, once a Corsican fruit slicer whom I discovered in a café in Ajaccio. I took him to Paris—I was then at the Provençal—trained and taught him, and made a good entrée man of him. He is now Laszio's first assistant at the Churchill. Laszio stole him from me in London in 1930. Stole my best pupil, and laughed at me! And now the brazen frog sends him to me with an invitation to lunch! Alberto appears before me in a morning coat, bows, and as if nothing had ever happened, delivers such a message in perfect English!"

"I take it you didn't go."

"Pah! Would I eat poison? I kicked Alberto out of the room." Berin shuddered. "I shall never forget—once in 1926, when I was ill and could not work, I came that close"—he held thumb and forefinger half an inch apart—"to giving Alberto the recipe for saucisse minuit. God above! If I had! He would be making it now for Laszio's menu! Horrible!"

Wolfe agreed. He had finished another bottle, and he now started on a suave speech of sympathy and understanding. It gave me a distinct pain. He might have seen it was wasted effort, that there wasn't a chance of his getting what he wanted; and it made me indignant to see him belittling himself trying to horn a favor out of that wild-eyed sausage cook. Besides, the train had made me so sleepy I couldn't keep my eyes open. I stood up.

Wolfe looked at me. "Yes, Archie?"

I said in a determined voice, "Club car," opened the door, and beat it.

It was after eleven o'clock, and half the chairs in the club car were empty. Two of the wholesome young fellows who pose for the glossy hair ads were there drinking highballs, and there was a scattering of the baldheads and streaked grays who had been calling porters George for thirty years. Vukcic and Miss Berin were seated with empty glasses in front of them, neither looking animated or entranced. Next to her on the other side was a square-jawed blue-eyed athlete in a quiet gray suit who would obviously be a self-made man in another ten years. I stopped in front of my friends and dropped a greeting on them. They replied. The blue-eyed athlete looked up from his book and made preparations to raise himself to give me a seat.

But Vukcic was up first. "Take mine, Goodwin. I'm sure Miss Berin won't mind the shift. I was up most of last night."

He said goodnights, and was off. I deposited myself, and flagged the steward when he stuck his nose out. It appeared that Miss Berin had fallen in love with American ginger ale, and I requested a glass of milk. Our needs were supplied and we sipped.

She turned the purple eyes on me. They looked darker than ever, and I saw that that question would not be settled until I met them in daylight. She said, with throat in her voice, "You really are a detective, aren't you? Mr. Vukcic has been telling me, he dines every month at Mr. Wolfe's house, and you live there. He says you are very brave and have saved Mr. Wolfe's life three times." She shook her head and let the eyes scold me. "But you shouldn't have told me that about watering the horses. You might have known I would ask about it and find out."

I said firmly, "Vukcic has only been in this country eight years and knows very little about the detective business."

"Oh, no!" She gurgled. "I'm not young enough to be such a big fool as that. I've been out of school three years."

"All right." I waved a hand. "Forget the horses. What kind of a school do girls go to over there?"

"A convent school. I did. At Toulouse."

"You don't look like any nun I ever saw."

She finished a sip of ginger ale and then laughed. "I'm not anything at all like a nun. I'm not a bit religious, I'm very worldly. Mother Cecilia used to tell us girls that a life of service to others was the purest and sweetest, but I thought about it and it seemed to me that the best way would be to enjoy life for a long while, until you got fat or sick or had a big family, and then begin on service to others. Don't you think so?"

I shook my head doubtfully. "I don't know, I'm pretty strong on service. But of course you shouldn't overdo it. You've been enjoying life so far?"

She nodded. "Sometimes. My mother died when I was young, and father has a great many rules for me. I saw how American girls acted when they came to San Remo, and I thought I would act the same way, but I found out I didn't know how, and anyway father heard about it when I sailed Lord Gerley's boat around the cape without a chaperon."

"Was Gerley along?"

"Yes, he was along, but he didn't do any of the work. He went to sleep and fell overboard and I had to tack three times to get him. Do you like Englishmen?"

I lifted a brow. "Well...I suppose I could like an Englishman, if the circumstances were exactly right. For instance, if it was on a desert island, and I had had nothing to eat for three days and he had just caught a rabbit—or, in case there were no rabbits, a wild boar or a walrus. Do you like Americans?"

"I don't know!" She laughed. "I have only met a few since I grew up, at San Remo and around there, and it seemed to me they talked funny and tried to act superior. I mean the men. I liked one I knew in London once, a rich one with a bad stomach who stayed at the Tarleton, and my father had special things prepared for him, and when he left he gave me nice presents. I think lots of them I have seen since I got to New York are very good-looking. I saw one at the hotel yesterday who was *quite* handsome. He had a nose something like yours, but his hair was lighter. I can't really tell whether I like people until I know them pretty well..."

She went on, but I was busy making a complicated discovery. When she had stopped to sip ginger ale my eyes had wandered away from her face to take in accessories, and as she had crossed her knees like American girls, without undue fuss as to her skirt, the view upward from a well-shaped foot and a custom-built ankle was as satisfactory as any I had ever seen. So far, so good; but the trouble was that I became aware that the blue-eyed athlete on the other side of her had one eye focused straight past the edge of his book, and its goal was obviously the same interesting object that I was studying, and my inner reaction to that fact was unsociable and alarming. Instead of being pleased at having a fellow man share a delightful experience with me, I became conscious of an almost uncontrollable impulse to do two things at once: glare at the athlete, and tell her to put her skirt down!

I pulled myself together inwardly, and considered it logically: there was only one theory by which I could possibly justify my resentment at his looking at that leg and my desire to make him stop, and that was that the leg belonged to me. Obviously, therefore, I was either beginning to feel that the leg was my property, or I was rapidly developing an intention to acquire it. The first was nonsense; it was *not* my property. The second was dangerous, since, considering the situation as a whole, there was only one practical and ethical method of acquiring it.

She was still talking. I gulped down the rest of the milk, which was not my habit, waited for an opening, and then turned to her without taking the risk of another dive into the dark purple eyes.

"Absolutely," I said. "It takes a long time to know people. How are you going to tell about anyone until you know them? Take love at first sight, for instance, it's ridiculous. That's not love, it's just an acute desire to get acquainted. I remember the first time I met my wife, out on Long Island, I hit her with my roadster. She wasn't hurt much, but I lifted her in and drove her home. It wasn't until after she sued me for $20,000 damages that I fell in what you might call love with her. Then the inevitable happened, and the children began to come, Clarence and Merton and Isabel and Melinda and Patricia and—"

"I thought Mr. Vukcic said you weren't married."

I waved a hand. "I'm not intimate with Vukcic. He and I have never discussed family matters. Did you know that in Japan it is bad form to mention your wife to another man or to ask him how his is? It would be the same as if you told him he was getting bald or asked him if he could still reach down to pull his socks on."

"Then you *are* married."

"I sure am. *Very* happily."

"What are the names of the rest of the children?"

"Well . . . I guess I told you the most important ones. The others are just tots."

I chattered on, and she chattered back, in the changed atmosphere, with me feeling like a man just dragged back from the edge of a perilous cliff, but with sadness in it too. Pretty soon something happened. I wouldn't argue about it, I am perfectly willing to admit the possibility that it was an accident, but all I can do is describe it as I saw it. As she sat talking to me, her right arm was extended along the arm of her chair on the side next to the blue-eyed athlete, and in

18

that hand was her half-full glass of ginger ale. I didn't see the glass begin to tip, but it must have been gradual and unobtrusive, and I'll swear she was looking at me. When I did see it, it was too late; the liquid had already begun to trickle onto the athlete's quiet gray trousers. I interrupted her and reached across to grab the glass; she turned and saw it and let out a gasp; the athlete turned red and went for his handkerchief. As I say, I wouldn't argue about it, only it was quite a coincidence that four minutes after she found out that one man was married she began spilling ginger ale on another one.

"Oh, I hope—does it stain? Si gauche! I am *so* sorry! I wasn't thinking... I wasn't looking..."

The athlete: "Quite all right—really—really—rite all kight—it doodn't stain—"

More of the same. I enjoyed it. But he was quick on the recovery, for in a minute he quit talking Chinese, collected himself, and spoke to me in his native tongue: "No damage at all, sir, you see there isn't. Really. Permit me; my name is Tolman. Barry Tolman, prosecuting attorney of Marlin County, West Virginia."

So he was a trouble-vulture and a politician. But in spite of the fact that most of my contacts with prosecuting attorneys had not been such as to induce me to keep their photographs on my dresser, I saw no point in being churlish. I described my handle to him and presented him to Constanza, and offered to buy a drink as compensation for us spilling one on him.

For myself, another milk, which would finish my bedtime quota. When it came I sat and sipped it and restrained myself from butting in on the progress of the new friendship that was developing on my right, except for occasional grunts to show that I wasn't sulking. By the time my glass was half empty Mr. Barry Tolman was saying:

"I heard you—forgive me, but I couldn't help hearing—I heard you mention San Remo. I've never been there. I was at Nice and Monte Carlo back in 1931, and someone, I forget who, told me I should see San Remo because it was more beautiful than any other place on the Riviera, but I didn't go. Now I... well... I can well believe it."

"Oh, you should have gone!" There was throat in her voice again, and it made me happy to hear it. "The hills and the vineyards and the sea!"

19

"Yes, of course. I'm very fond of scenery. Aren't you, Mr. Goodwin? Fond of—" There was a concussion of the air and a sudden obliterating roar as we thundered past a train on the adjoining track. It ended. "Fond of scenery?"

"You bet." I nodded, and sipped.

Constanza said, "I'm so sorry it's night. I could be looking out and seeing America. Is it rocky—I mean, is it the Rocky Mountains?"

Tolman didn't laugh. I didn't bother to glance to see if he was looking at the purple eyes; I knew that must be it. He told her no, the Rocky Mountains were 1500 miles away, but that it was nice country we were going through. He said he had been in Europe three times, but that on the whole there was nothing there, except of course the historical things, that could compare with the United States. Right where he lived, in West Virginia, there were mountains that he would be willing to put alongside Switzerland and let anyone take their pick. He had never seen anything anywhere as beautiful as his native valley, especially the spot in it where they had built Kanawha Spa, the famous resort. That was in his county.

Constanza exclaimed, "But that's where I'm going! Of course it is! Kanawha Spa!"

"I . . . I hope so." His cheek showed red. "I mean, three of these pullmans are Kanawha Spa cars, and I thought it likely . . . I thought it possible I might have a chance of meeting you, though of course I'm not in the social life there . . ."

"And then we met on the train. Of course, I won't be there very long. But since you think it's nicer than Europe, I can hardly wait to see it, but I warn you I love San Remo and the sea. I suppose on your trips to Europe you take your wife and children along?"

"Oh, now!" He was groggy. "Now, really! Do I look old enough to have a wife and children?"

I thought, you darned nut, cover up that chin! My milk was finished. I stood up.

"If you folks will excuse me, I'll go and make sure my boss hasn't fallen off the train. I'll come back soon, Miss Berin, and take you to your father. You can't be expected to learn the knack of acting like the American girls the first day out."

Neither of them broke into tears to see me go.

In the first car ahead I met Jerome Berin striding down the passage. He stopped and of course I had to.

He roared, "My daughter? Vukcic left her!"

"She's perfectly all right." I thumbed to the rear. "She's back in the club car talking with a friend of mine I introduced to her. Is Mr. Wolfe okay?"

"Okay? I don't know. I just left him."

He brushed past me and I went on.

Wolfe was alone in the room, still on the seat, the picture of despair, gripping with his hands, his eyes wide open. I stood and surveyed him.

I said, "See America first. Come and play with us in vacationland! Not a draft on the train and sailing like a gull!"

He said, "Shut up!"

He couldn't sit there all night. The time had come when it must be done. I rang the bell for the porter to do the bed. Then I went up to him—but no. I remember in an old novel I picked up somewhere it described a lovely young maiden going into her bedroom at night and putting her lovely fingers on the top button of her dress and then it said, "But now we must leave her. There are some intimacies which you and I, dear reader, must not venture to violate; some girlish secrets which we must not betray to the vulgar gaze. Night has drawn its protecting veil; let us draw ours!"

Okay by me.

2

I SAID, "I wouldn't have thought this was a job for a house dick, watching for a kid to throw stones. Especially a ritzy house dick like you."

Gershom Odell spit through his teeth at a big fern ten feet away from where we sat on a patch of grass. "It isn't. But I told you. These birds pay from fifteen to fifty bucks a day to stay at this caravansary and to write letters on Kanawha Spa stationery, and they don't like to have niggers throwing stones at them when they go horseback riding. I didn't say a kid, I said a nigger. They suspect it was one that got fired from the garage about a month ago."

The warm sun was on me through a hole in the trees, and I yawned. I asked, to show I wasn't bored, "You say it happened about here?"

He pointed. "Over yonder, from the other side of the path. It was old Crisler that got it both times, you know, the fountain pen Crisler, his daughter married Ambassador Willetts."

There were sounds from down the way. Soon the hoofbeats were plainer, and in a minute a couple of genteel but good-looking horses came down the path from around a curve, and trotted by, close enough so that I could have tripped them with a fishing pole. On one of them was a dashing chap in a loud-checked jacket, and on the other a dame plenty old and fat enough to start on service to others any time the spirit moved her.

Odell said, "That was Mrs. James Frank Osborn, the Baltimore Osborn, ships and steel, and Dale Chatwin, a good bridge player on the make. See him worry his horse? He can't ride worth a damn."

"Yeah? I didn't notice. You sure are right there on the social list."

"Got to be, on this job." He spit at the fern again, scratched the back of his head, and plucked a blade of grass and stuck it in his mouth. "I guess nine out of ten that come to this joint, I know 'em without being told. Of course sometimes there's strangers. For instance, take your crowd. Who the hell are they? I understand they're a bunch of good cooks that the chef invited. Looks funny to me. Since when was Kanawha Spa a domestic science school?"

I shook my head. "Not my crowd, mister."

"You're with 'em."

"I'm with Nero Wolfe."

"He's with 'em."

I grinned. "Not this minute, he ain't. He's in Suite 60, on the bed fast asleep. I think I'll have to chloroform him Thursday to get him on the train home." I stretched in the sun. "At that, there's worse things than cooks."

"I suppose so," he admitted. "Where do they all come from, anyway?"

I pulled a paper from my pocket—a page I had clipped from the magazine section of the *Times*—and unfolded it and glanced at the list again before passing it across to him:

LES QUINZE MAITRES

Jerome Berin, the Corridona, San Remo.
Leon Blanc, the Willow Club, Boston.

Ramsey Keith, Hotel Hastings, Calcutta.
Phillip Laszio, Hotel Churchill, New York.
Domenico Rossi, Empire Café, London.
Pierre Mondor, Mondor's, Paris.
Marko Vukcic, Rusterman's Restaurant, New York.
Sergei Vallenko, Chateau Montcalm, Quebec.
Lawrence Coyne, The Rattan, San Francisco.
Louis Servan, Kanawha Spa, West Virginia.
Ferid Khaldah, Café de l'Europe, Istanbul.
Henri Tassone, Shepheard's Hotel, Cairo.

DECEASED:

Armand Fleury, Fleury's, Paris.
Pasquale Donofrio, the Eldorado, Madrid.
Jacques Baleine, Emerald Hotel, Dublin.

Odell took a look at the extent of the article, made no offer
to read it, and then went over the names and addresses with
his head moving slowly back and forth. He grunted. "Some
bunch of names. You might think it was a Notre Dame
football team. How'd they get all the press? What does that
mean at the top, less quinzy something?"

"Oh, that's French." I pronounced it adequately. "It means
'The Fifteen Masters.' These babies are famous. One of them
cooks sausages that people fight duels over. You ought to see
him and tell him you're a detective and ask him to give you
the recipe; he'd be glad to. They meet every five years on the
home grounds of the oldest one of their number; that's why
they came to Kanawha Spa. Each one is allowed to bring one
guest—it's all there in the article. Nero Wolfe is Servan's
guest, and Vukcic invited me so I could be with Wolfe.
Wolfe's the guest of honor. Only ten of 'em are here. The last
three died since 1932, and Khaldah and Tassone couldn't
come. They'll do a lot of cooking and eating and drinking, and
tell each other a lot of lies, and elect three new members,
and listen to Nero Wolfe make a speech—and oh yeah, one of
'em's going to get killed."

"That'll be fun." Odell spit through his teeth again. "Which
one?"

"Phillip Laszio, Hotel Churchill, New York. The article
says his salary is sixty thousand berries per annum."

"Which may be. Who's going to kill him?"

"They're going to take turns. If you want tickets for the

series, I'd be glad to get you a couple of ringsides, and here's a tip, you'd better tell the desk to collect for his room in advance, because you know how long it takes—well God bless my eyes! All with a few spoonfuls of ginger ale!"

A horseman and horsewoman had cantered by on the path, looking sideways at each other, laughing, their teeth showing and their faces flushed. As their dust drifted toward us I asked Odell, "Who's that happy pair?"

He grunted. "Barry Tolman, prosecuting attorney of this county. Going to be president some day, ask him. The girl came with your crowd, didn't she? Incidentally, she's easy on the eyes. What was the crack about ginger ale?"

"Oh, nothing." I waved a hand. "Just an old quotation from Chaucer. It wouldn't do any good to throw stones at them, they wouldn't notice anything less than an avalanche.—By the way, what is this stone-throwing gag?"

"No gag. Just part of the day's work."

"You call this work? I'm a detective. In the first place, do you suppose anyone is going to start a bombardment with you and me sitting here in plain sight? And this bridle path winds around here for six miles, and why couldn't he pick another spot? Secondly, you told me that a Negro that got fired from the garage is suspected of doing it to annoy the management, but in that case it was just a coincidence that he picked fountain pen Crisler for a target both times? It's a phony. You didn't show me the bottom. Not that it's any of my business, but just for fun I thought I'd demonstrate that I'm only dumb on Sundays and holidays."

He looked at me with one eye. Then with both, and then he grinned at me. "You seem to be a good guy."

I said warmly, "I am."

He was still grinning. "Honest to God, it's too good not to tell you. You would enjoy it better if you knew Crisler. But it wasn't only him. Another trouble was that I never get any time to myself around here. Sixteen hours a day! That's the way it works out. I've only got one assistant, and you ought to see him, he's somebody's nephew. I had to be on duty from sunrise to bedtime. Then there was Crisler, just a damn bile factory. He had it in for me because I caught his chauffeur swiping grease down at the garage, and boy, when he was mean he was mean. The nigger that helped me catch the chauffeur, Crisler had him fired. He was after my scalp too. I made my plans and they worked."

Odell pointed. "See that ledge up there? No, over yonder, the other side of those firs. That's where I was when I threw stones at him. I hit him both times."

"I see. Hurt him much?"

"Not enough. His shoulder was pretty sore. I had fixed up a good alibi in case of suspicions. Crisler checked out. That was one advantage. Another was that almost whenever I want to I can say I'm going out for the stone thrower, and come to the woods for an hour or two and be alone and spit and look at things. Sometimes I let them see me from the bridle path, and they think they're being protected and that's jake."

"Pretty good idea. But it'll play out. Sooner or later you'll either have to catch him or give it up. Or else throw some more stones."

He grinned. "Maybe you think it wasn't a good shot the time I got him in the shoulder! See how far away that ledge is? I don't know whether I'll try it again or not, but if I do, I know damn well who I'll pick. I'll point her out to you." He glanced at his wrist. "Jumping Jesus, nearly five o'clock. I've got to get back."

He scrambled up and started off headlong, and as I was in no hurry I let him go, and moseyed idly along behind. As I had already discovered, wherever you went around Kanawha Spa, you were taking a walk in the garden. I don't know who kept the woods swept and dusted off the trees for what must have been close to a thousand acres, but it was certainly model housekeeping. In the neighborhood of the main hotel, and the pavilions scattered around, and the building where the hot springs were, it was mostly lawns and shrubs and flowers, with three classy fountains thirty yards from the main entrance. The things they called pavilions, which had been named after the counties of West Virginia, were nothing to sneeze at themselves in the matter of size, with their own kitchens and so forth, and I gathered that the idea was that they offered more privacy at an appropriate price. Two of them, Pocahontas and Upshur, only a hundred yards apart and connected by a couple of paths through trees and shrubs, had been turned over to the fifteen masters—or rather, ten—and our Suite 60, Wolfe's and mine, was in Upshur.

I strolled along carefree. There was lots of junk to look at if you happened to be interested in it—big clusters of pink flowers everywhere on bushes which Odell had said was

25

mountain laurel, and a brook zipping along with little bridges across it here and there, and some kind of wild trees in bloom, and birds and evergreens and so on. That sort of stuff is all right, I've got nothing against it, and of course out in the country like that something might as well be growing or what would you do with all the space, but I must admit it's a poor place to look for excitement. Compare it, for instance, with Times Square or the Yankee Stadium.

Closer to the center of things, in the section where the pavilions were, and especially around the main building and the springs, there was more life. Plenty of folks, such as they were, coming and going in cars or on horseback and sometimes even walking. Most of those walking were Negroes in the Kanawha Spa uniform, black breeches and bright green jackets with big black buttons. Off on a side path you might catch one of them grinning, but out in the open they looked as if they were nearly overcome by something they couldn't tell you, like bank tellers.

It was a little after five when I got to the entrance of Upshur Pavilion and went in. Suite 60 was in the rear of the right wing. I opened its door with care and tiptoed across the hall so as not to wake the baby, but opening another door with even more care I found that Wolfe's room was empty. The three windows I had left partly open were closed, the hollow in the center of the bed left no doubt as to who had been on it, and the blanket I had spread over him was hanging at the foot. I glanced in the hall again; his hat was gone. I went to the bathroom and turned on the faucet and began soaping my hands. I was good and sore. For ten years I had been accustomed to being as sure of finding Nero Wolfe where I had left him as if he had been the Statue of Liberty, unless his house had burned down, and it was upsetting, not to mention humiliating, to find him flitting around like a hummingbird for a chance to lick the boots of a dago sausage cook.

After splashing around a little and changing my shirt, I was tempted to wander over to the hotel and look-to-see around, but I knew Fritz and Theodore would murder me if I didn't bring him back in one piece, so instead I left by the side entrance and followed the path to Pocahontas Pavilion.

Pocahontas was much more ambitious than Upshur, with four good-sized public rooms centrally on the ground floor, and suites in the wings and the upper story. I heard noises before I got inside, and, entering, found that the masters were having a good time. I had met the whole gang at lunch, which had been cooked at the pavilion and served there, with five different ones contributing a dish, and I admit it hadn't been hard to get down—which, since Fritz Brenner's cooking under Nero Wolfe's supervision had been my steady diet for ten years, would be a tribute for anyone.

I let a greenjacket open the door for me and trusted my hat to another one in the hall, and began the search for my lost hummingbird. In the parlor on the right, which had dark wooden things with colored rugs and stuff around everywhere—Pocahontas was all Indian as to furnishings—three couples were dancing to a radio. A medium brunette about my age, medium also as to size, with a high white brow and long sleepy eyes, was fastened onto Sergei Vallenko, a blond Russian ox around fifty with a scar under one ear. She was Dina Laszio, daughter of Domenico Rossi, onetime wife of Marko Vukcic, and stolen from him, according to Jerome Berin, by Phillip Laszio. A short middle-aged woman built like a duck, with little black eyes and fuzz on her upper lip, was Marie Mondor, and the pop-eyed chap with a round face, maybe her age and as plump as her, was her husband, Pierre Mondor. She couldn't speak English, and I saw no reason why she should. The third couple consisted of Ramsey Keith, a little sawed-off Scotchman at least sixty with a face like a sunset preserved in alcohol, and a short and slender black-eyed affair who might have been anything under 35 to my limited experience, because she was Chinese. To my surprise, when I had met her at lunch, she had looked dainty and mysterious, just like the geisha propaganda pictures. I believe geishas are Japs, but it's all the same. Anyway, she was Lio Coyne, the fourth wife of Lawrence Coyne; and hurrah for Lawrence, since he was all of three score and ten and as white as a snowbank.

I tried the parlor on the left, a smaller one. The pickings there were scanty. Lawrence Coyne was on a divan at the far end, fast asleep, and Leon Blanc, dear old Leon, was standing in front of a mirror, apparently trying to decide if he needed a shave. I ambled on through to the dining room. It was big and somewhat cluttered. Besides the long table and a slew of chairs, there were two serving tables and a cabinet full of paraphernalia, and a couple of huge screens with pictures of Pocahontas saving John Smith's life and other things. There were four doors: the one I had come in by, a double one to the large parlor, a double glass one to a side terrace, and one out to the pantry and the kitchen.

There were also, as I entered, people. Marko Vukcic was on a chair by the long table, with a cigar in his mouth, shaking his head at a telegram he was reading. Jerome Berin was standing with a wineglass in his hand, talking with a dignified old bird with a gray mustache and a wrinkled face—that being Louis Servan, dean of the fifteen masters and their host at Kanawha Spa. Nero Wolfe was on a chair too small for him over by the glass door to the terrace, which stood open, leaning back uncomfortably so that his half-open eyes could take in the face of the man standing looking down at him. It was Phillip Laszio—chunky, not much gray in his hair, with clever eyes and a smooth skin and slick all over. Alongside Wolfe's chair was a little stand with a glass and a couple of beer bottles, and at his other elbow, almost sitting on his knee, with a plate of something in her hand, was Lisette Putti. Lisette was as cute as they come, and had already made friends, in spite of a question of irregularity regarding her status. She was the guest of Ramsey Keith, who, coming all the way from Calcutta, had introduced her as his niece. Vukcic had told me that Marie Mondor's sputterings after lunch had been to the effect that Lisette was a coquine and Keith had picked her up in Marseilles, but after all, Vukcic said, it was physically possible for a man named Keith to have a niece named Putti, and even if it was a case of mistaken identity, it was Keith who was paying the bills. Which sounded like a loose statement, but it was none of my affair.

As I approached, Laszio finished some remark to Wolfe and Lisette began spouting to him in French, something about the stuff she had on the plate, which looked like fat brown crackers; but just then there was a yell from the direction of the kitchen, and we all turned to see the swinging door open and Domenico Rossi come leaping through with a steaming dish in one hand and a long-handled spoon in the other.

"It curdled!" he shrieked. He rushed across to us and thrust the dish at Laszio. "Look at that dirty mud! What did I tell you? By God, look! You owe me a hundred francs! A devil

28

of a son-in-law you are, and twice as old as I am anyhow, and ignorant of the very first essentials!"

Laszlo quietly shrugged. "Did you warm the milk?"

"Me? Do I look like an egg-freezer?"

"Then perhaps the eggs were old."

"Louis!" Rossi whirled and pointed the spoon at Servan. "Do you hear that? He says you have old eggs!"

Servan chuckled. "But if you did it the way he said to, and it curdled, you have won a hundred francs. Where is the objection to that?"

"But everything wasted! Look: mud!" Rossi puffed. "These damn modern ideas! Vinegar is vinegar!"

Laszlo said quietly, "I'll pay. To-morrow I'll show you how." He turned abruptly and went to the door to the large parlor and opened it, and the sound of the radio came through. Rossi trotted around the table with the dish of mud to show it to Servan and Berin. Vukcic stuffed his telegram in his pocket and went over to look at it. Lisette became aware of my presence and poked the plate at me and said something. I grinned at her and replied, "Jack Spratt could eat no fat, his wife could—"

"Archie!" Wolfe opened his eyes. "Miss Putti says that those wafers were made by the two hands of Mr. Keith, who brought the ingredients from India."

"Did you try them?"

"Yes."

"Are they any good?"

"No."

"Then will you kindly tell her that I never eat between meals?"

I wandered over to the parlor door and stood beside Phillip Laszlo, looking at the three couples dancing—only it was apparent that he was only seeing one. Mamma and papa Mondor were panting but game, Ramsey Keith and the geisha were funny to look at but obviously not concerned with that aspect of the matter, and Dina Laszlo and Vallenko apparently hadn't changed holds since my previous view. However, they soon did. Something was happening beside me. Laszlo said nothing, and made no gesture that I saw, but he must have achieved some sort of communication, for the two stopped abruptly, and Dina murmured something to her partner and then alone crossed the floor to her husband. I sidestepped a couple of paces to give them room, but they weren't paying any attention to me.

She asked him, "Would you like to dance, dear?"

"You know I wouldn't. You weren't dancing."

"But what—" She laughed. "They call it dancing, don't they?"

"They may. But you weren't dancing." He smiled—that is, technically; it looked more like a smile to end smiles.

Vallenko came up. He stopped close to them, looked from his face to hers and back again, and all at once burst out laughing. "Ah, Laszio!" He slapped him on the back, not gently. "Ah, my friend!" He bowed to Dina. "Thank you, madame." He strode off.

She said to her husband, "Phillip dear, if you don't want me to dance with your colleagues you might have said so. I don't find it so great a pleasure—"

It didn't seem likely that they would need me to help out, so I went back out to the dining room and sat down. For half an hour I sat there and watched the zoo. Lawrence Coyne came in from the small parlor, rubbing his eyes and trying to comb his white whiskers with his fingers. He looked around and called "Lio!" in a roar that shook the windows, and his Chinese wife came trotting from the other room, got him in a chair and perched on his knee. Leon Blanc entered, immediately got into an argument with Berin and Rossi, and suddenly disappeared with them into the kitchen. It was nearly six o'clock when Constanza blew in. She had changed from her riding things. She looked around and offered a few greetings which nobody paid much attention to, then saw Vukcic and me and came over to us and asked where her father was. I told her, in the kitchen fighting about lemon juice. In the daylight the dark purple eyes were all and more than I had feared.

I observed, "I saw you and the horses a couple of hours ago. Will you have a glass of ginger ale?"

"No, thanks." She smiled as to an indulgent uncle. "It was very nice of you to tell father that Mr. Tolman is your friend."

"Don't mention it. I could see you were young and helpless, and thought I might as well lend a hand. Are things beginning to shape up?"

"Shape up?"

"It doesn't matter." I waved a hand. "As long as you're happy."

"Certainly I'm happy. I *love* America. I believe I'll have some ginger ale after all. No, don't move, I'll get it." She moved around the table toward a button.

I don't believe Vukcic, right next to me, heard any of it, because he had his eyes on his former wife as she sat with Laszio and Servan talking to Wolfe. I had noticed that tendency in him during lunch. I had also noticed that Leon Blanc unobtrusively avoided Laszio and had not once spoken to him who, according to Berin, had stolen Blanc's job at the Hotel Churchill; whereas Berin himself was inclined to find opportunities for glaring at Laszio at close quarters, but also without speaking. There was undoubtedly a little atmosphere around, what with Mamma Mondor's sniffs at Lisette Putti and a general air of comradely jealousy and arguments about lettuce and vinegar and the thumbs down clique on Laszio, and last but not least, the sultry mist that seemed to float around Dina Laszio. I have always had a belief that the swamp-woman—the kind who can move her eyelids slowly three times and you're stuck in a marsh and might as well give up—is never any better than a come-on for suckers; but I could see that if Dina Laszio once got you alone and she had her mind on her work and it was raining outdoors, it would take more than a sense of humor to laugh it off. She was way beyond the stage of spilling ginger ale on lawyers.

I watched the show and waited for Wolfe to display signs of motion. A little after six he made it to his feet, and I followed him onto the terrace and along the path to Upshur. Considering the terrible hardships of the train, he was navigating fine. In Suite 60 there had been a chambermaid around, for the bed was smoothed out again and the blanket folded up and put away. I went to my room, and a little later rejoined Wolfe in his. He was in a chair by the window which was almost big enough for him, leaning back with his eyes closed and a furrow in his brow, with his fingers meeting at the center of his paunch. It was a pathetic sight. No Fritz, no atlas to look at, no orchids to tend to, no bottle caps to count! I was sorry that the dinner was to be informal, since three or four of the masters were cooking it, because the job of getting into dinner clothes would have made him so mad that it would have taken his mind off of other things and really been a relief to him. As I stood and surveyed him he heaved a long deep shuddering sigh, and to keep the tears from coming to my eyes I spoke.

"I understand Berin is going to make saucisse minuit for lunch to-morrow. Huh?"

No score. I said, "How would you like to go back in an airplane? They have a landing field right here. Special service, on call, sixty bucks to New York, less than four hours."

Nothing doing. I said, "They had a train wreck over in Ohio last night. Freight. Over a hundred pigs killed."

He opened his eyes and started to sit up, but his hand slipped on the arm of the foreign chair and he slid back again. He declared, "You are dismissed from your job, to take effect upon our arrival at my house in New York. I *think* you are. It can be discussed after we get home."

That was more like it. I grinned at him. "That will suit me fine. I'm thinking of getting married anyhow. The little Berin girl. What do you think of her?"

"Pfui."

"Go on and phooey. I suppose you think living with you for ten years has destroyed all my sentiment. I suppose you think I am no longer subject—"

"Pfui!"

"Very well. But last night in the club car it came to me. I don't suppose you realize what a pippin she is, because you seem to be immune. And of course I haven't spoken to her yet, because I couldn't very well ask her to marry a—well, a detective. But I think if I can get into some other line of work and prove that I can make myself worthy of her—"

"Archie." He was sitting up now, and his tone was a menacing murmur. "You are lying. Look at me."

I gave him as good a gaze as I could manage, and I thought I had him. But then I saw his lids begin to droop, and I knew it was all off. So the best I could do was grin at him.

"Confound you!" But he sounded relieved at that. "Do you realize what marriage means? Ninety percent of men over thirty are married, and look at them! Do you realize that if you had a wife she would insist on cooking for you? Do you know that all women believe that the function of food begins when it reaches the stomach? Have you any idea that a woman can ever—what's that?"

The knocking on the outer door of the suite had sounded

twice, the first time faintly, and I had ignored it because I didn't want to interrupt him. Now I went out and through the inner hall and opened up. Whereupon I, who am seldom surprised, was close to astonished. There stood Dina Laszio.

Her eyes looked larger than ever, but not quite so sleepy. She asked in a low voice, "May I come in? I wish to see Mr. Wolfe."

I stood back, she went past, and I shut the door. I indicated Wolfe's room, "In there, please," and she preceded me. The only perceptible expression on Wolfe's face as he became aware of her was recognition.

He inclined his head. "I am honored, madam. Forgive me for not rising; I permit myself that discourtesy. That chair around, Archie?"

She was nervous. She looked around. "May I see you alone, Mr. Wolfe?"

"I'm afraid not. Mr. Goodwin is my confidential assistant."

"But I..." She stayed on her feet. "It is hard to tell even you..."

"Well, madam, if it is too hard..." Wolfe let it hang in the air.

She swallowed, looked at me again, and took a step toward him. "But it would be harder... I must tell someone. I have heard much of you, of course... in the old days, from Marko... and I must tell someone, and there is no one but you to tell. Somebody is trying to poison my husband."

"Indeed." Wolfe's eyes narrowed faintly. "Be seated. Please. It's easier to talk sitting down, don't you think, Mrs. Laszio?"

3

THE SWAMP-WOMAN lowered it into the chair I had placed. Needless to say, I leaned against the bedpost not as nonchalant as I looked. It sounded as if this might possibly be something that would help to pass the time, and justify my foresight in chucking my pistol and a couple of notebooks into my bag when I had packed.

She said, "Of course... I know you are an old friend of

Marko's. You probably think I wronged him when I . . . left him. But I count on your sense of justice . . . your humanity. . . ."

"Weak supports, madam." Wolfe was brusque. "Few of us have enough wisdom for justice, or enough leisure for humanity. Why do you mention Marko? Do you suggest that he is poisoning Mr. Laszio?"

"Oh, no!" Her hand fluttered from her lap and came to rest on the arm of her chair. "Only I am sorry if you are prejudiced against my husband and me, for I have decided that I must tell someone, and there is no one but you to tell. . . ."

"Have you informed your husband that he is being poisoned?"

She shook her head, with a little twist on her lips. "He informed me. To-day. You know, of course, that for luncheon several of them prepared dishes, and Phillip did the salad, and he had announced that he was going to make Meadowbrook dressing, which he originated. They all know that he mixes the sugar and lemon juice and sour cream an hour ahead of time, and that he always tastes in spoonfuls. He had the things ready, all together on a corner table in the kitchen, lemons, bowl of cream, sugar shaker. At noon he started to mix. From habit he shook sugar on to the palm of his hand and put his tongue to it, and it seemed gritty and weak. He shook some on to a pan of water, and little particles stayed on top, and when he stirred it some still stayed. He put sherry in a glass and stirred some of it into that, and only a small portion of it would dissolve. If he had mixed the dressing and tasted a spoonful or two, as he always does, it would have killed him. The sugar was mostly arsenic."

Wolfe grunted. "Or flour."

"My husband said arsenic. There was no taste of flour."

Wolfe shrugged. "Easily determined, with a little hydrochloric acid and a piece of copper wire. You do not appear to have the sugar shaker with you. Where is it?"

"I suppose, in the kitchen."

Wolfe's eyes opened wide. "Being used for our dinner, madam? You spoke of humanity—"

"No. Phillip emptied it down the sink and had it refilled by one of the Negroes. It was sugar, that time."

"Indeed." Wolfe settled, and his eyes were again half shut. "Remarkable. Though he was sure it was arsenic? He didn't turn it over to Servan? Or report it to anyone but you? Or preserve it as evidence? Remarkable."

34

"My husband is a remarkable man." A ray of the setting sun came through the window to her face, and she moved a little. "He told me that he didn't want to make things difficult for his friend, Louis Servan. He forbade me to mention it. He is a strong man and he is very contemptuous. That is his nature. He thinks he is too strong and competent and shrewd to be injured by anyone." She leaned forward and put out a hand, palm up. "I come to you, Mr. Wolfe! I am afraid!"

"What do you want me to do? Find out who put the arsenic in the sugar shaker?"

"Yes." Then she shook her head. "No. I suppose you couldn't, and even if you did, the arsenic is gone. I want to protect my husband."

"My dear madam." Wolfe grunted. "If anyone not a moron has determined to kill your husband, he will be killed. Nothing is simpler than to kill a man; the difficulties arise in attempting to avoid the consequences. I'm afraid I have nothing to suggest to you. It is doubly difficult to save a man's life against his will. Do you think you know who poisoned the sugar?"

"No. Surely there is something—"

"Does your husband think he knows?"

"No. Surely you can—"

"Marko? I can ask Marko if he did it?"

"No! Not Marko! You promised me you wouldn't mention—"

"I promised nothing of the sort. Nothing whatever. I am sorry, Mrs. Laszio, if I seem rude, but the fact is that I hate to be taken for an idiot. If you think your husband may be poisoned, what you need is a food taster, and that is not my profession. If you fear bodily violence for him, the best thing is a bodyguard, and I am not that either. Before he gets into an automobile, every bolt and nut and connection must be thoroughly tested. When he walks the street, windows and tops of buildings must be guarded, and passersby kept at a distance. Should he attend the theater—"

The swamp-woman got up. "You make a joke of it. I'm sorry."

"It was you who started the joke—"

But she wasn't staying for it. I moved to open the door, but she had the knob before I got to it, and since she felt that way about it I let her go on and do the outside one too. I saw that it was closed behind her, and then returned to Wolfe's room

35

and put on a fake frown for him which was wasted, because he had his eyes shut. I told his big round face:

"That's a fine way to treat a lady client who comes to you with a nice straight open-and-shut proposition like that. All we would have to do would be go down to the river where the sewer empties and swim around until we tasted arsenic—"

"Arsenic has no taste."

"Okay." I sat down. "Is she fixing up to poison him herself and preparing a line of negative presumptions in advance? Or is she on the level and just poking around trying to protect her man? Or is Laszio making up tales to show her how cute he is? You should have seen him looking at her when she was dancing with Vallenko. I suppose you've observed Vukcic lamping her with the expression of a moth in a cage surrounded by klieg lights. Or was someone really gump enough to endanger all our lives by putting arsenic in the sugar shaker? Incidentally, it'll be dinnertime in ten minutes, and if you intend to comb your hair and tuck your shirt in—did you know that you can have one of these greenjackets for a valet for an extra five bucks per diem? I swear to God I think I'll try it for half a day. I'd be a different person if I took proper care of myself."

I stopped to yawn. Insufficient sleep and outdoor sunshine had got me. Wolfe was silent. But presently he spoke:

"Archie. Have you heard of the arrangement for this evening?"

"No. Anything special?"

"Yes. It seems to have come about through a wager between Mr. Servan and Mr. Keith. After the digestion of dinner there is to be a test. The cook will roast squabs, and Mr. Laszio, who volunteered for the function, will make a quantity of Sauce Printemps. That sauce contains nine seasonings, besides salt: cayenne, celery, shallots, chives, chervil, tarragon, peppercorn, thyme and parsley. Nine dishes of it will be prepared, and each will lack one of the seasonings, a different one. The squabs and sauce dishes will be arrayed in the dining room, and Mr. Laszio will preside. The gathering will be in the parlor, and each will go to the dining room, singly to prevent discussion, taste the sauces on bits of squab, and record which dish lacks chives, which peppercorn, and so on. I believe Mr. Servan has wagered on an average of eighty percent correct."

"Well." I yawned again. "I can pick the one that lacks squab."

"You will not be included. Only the members of Les Quinze Maîtres and myself. It will be an instructive and interesting experiment. The chief difficulty will be with chives and shallots, but I believe I can distinguish. I shall drink wine with dinner, and of course no sweet. But the possibility occurred to me of a connection between this affair and Mrs. Laszio's strange report. Mr. Laszio is to make the sauce. You know I am not given to trepidation, but I came here to meet able men, not to see one or more of them murdered."

"You came here to learn how to make sausage. But forget it; I guess that's out. But how could there be a connection? It's Laszio that's going to get killed, isn't it? The tasters are safe. Maybe you'd better go last. If you get sick out here in the jungle I will have a nice time."

He shut his eyes. Soon he opened them again. "I don't like stories about arsenic in food. What time is it?"

Too darned lazy to reach in his pocket. I told him, and he sighed and began preparations for getting himself upright.

The dinner at Pocahontas Pavilion that evening was elegant as to provender, but a little confused in other respects. The soup, by Louis Servan, looked like any consommé, but it wasn't just any. He had spread himself, and it was nice to see his dignified old face get red with pleasure as they passed remarks to him. The fish, by Leon Blanc, was little six-inch brook trout, four to a customer, with a light brown sauce with capers in it, and a tang that didn't seem to come from lemon or any vinegar I had ever heard of. I couldn't place it, and Blanc just grinned at them when they demanded the combination, saying he hadn't named it yet. All of them, except Lisette Putti and me, ate the trout head and bones and all, even Constanza Berin, who was on my right. She watched me picking away and smiled at me and said I would never make a gourmet, and I told her not eating fishes' faces was a matter of sentiment with me on account of my pet goldfish. Watching her crunch those trout heads and bones with her pretty teeth, I was glad I had put the kibosh on my attack of leg-jealousy.

The entrée, by Pierre Mondor, was of such a nature that I imitated some of the others and had two helpings. It appeared to be a famous creation of his, well-known to the others, and Constanza told me that her father made it very well and that the main ingredients were beef marrow, cracker crumbs, white wine and chicken breast. In the middle of my second portion I caught Wolfe's eye across the table and winked at him, but he ignored me and hung on to solemn bliss. As far as he was concerned, we were in church, and Saint Peter was speaking. It was during the consumption of the entrée that Mondor and his plump wife, without any warning, burst into a screaming argument which ended with him bouncing up and racing for the kitchen, and her hot on his tail. I learned afterward that she had heard him ask Lisette Putti if she liked the entrée. She must have been abnormally moral for a Frenchwoman.

The roast was young duck à la Mr. Richards, by Marko Vukcic. This was one of Wolfe's favorites and I was well acquainted with the Fritz Brenner-Nero Wolfe version of it, and by the time it arrived I was so nearly filled that I was in no condition to judge, but the other men took a healthy gulp of Burgundy for a capital letter to start the new paragraph, and waded in as if they had been waiting for some such little snack to take the edge off their appetite. I noticed that the best the women could do was peck, particularly Lio, Lawrence Coyne's Chinese wife, and Dina Laszio. I also noticed that the greenjacket waiters were aware that they were looking on at a gastronomical World's Series, though they were trying not to show it. Before it was over those birds disposed of nine ducks. It looked to me as if Vukcic was overdoing it a little on the various brands of wine, and maybe that was why he was so quick on the trigger when Phillip Laszio began making remarks about duck stuffings which he regarded as superior to Mr. Richards' and proceeded from that to comments on the comparative discrimination of the clientele of the Hotel Churchill and Rusterman's Restaurant. I had come as Vukcic's guest, and anyway I liked him, and it was embarrassing to me when he hit Laszio square in the eye with a hunk of bread. The others seemed to resent it chiefly as an interruption, and Servan, next to Laszio, soothed him, and Vukcic glared at their remonstrances and drank more Burgundy, and a greenjacket retrieved the bread from the floor, and they went back to the duck.

The salad, by Domenico Rossi, was attended by something of an uproar. In the first place, Phillip Laszio left for the kitchen while it was being served and Rossi had feelings about that and continued to express them after Servan had explained that Laszio must attend to the preparation of the Sauce Printemps for the test that had been arranged. Rossi didn't stop his remarks about sons-in-law twice his age. Then he noticed that Pierre Mondor wasn't pretending to eat, and wanted to know if perchance he had discovered things crawling on the lettuce. Mondor replied, friendly but firm, that the juices necessary to impart a flavor to salads, especially vinegar, were notoriously bad companions for wine, and that he wished to finish his Burgundy.

Rossi said darkly, "There is no vinegar. I am not a barbarian."

"I have not tasted it. I smell salad juice, that is why I pushed it away."

"I tell you there is no vinegar! That salad is mostly by the good God, as He made things! Mustard sprouts, cress sprouts, lettuce! Onion juice with salt! Bread crusts rubbed with garlic! In Italy we eat it from bowls, with Chianti, and we thank God for it!"

Mondor shrugged. "In France we do not. France, as you well know, my dear Rossi, is supreme in these things. In what language—"

"Ha!" Rossi was on his hind legs. "Supreme because we taught you! Because in the sixteenth century you came and ate our food and copied us! Can you read? Do you know the history of gastronomy? Any history at all? Do you know that of all the good things in France, of which there are a certain number, the original is found in Italy? Do you know—"

I suppose that's how the war will start. On that occasion it petered out. They kept Mondor from firing up and got Rossi started on his own salad, and we had peace.

Coffee was served in the two parlors. Two, because Lawrence Coyne got stretched out on the divan in the small one again, and Keith and Leon Blanc sat by him and talked. I'm always more comfortable on my feet after a meal, and I wandered around. Back in the large parlor, Wolfe and Vukcic and Berin and Mondor were in a group in a corner, discussing the duck. Mamma Mondor came waddling in from the hall with a bag of knitting and got settled under a light. Lio Coyne was on a big chair with her feet tucked under her, listening to Vallenko tell her stories. Lisette Putti was filling Servan's coffee cup, and Rossi stood frowning at an Indian blanket thrown over a couch as if he suspected it was made in France.

I couldn't see Dina Laszio anywhere, and wondered idly whether she was off somewhere mixing poison or had merely gone to her room, which was in the left wing of Pocahontas, for some bicarbonate. Or maybe out in the kitchen helping her husband? I moseyed out there. In the dining room, as I went through, they were getting ready for the sauce test, with the chairs moved back to the walls, and the big screens in front of the serving tables, and a fresh cloth on the long table. I sidestepped a couple of greenjackets and proceeded. Dina wasn't in the kitchen. Half a dozen people in white aprons paid no attention to me, since in the past twelve hours they had got accustomed to the place being cluttered up with foreign matter. Laszio, also in an apron, was at the big range stirring and peering into a pan, with a shine at each elbow waiting for commands. The place smelled sort of unnecessary on account of what I still had in me, and I went out again and down the pantry hall and back to the parlor. Liqueurs were being passed, and I snared myself a stem of cognac and sought a seat and surveyed the scene.

It occurred to me that I hadn't noticed Constanza around. In a little while she came in, from the hall, ran her eyes over the room, and came and sat down beside me and crossed her knees flagrantly. I saw signs on her face, and leaned toward her to make sure.

"You've been crying."

She nodded. "Of course I have! There's a dance at the hotel, and Mr. Tolman asked me to go and my father won't let me! Even though we're in America! I've been in my room crying." She hitched her knee up a little. "Father doesn't like me to sit like this, that's why I'm doing it."

I grunted, "Leg-jealousy. Parental type."

"What?"

"Nothing. You might as well make yourself comfortable, he isn't looking at you. Can I get you some cognac?"

We whiled away a pleasant hour, punctuated by various movements and activities outside our little world. Dina Laszio came in from the hall, got herself a liqueur, stopped for a few words with Mamma Mondor, and then moved on to the little stool in front of the radio. She sipped the liqueur and monkeyed with the dials, but got nothing on it. In a minute or two Vukcic came striding across the room, pulled a chair up beside the stool, and sat down. Her smile at him, as he spoke to her, was very good, and I wondered if he was in any condition to see how good it was. Coyne and Keith and Blanc came in from the small parlor. Around ten o'clock we had a visitor—nothing less than Mr. Clay Ashley, the manager of Kanawha Spa. He was fifty, black-haired with no gray, polished inside and out; and had come to make a speech. He wanted us to know that Kanawha Spa felt itself deeply honored by this visit from the most distinguished living representatives of one of the greatest of the arts. He hoped we would enjoy and so forth. Servan indicated Nero Wolfe, the guest of honor, as the appropriate source of the reply, and for once Wolfe had to get up out of his chair without intending to go anywhere. He offered a few remarks, and thanks to Mr. Ashley, saying nothing about train rides and sausages, and Mr. Ashley went, after being presented to those he hadn't met.

It was then time for another little speech, this time by Louis Servan. He said everything was in readiness for the test and explained how it would be. On the dining table would be nine dishes of Sauce Printemps on warmers, each lacking one of the nine seasonings, also a server of squabs, and plates and other utensils. Each taster would slice his own bits of squab; it was not permitted to taste any sauce without squab. Water would be there to wash the palate. Only one taste from each dish was allowed. In front of each dish would be a number on a card, from 1 to 9. Each taster would be provided with a slip of paper on which the nine seasonings were listed, and after each seasoning he would write the number of the dish in which that was lacking. Laszio, who had prepared the sauce, would be in the dining room to preside. Those who had tasted were not to converse with those who had not tasted until all were finished. To avoid confusion the tasting would be done in this order—Servan read it from a slip:

> Mondor
> Coyne
> Keith
> Blanc
> Servan
> Berin
> Vukcic
> Vallenko
> Rossi
> Wolfe

Right away there was a little hitch. When the slips were passed out and it came to Leon Blanc, he shook his head. He told Servan apologetically but firmly, "No, Louis, I'm sorry. I have tried not to let my opinion of Phillip Laszio make discomfort for any of you, but under no circumstances will I eat anything prepared by him. He is...all of you know...but I'd better not say...."

He turned on his heel and beat it from the room, to the hall. The only thing that ruptured the silence was a long low growl from Jerome Berin, who had already accepted his slip.

Ramsey Keith said, "Too bad for him. Dear old Leon. We all know—but what the devil! Are you first, Pierre? I hope to God you miss all of 'em! Is everything ready in there, Louis?"

Mamma Mondor came trotting up to face her husband, holding her knitting against her tummy, and squeaked something at him in French. I asked Constanza what it was, and she said she told him if he made one mistake on such a simple thing there would be no forgiveness either by God or by her. Mondor patted her on the shoulder impatiently and reassuringly and trotted for the door to the dining room, closing it behind him. In ten minutes, maybe fifteen, the door opened again and he reappeared.

Keith, who had made the bet with Servan which had started it, approached Mondor and demanded, "Well?"

Mondor was frowning gravely. "We have been instructed not to discuss. I can say, I warned Laszio against an excess of salt and he ignored it. Even so, it will be utterly astounding if I have made a mistake."

Keith turned and roared across the room, "Lisette, my dearest niece! Give all of them cordials! Insist upon it! Seduce them!"

Servan, smiling, called to Coyne, "You next, Lawrence."

The old snowbank went. I could see it would be a long drawn out affair. Constanza had been called across to her father. I wondered what it would be like to dance with a swamp-woman, and went to where Dina Laszio still sat on the radio stool and Vukcic beside her, but got turned down. She gave me an indifferent glance from the long sleepy eyes and said she had a headache. That made me stubborn and I looked around for another partner, but it didn't look promising. Coyne's Chinese wife, Lio, wasn't there, though I hadn't noticed her leave the room. Lisette had taken Keith's command literally and was on a selling tour with a tray of cordials. I didn't care to tackle Mamma Mondor for fear Pierre would get jealous. As for Constanza—well, I thought of all the children at home, and then I considered her, with her eyes close to me and my arm around her and that faint fragrance which made it seem absolutely necessary to get closer so you could smell it better, and I decided it wouldn't be fair to my friend Tolman. I cast another disapproving glance at Vukcic as he sat glued to the chair alongside Dina Laszio, and went over and copped the big chair where Lio Coyne had been.

I'm pretty sure I didn't go to sleep, because I was conscious of the murmur of the voices all the time, but there's no question that my eyes were closed for a spell, and I was so comfortable otherwise that it annoyed me that I couldn't keep from worrying about how those guys could swallow the squabs and sauces less than three hours after the flock of ducks had gone down. It was the blare of the radio starting that woke me—I mean made me open my eyes. Dina Laszio was on her feet, leaning over twisting the dial, and Vukcic was standing waiting for her. She straightened up and melted into him and off they went. In a minute Keith and Lisette Putti were also dancing, and then Louis Servan with Constanza. I looked around. Jerome Berin wasn't there, so apparently they had got down to him on the tasting list. I covered a yawn, and stretched without putting my arms out, and arose and moseyed over to the corner where Nero Wolfe was talking with Pierre Mondor and Lawrence Coyne. There was an extra chair, and I took it.

Pretty soon Berin entered from the dining room and crossed the room to our corner. I saw Servan, without interrupting his dancing, make a sign to Vukcic that he was next, and Vukcic nodded back but showed no inclination to break his clinch with Dina. Berin was scowling. Coyne asked him:

"How about it, Jerome? We've both been in. Number 3 is shallots. No?"

Mondor protested, "Mr. Wolfe hasn't tried it yet. He goes last."

Berin growled, "I don't remember the numbers. Louis has my slip. God above, it was an effort I tell you, with that dog of a Laszio standing there smirking at me." He shook himself. "I ignored him. I didn't speak to him."

They talked. I listened with only one ear, because of a play

43

I was enjoying out front. Servan had highballed Vukcic twice more to remind him it was his turn to taste, without any result. I could see Dina smile into Vukcic's face, and I noticed that Mamma Mondor was also seeing it and was losing interest in her knitting. Finally Servan parted from Constanza, bowed to her, and approached the other couple. He was too polite and dignified to grab, so he just got in their way and they had to stop. They untwined.

Servan said, "Please. It is best to keep the order of the list. If you don't mind."

Apparently Vukcic was no longer lit, and anyway he wouldn't have been rude to Servan. With a toss of his head he shook his hair-tangle back, and laughed. "But I think I won't do it. I think I shall join the revolt of Leon Blanc." He had to speak loud on account of the radio.

"My dear Vukcic!" Servan was mild. "We are civilized people, are we not? We are not children."

Vukcic shrugged. Then he turned to his dancing partner. "Shall I do it, Dina?" Her eyes were up to him, and her lips moved, but in too low a voice for me to catch it. He shrugged again, and turned and headed for the dining room door and opened it and went in, with her watching his back. She went back to the stool by the radio, and Servan resumed with Constanza. Pretty soon, at eleven-thirty, there was a program change and the radio began telling about chewing gum, and Dina switched it off.

She asked, "Shall I try another station?"

Apparently they had had enough, so she left it dead. In our corner, Wolfe was leaning back with his eyes shut and Coyne was telling Berin about San Francisco Bay, when his Chinese wife entered from the hall, looked around and saw us and trotted over, and stuck her right forefinger into Coyne's face and told him to kiss it because she had got it caught in a door and it hurt.

He kissed it. "But I thought you were outside looking at the night."

"I was. But the door caught me. Look! It hurts."

He kissed the finger again. "My poor little blossom!" More kisses. "My flower of Asia! Now we're talking, run away and let us alone."

She went off pouting.

Vukcic entered from the dining room, and came straight

across to Dina Laszio. Servan told Vallenko he was next. Vukcic turned to him:

"Here's my slip. I tasted each dish once. That's the rule, eh? Laszio isn't there."

Servan's brows went up. "Not there? Where is he?"

Vukcic shrugged. "I didn't look for him. Perhaps in the kitchen."

Servan called to Keith: "Ramsey! Phillip has left his post! Only Vallenko and Rossi and Mr. Wolfe are left. What about it?"

Keith said he would trust them if Servan would, and Vallenko went in. In due time he was back, and it was Rossi's turn. Rossi hadn't been in a scrap for over three hours, and I pricked my ears in expectation of hearing through the closed door some hot remarks about sons-in-law, in case Laszio had got back on the job, but there was so much jabber in the parlor that I wouldn't have heard it anyway. When Rossi returned he announced to the gathering that no one but a fool would put as much salt as that in Sauce Printemps, but no one paid any attention to him. Nero Wolfe, last but not least, pried himself loose from his chair and, as the guest of honor, was conducted to the door by Louis Servan. I was darned glad that at last I could see bedtime peeping over the horizon.

In ten minutes the door opened and Wolfe reappeared. He stood on the threshold and spoke:

"Mr. Servan! Since I am the last, would you mind if I try an experiment with Mr. Goodwin?"

Servan said no, and Wolfe beckoned to me. I was already on my feet, because I knew something was up. There are various kinds of experiments that Wolfe might try with me as the subject, but none of them would be gastronomical. I crossed the parlor and followed him into the dining room, and he shut the door. I looked at the table. There were the nine dishes, with numbered cards in front of them, and a big electric server, covered, and a pitcher of water and glasses, and plates and forks and miscellany.

I grinned at Wolfe. "Glad to help you out. Which one did you get stuck on?"

He moved around the table. "Come here." He went on, to the right, to the edge of the big Pocahontas screen standing there, and I followed him. Behind the screen he stopped, and pointed at the floor. "Look at that confounded mess."

I stepped back a step, absolutely surprised. I had discounted all the loose talk about killing on account of its being dagoes, and whatever I might have thought about the swamp-woman's little story, at least it hadn't prepared me for blood. But there was the blood, though there wasn't much of it, because the knife was still sticking in the left middle of Phillip Laszio's back, with only the hilt showing. He was on his face, with his legs straight out, so that you might have thought he was asleep if it hadn't been for the knife. I moved across and bent over and twisted the head enough to get a good look at one eye. Then I got up and looked at Wolfe.

He said bitterly, "A pleasant holiday! I tell you, Archie—but no matter. Is he dead?"

"Dead as a sausage."

"I see. Archie. We have never been guilty of obstructing justice. That's the legal term, let them have it. But this is not our affair. And at least for the present—what do you remember about our trip down here?"

"I think I remember we came on a train. That's about as far as I could go."

He nodded. "Call Mr. Servan."

4

AT THREE O'CLOCK in the morning I sat in the small parlor of Pocahontas Pavilion. Across a table from me sat my friend Barry Tolman, and standing back of him was a big-jawed squint-eyed ruffian in a blue serge suit, with a stiff white collar, red tie and pink shirt. His name and occupation had not been kept a secret: Sam Pettigrew, sheriff of Marlin County. There were a couple of nondescripts, one with a stenographer's notebook at the end of the table, and a West Virginia state cop was on a chair tilted against the wall. The door to the dining room stood open and there was still a faint smell of photographers' flashlight bombs, and a murmur of voices came through from sleuths doing fingerprints and similar chores.

The blue-eyed athlete was trying not to sound irritated: "I know all that, Ashley. You may be the manager of Kanawha

Spa, but I'm the prosecuting attorney of this county, and what do you want me to do, pretend he fell on the damn knife by accident? I resent your insinuation that I'm making a grab for the limelight—"

"All right, Barry. Forget it." Clay Ashley, standing beside me, slowly shook his head. "Of all the rotten breaks! I know you can't suppress it, of course. But for God's sake get it over with and get 'em out of here—all right, I know you will as soon as you can. Excuse me if I said things. . . . I'm going to try to get some sleep. Have them call me if I can do anything."

He beat it. Someone came from the dining room to ask Pettigrew a question, and Tolman shook himself and rubbed his bloodshot eyes with his fingers. Then he looked at me:

"I sent for you again, Mr. Goodwin, to ask if you have thought of anything to add to what you told me before."

I shook my head. "I gave you the crop."

"You haven't remembered anything at all that happened, in the parlor or anywhere else, any peculiar conduct, any significant conversation?"

I said no.

"Anything during the day, for instance?"

"Nope. Day or night."

"When Wolfe called you secretly into the dining room and showed you Laszio's body behind the screen, what did he say to you?"

"He didn't call me secretly. Everybody heard him."

"Well, he called you alone. Why?"

I lifted the shoulders and let them drop. "You'll have to ask him."

"What did he say?"

"I've already told you. He asked me to see if Laszio was dead, and I saw he was, and he asked me to call Servan."

"Was that all he said?"

"I think he remarked something about it being a pleasant holiday. Sometimes he's sarcastic."

"He seems also to be cold-blooded. Was there any special reason for his being cold-blooded about Laszio?"

I put my foot down a little harder on the brake. Wolfe would never forgive me if by some thoughtless but relevant remark I got this buzzard really down on us. I knew why Wolfe had bothered to get me in the dining room alone and inquire about my memory before broadcasting the news: it had occurred to him that in a murder case a material witness may be required to furnish bond not to leave the state without permission, or to return to testify at the trial, and it was contrary to his idea of the good life to do either one. It wasn't easy to maintain outward respect for a guy who had been boob enough to fall for that ginger ale act in the club car, but while I had nothing at all against West Virginia I wasn't much more anxious to stay there or return there than Wolfe was.

I said, "Certainly not. He had never met Laszio before."

"Had anything happened during the day to make him—er, indifferent to Laszio's welfare?"

"Not that I know of."

"And had you or he knowledge of a previous attempt on Laszio's life?"

"You'll have to ask him. Me, no."

My friend Tolman forsook friendship for duty. He put an elbow on the table and pointed a finger at me and said in a nasty tone, "You're lying." I also noticed that the squint-eyed sheriff had a scowl on him not to be sneezed at, and the atmosphere of the whole room was unhealthy.

I put my brows up. "Me lying?"

"Yes, you. What did Mrs. Laszio tell you and Wolfe when she called at your suite yesterday afternoon?"

I hope I didn't gulp visibly. I know my brain gulped, but only once. No matter how he had found out, or how much, there was but one thing to do. I said, "She told us that her husband told her that he found arsenic in the sugar shaker and dumped it in the sink, and she wanted Wolfe to protect her husband. She also said that her husband had instructed her not to mention it to anyone."

"What else?"

"That's all."

"And you just told me that you had no knowledge of a previous attempt on Laszio's life. Didn't you?"

"I did."

"Well?" He stayed nasty.

I grinned at him. "Look, Mr. Tolman. I don't want to try to get smart with you, even if I knew how. But consider a few things. In the first place, without any offense—you're just a young fellow in your first term as a prosecutor—Nero Wolfe has solved more tough ones than you've even heard about. You know that, you know his reputation. Even if either of us

48

knew anything that would give you a trail, which we don't, it wouldn't pay you to waste time trying to squeeze juice out of us without our consent, because we're old hands. I'm not bragging, I'm just stating facts. For instance, about my knowing about an attempt to kill Laszio, I repeat I didn't. All I knew was that Mrs. Laszio told us that her husband told her that he found something in the sugar shaker besides sugar. How could he have been sure it was arsenic? Laszio wasn't poisoned, he was stabbed. In my experience—"

"I'm not interested in your experience." Still nasty. "I asked you if you remember anything that might have any significance regarding this murder. Do you?"

"I've told you what Mrs. Laszio told us—"

"So has she. Pass that for the moment. Anything else?"

"No."

"You're sure?"

"Yes."

Tolman told the state cop, "Bring Odell in."

It came to me. So that was it. A fine bunch of friends I had made since entering the dear old Panhandle State—which nickname I had learned from my pal Gershom Odell, house dick of Kanawha Spa. My brain was gulping again, and this time I wasn't sure whether it would get it down or not. The process was interrupted by the entry of my pal, ushered in by the cop. I turned a stare on him which he did not meet. He came and stood near me at the table, so close I could have smacked him one without getting up.

Tolman said, "Odell, what was it this man told you yesterday afternoon?"

The house dick didn't look at me. He sounded gruff. "He told me Phillip Laszio was going to be killed by somebody, and when I asked him who was going to do it he said they were going to take turns."

"What else?"

"That's all he said."

Tolman turned to me, but I beat the gun. I gave Odell a dig in the ribs that made him jump. "Oh, that's it!" I laughed. "I remember now, when we were out by the bridle path throwing stones, and you pointed out that ledge to me and told me—sure! Apparently you didn't tell Mr. Tolman *everything* we said, since he thinks—Did you tell him how I was talking about those dago and polack cooks, and how they're so jealous of each other they're apt to begin killing each other off any time, and how Laszio was the highest paid of the bunch, sixty thousand bucks a year, so they would be sure to pick on him first, and how they would take turns killing him first and then begin on the next one—and then I remember you began telling me about the ledge and how it happened you could leave the hotel at that time of day—" I turned to Tolman. "That's all that was, just a couple of guys talking to pass the time. You're welcome to any significance you can find in it. If I told you what Odell told me about that ledge—" I laughed and poked my pal in the ribs again.

Tolman was frowning, but not at me. "What about it, Odell? That's not the way you told it. What about it?"

I had to hand it to Odell for a good poker face, at that. He was the picture of a Supreme Court justice pretending that he had no personal interest in the matter. Still he didn't glance at me, but he looked Tolman quietly in the eye. "I guess my tongue kinda ran away with me. I guess it was about like he says, just shootin' off. But of course I remembered the name, Phillip Laszio, and any detective would jump at a chance to have a hot one on a murder. . . ."

The squint-eyed ruffian spoke, in a thin mild drawl that startled me. "You sound pretty inaccurate to me, Odell. Maybe you ought to do less guessin'?"

Tolman demanded, "Did he or did he not tell you Laszio was going to be killed?"

"Well . . . the way he just said it, yes. I mean about them all being jealous dagoes, and Laszio getting sixty thousand—I'm sure he said that. I guess that's all there was to it."

"What about it, Goodwin? Why did you pick on Laszio?"

I showed a palm. "I didn't pick on him. I happened to mention him because I knew he was the tops—in salary, anyhow. I had just read an article—want to see it?"

The sheriff drawled, "We're wastin' time. Get the hell out of here, Odell."

My pal, without favoring me with a glance, turned and made for the door. Tolman called to the cop:

"Bring Wolfe in."

I sat tight. Except for the little snags that had threatened to trip me up, I was enjoying myself. I was wondering what Inspector Cramer of the New York Homicide Squad would say if he could see Nero Wolfe letting himself be called in for a grilling by small town snoops at half-past three in the morning, because he didn't want to offend a prosecuting attorney! He hadn't been up as late as that since the night Clara Fox slept in his house in my pajamas. Then I thought I might as well offer what help I could, and got up and brought a big armchair from the other end of the room and put it in position near the table.

The cop returned, with my boss. Tolman asked the cop who was left out there, and the cop said, "That Vookshish or whatever it is, and Berin and his daughter. They tried to shoo her off to bed, but she wouldn't go. She keeps making passes to come in here."

Tolman was chewing his lip, and I kept one sardonic eye on him while I used the other one to watch Nero Wolfe getting himself into the chair I had placed. Finally Tolman said, "Send them to their rooms. We might as well knock off until morning. All right, Pettigrew?"

"Sure. Bank it up and sleep on it." He squinted at the cop. "Tell Plank to wait out there until we see what arrangements he's made. This is no time of night for anyone to be taking a walk."

The cop departed. Tolman rubbed his eyes, then, chewing at his lip again, leaned back and looked at Wolfe. Wolfe seemed placid enough, but I saw his forefinger tapping on the arm of his chair and knew what a fire was raging inside of him. He offered as a bit of information, "It's nearly four o'clock, Mr. Tolman."

"Thanks." Tolman sounded peevish. "We won't keep you long. I sent for you again because one or two things have come up." I observed that he and the sheriff both had me in the corner of their eyes, and I'd have sworn they were putting over a fast one and trying to catch me passing some kind of a sign to Wolfe. I let myself look sleepy, which wasn't hard.

Wolfe said, "More than one or two, I imagine. For instance, I suppose Mrs. Laszio has repeated to you the story she told me yesterday afternoon. Hasn't she?"

"What story was that?"

"Come now, Mr. Tolman." Wolfe stopped tapping with the finger and wiggled it at him. "Don't be circuitous with me. She was in here with you over half an hour, she must have told you that story. I figured she would. That was why I didn't mention it; it seemed preferable that you should get it fresh from her."

"What do you mean, you figured she would?"

"Only an assumption." Wolfe was mild and inoffensive. "After all, she is a participant in this tragedy, while I am merely a bystander—"

"Participant?" Tolman was frowning. "Do you mean she had a hand in it? You didn't say that before."

"Nor do I say it now. I merely mean, it was her husband who was murdered, and she seems to have had, if not premonition, at least apprehension. You know more about it than I do, since you have questioned her. She informed you, I presume, that her husband told her that at noon yesterday, in the kitchen of this place, he found arsenic in a sugar shaker which was intended for him; and that without her husband's knowledge or consent she came to ask my assistance in guarding him from injury and I refused it."

"Why did you refuse it?"

"Because of my incompetence for the task. As I told her, I am not a food taster or a body guard." Wolfe stirred a little; he was boiling. "May I offer advice, Mr. Tolman? Don't waste your energy on me. I haven't the faintest idea who killed Mr. Laszio, or why. It may be that you have heard of me; I don't know; if so, you have perhaps got the impression that when I am engaged on a case I am capable of sinuosities, though you wouldn't think it to look at me. But I am not engaged on this case, I haven't the slightest interest in it, I know nothing whatever about it, and you are as apt to receive pertinent information from the man in the moon as you are from me. My connection with it is threefold. First, I happened to be here; that is merely my personal misfortune. Second, I discovered Mr. Laszio's body; as I told you, I was curious as to whether he was childishly keeping secret surveillance over the table, and I looked behind the screen. Third, Mrs. Laszio told me someone was trying to poison her husband and asked me to prevent it; you have that fact; if there is a place for that piece in your puzzle, fit it in. You have, gentlemen, my sympathy and my best wishes."

Tolman, who after all wasn't much more than a kid, twisted his head to get a look at the sheriff, who was slowly scratching his cheek with his middle finger. Pettigrew looked back at him and finally turned to Wolfe:

"Look, mister, you've got us wrong I think. We're not aiming to make you any trouble or any inconvenience. We don't regard you as one of that bunch that if they knew anything they wouldn't tell us if they could help it. But you say maybe we've heard of you. That's right. We've heard of you. After all, you was around with this bunch all day talking with 'em. You know? I don't know what Tolman here thinks, but it's my opinion it wouldn't hurt any to tell you what we've found out and get your slant on it. Since you say you've got no interest in it that might conflict. All right, Barry?"

Wolfe said, "You'd be wasting your time. I'm not a wizard. When I get results, I get them by hard work, and this isn't my case and I'm not working on it."

I covered a grin. Tolman put in, "The sooner this thing is cleaned up, the better for everybody. You realize that. If the sheriff—"

Wolfe said brusquely, "Very well. To-morrow."

"It's already to-morrow. God knows how late you'll sleep in the morning, but I won't. There's one thing in particular I want to ask you. You told me that the only one of these people you know at all well is Vukcic. Mrs. Laszio told me about her being married to Vukcic and getting divorced from him some years ago to marry Laszio. Could you tell me how Vukcic has been feeling about that?"

"No. Mrs. Laszio seems to have been quite informative."

"Well, it was her husband that got killed. Why? Have you got anything against her? That's the second dig you've taken at her."

"Certainly I have something against her. I don't like women asking me to protect their husbands. It is beneath the dignity of a man to rely, either for safety or salvation, on the interference of a woman. Pfui!"

Of course Wolfe wasn't in love. I hoped Tolman realized that. He said:

"I asked you that question, obviously, because Vukcic was one of the two who had the best opportunity to kill him. Most of them are apparently out of it, by your own testimony among others." He glanced at one of the papers on the table. "The ones who were in the parlor all the time, according to present information, are Mrs. Laszio, Mrs. Mondor, Lisette Putti and Goodwin. Servan says that when he went to the dining room to taste those sauces Laszio was there alive and nothing wrong, and at that time Mondor, Coyne and Keith had already been in, and it is agreed that none of them left the parlor again. They too are apparently out of it. The next two were Berin and Vukcic. Berin says that when he left the dining room Laszio was still there and still nothing wrong,

53

and Vukcic says that when he entered, some eight or ten minutes later on account of a delay, Laszio was gone and he saw nothing of him and noticed nothing wrong. The three who went last, Vallenko and Rossi and you, are also apparently out of it, but not as conclusively as the others, since it is quite possible that Laszio had merely stepped out to the terrace or gone to the toilet, and returned after Vukcic left the dining room. According to the cooks, he had not appeared in the kitchen, so he had not gone there."

Tolman glanced at the paper again. "That makes two probabilities, Berin and Vukcic, and three possibilities, Vallenko and Rossi and you. Besides that, there are three other possibilities. Someone could easily have entered the dining room from the terrace at any time; the glass doors were closed and the shades drawn, but they were not locked. And there were three people who could have done that: Leon Blanc, who refused to take part on account of animosity toward Laszio and was absent; Mrs. Coyne, who was outdoors alone for nearly an hour, including the interval between Berin's visit to the dining room and that of Vukcic; and Miss Berin. Blanc claims he went to his room and didn't leave it, and the hall attendants didn't see him go out, but there is a door to the little side terrace at the end of the left wing corridor which he could have used without observation. Mrs. Coyne says she was on the paths and lawns throughout her absence, was not on the dining room terrace, and re-entered by the main entrance and went straight to the parlor. As for Miss Berin, she returned to the parlor, from the room, before the tasting of the sauces began, and did not again leave; I mentioned her absence only to have the record complete."

I thought to myself, you cold-blooded hound! She was in her room crying for you, that was her absence, and you make it just part of a list!

"You were there, Mr. Wolfe. That covers it, doesn't it?"

Wolfe grunted. Tolman resumed, "As for motive, with some of them there was enough. With Vukcic, the fact that Laszio had taken his wife. And immediately preceding Vukcic's trip to the dining room he had been talking with Mrs. Laszio and gazing at her and dancing with her—"

Wolfe said sharply, "A woman told you that."

"By God," the sheriff drawled, "you seem to resent the few little things we have found out. I thought you said you weren't interested."

"Vukcic is my friend. I'm interested in him. I'm not interested in this murder, with which he had no connection."

"Maybe not." Tolman looked pleased, I suppose because he had got a rise out of Nero Wolfe. "Anyway, my talk with Mrs. Mondor was my first chance to make official use of my French. Next there is Berin. I got this not from Mrs. Mondor, but from him. He declares that Laszio should have been killed long before now, that he himself would have liked to do it, and that if he has any opportunity to protect the murderer he will do so."

Wolfe murmured, "Berin talks."

"I'll say he does. So does that little Frenchman Leon Blanc, but not the same style. He admits that he hated Laszio because he cheated him out of his job at the Hotel Churchill some years ago, but he says he wouldn't murder anybody for anything. He says that it does not even please him that Laszio is dead, because death doth not heal, it amputates. Those were his words. He's soft-spoken and he certainly doesn't seem aggressive enough to stab a man through the heart, but he's no fool and possibly he's smooth.

"There's the two probabilities and one possibility with motives. Of the four other possibilities, I guess you didn't do it. If Rossi or Vallenko had any feelings that might have gone as far as murder, I haven't learned it yet. As for Mrs. Coyne, she never saw Laszio before, and I can't discover that she has spoken to him once. So until further notice we have Berin and Vukcic and Blanc. Any of them could have done it, and I think one of them did. What do you think?"

Wolfe shook his head. "Thank heaven, it isn't my problem, and I don't have to think."

Pettigrew put in, in his mild drawl, "Do you suppose there's any chance you suspect your friend Vukcic did it and so you'd rather not think about it?"

"Chance? Certainly. Remote. If Vukcic did it, I hope with all my heart he left no rope for you to hang him by. And as for information regarding it, I have none, and if I had I wouldn't reveal it."

Tolman nodded. "That's frank, but not very helpful. I don't have to point out to you that if you're interested in your friend Vukcic and think he didn't do it, the quickest way to clear him is to find out who did. You were right there on the spot; you saw everyone and heard everything that was said. It seems to me that under those circumstances a man of your reputation and ability should find it possible to offer some help. If you don't it's bound to put more suspicion on your friend Vukcic, isn't it?"

"I don't know. Your suspicions are your affair; I can't regulate them. Confound it, it's four o'clock in the morning!" Wolfe sighed. Then he compressed his lips. He sat that way, and finally muttered, "Very well, I'll help for ten minutes. Tell me about the routine—the knife, fingerprints, anything found—"

"Nothing. There were two knives on the table for slicing the squab, and it was one of them. You saw for yourself there was not the slightest sign of a struggle. Nothing anywhere. No prints that seem to mean anything; those on the knife handle were all smudged. The levers on the door to the terrace are rough wrought iron. Men are still in there working it over, but that angle looks hopeless."

Wolfe grunted. "You've omitted possibilities. The cooks and waiters?"

"They've all been questioned by the sheriff, who knows how to deal with niggers. None of them went to the dining room, and they didn't see or hear anything. Laszio had told them he would ring if anything was wanted."

"Someone could have gone from the large parlor to the small one and from there entered the dining room and killed him. You should establish beyond doubt the presence of everyone in the large parlor, especially during the interim between Berin's leaving the dining room and Vukcic's entering it, which, as you say, was some eight or ten minutes."

"I have done so. Of course, I covered everybody pretty fast."

"Then cover them again. Another possibility: someone could have been concealed behind either of the screens and struck from there when the opportunity offered."

"Yeah? Who?"

"I'm sure I couldn't say." Wolfe frowned. "I may as well tell you, Mr. Tolman, I am extremely skeptical regarding your two chief suspects, Mr. Berin and Mr. Vukcic. That is putting it with restraint. As for Mr. Blanc, I am without an opinion; as you have pointed out, he could unquestionably have left his room, made an exit at the end of the left wing corridor, circled the building, entered by the dining room terrace, achieved his purpose, and returned the way he had come. In that case, might he not have been seen by Mrs. Coyne, who was outdoors at the time, looking at the night?"

Tolman shook his head. "She says not. She was at the front and the side both. She was no one but a nigger in uniform, and stopped him and asked him what the sound of a whippoorwill was. We've found him—one of the boys from the spring on his way to Mingo Pavilion."

"So. As for Berin and Vukcic, if I were you I would pigeonhole them for the present. Or at least—I offer a suggestion: get the slips, the tasting reports, from Mr. Servan—"

"I have them."

"Good. Compare them with the correct list, which you also got from Mr. Servan no doubt—"

"He didn't have it. It was in Laszio's pocket."

"Very well. Compare each list with it, and see how nearly each taster was correct."

Sheriff Pettigrew snorted. Tolman asked dryly, "You call that being helpful, do you?"

"I do. I am already—by the way!" Wolfe straightened a little. "If you have the correct list there—the one you took from Laszio's pocket—do you mind if I look at it a moment?"

Tolman, with his brows up, shuffled through the papers before him, extracted one, handed it to me, and I passed it to Wolfe. Wolfe looked at it with his forehead wrinkled, and exclaimed, "Good God!" He looked at it again, and turning to me, shaking the paper in his hand. "Archie. Coyne was right! Number 3 was shallots!"

Tolman asked sarcastically, "Comedy relief? Much obliged for *that* help."

I grinned at him. "Comedy hell, he won't sleep for a week, he guessed wrong."

Wolfe reproved me: "It was not a guess. It was a deliberate conclusion, and it was wrong." He handed me the paper. "Pardon me, Mr. Tolman, I've had a blow. Actually. I wouldn't expect you to appreciate it. As I was saying, I am already more than skeptical regarding Berin and Vukcic. I have known Mr. Vukcic all my life. I can conceive of his stabbing a man, under hypothetical conditions, but I am sure that if he did you wouldn't find the knife in the man's back. I don't know Mr. Berin well, but I saw him at close range and heard him speak less than a minute after he left the dining room last night, and I would stake something that he wasn't fresh from the commission of a cowardly murder. He had but a moment before sunk a knife in Mr. Laszio's back, and I detected no residue of that experience in his posture, his hands, his eyes, his voice? I don't believe it."

"And about comparing these lists—"

"I'm coming to that. I take it that Mr. Servan has described the nature of that test to you—each sauce lacking one or another of the seasonings. We were permitted but one taste from each dish—only one! Have you any conception of the delicacy and sensitivity required? It took the highest degree of concentration and receptivity of stimuli. To detect a single false note in one of the wood winds in a symphonic passage by full orchestra would be the same. So, compare those lists. If you find that Berin and Vukcic were substantially correct— say seven or eight out of nine—they are eliminated. Even six. No man about to kill another, or just having done so, could possibly control his nervous system sufficiently to perform such a feat. I assure you this is not comedy."

Tolman nodded. "All right, I'll compare them."

"It would be instructive to do so now."

"I'll attend to it. Any other suggestions?"

"No." Wolfe got his hands on the chair arms, pulled his feet back, braced, and arose. "The ten minutes are up." He did his little bow. "I offer you again, gentlemen, my sympathy and best wishes."

The sheriff said, "I understand you're sleepin' in Upshur. Of course you realize you're free to go anywhere you want to around the grounds here."

"Thank you, sir." Wolfe sounded bitter. "Come, Archie."

Not to crowd the path, I let him precede me among the greenery back to Upshur Pavilion. We didn't go through darkness, but through the twilight of dawn, and there were so many birds singing you couldn't help noticing it. In the main hall of the pavilion the lights were turned on, and a couple of state cops were sitting there. Wolfe passed them without a glance.

I went to his room with him to make sure that everything was jake. The bed had been turned down, and the colored rugs and things made it bright and pleasant, and the room was big and classy enough to make it worth at least half of the twenty bucks a day they charged for it, but Wolfe frowned around as if it had been a pigpen.

I inquired, "Can I help on the disrobing?"

"No."

"Shall I bring a pitcher of water from the bathroom?"

"I can walk. Goodnight."

"Goodnight, boss." I went.

His voice halted me at the door. "Archie. This Mr. Laszio seems to have had unpleasant characteristics. Do you suppose there is any chance he deliberately made that list incorrect, to disconcert his colleagues—and me?"

"Huh-uh. Not the faintest. Professional ethics, you know. Of course I'm sorry you got so many wrong—"

"Two! Shallots and chives! Leave me! Get out!"

He sure was one happy detective that night.

5

AT TWO O'CLOCK the next day, Wednesday, I was feeling pretty screwy and dissatisfied with life, but in one way completely at home. Getting to bed too late, or having my sleep disturbed unduly, poisons my system, and I had had both to contend with. Having neglected to hang up a notice, a damn fool servant had got me to the door of our suite at nine o'clock to ask if we wanted baths drawn or any other little service, and I had told him to return at sundown. At ten-thirty the phone woke me; my friend Barry Tolman wanted to speak to Wolfe. I explained that Wolfe's first exposure to the light of day would have to be on his own initiative, and told the operator no more calls until further notice. In spite of that, an hour later the phone rang again and kept on ringing. It was Tolman, and he just had to speak to Wolfe. I told him absolutely nothing doing, without a search and seizure warrant, until Wolfe had announced himself as conscious. But that time I was roused enough to become aware of other necessities besides sleep, so I bathed and shaved and dressed and phoned Room Service for some breakfast, since I couldn't go and get it under the circumstances. I had finished the third cup of coffee when I heard Wolfe yelling for me. He was certainly getting demoralized. At home in New York, I hadn't heard him yell more than three times in ten years.

He gave me his breakfast order, which I phoned, and then issued the instructions which made me feel at home. It was his intention to confine his social contacts for that afternoon exclusively to me. Business and professional contacts were out. The door was to be kept locked, and any caller, unless it should happen to be Marko Vukcic, was to be told that Wolfe was immersed in something, no matter what. Telephone calls were to be handled by me, since he knew nothing that I didn't know. (This jarred my aplomb, since it was the first time he had ever admitted it.) Should I feel the need of more fresh air than was obtainable through open windows, which was idiotic but probable, the DO NOT DISTURB card was to be hung on the door and the key kept in my pocket.

I phoned for whatever morning papers were available, and when they came passed a couple to Wolfe and made myself comfortable on a couch with the remainder. Those from New York and Pittsburgh and Washington, being early train editions, had no mention of the Laszio murder, but there were big headlines and a short piece in the Charleston *Journal*, which had only sixty miles to come.

But before the day was out Wolfe's arrangements for peaceful privacy got shot full of holes. The first and least important of the upsets came before he had finished with the newspapers when, around two o'clock, there were sounds at the outer door and I went and opened it a discreet twelve inches to find myself confronted by two gentlemen who did not look local and whom I had never seen before. One was shorter than me and somewhat older, dark-skinned, wiry and compact, in a neat gray herringbone with padded shoulders and cut-in waist; the other, medium both in age and size, wore his hairline well above his temples and had small gray eyes that looked as if nobody would ever have to irritate him again because he was already irritated for good. But he spoke and listened politely as he asked me if that was Mr. Nero Wolfe's suite and I informed him it was, and announced that he was Mr. Liggett and the padded specimen was Mr. Malfi, and he would like to see Wolfe. I explained that Wolfe was immersed, and he looked impatient and dug an envelope from his pocket and handed it to me. I apologized for shutting them in the hall before I did so, and returned to the pigpen.

"Two male strangers, vanilla and caramel. To see you."

Wolfe's eyes didn't leave his newspapers. "If either of them was Mr. Vukcic, I presume you would have recognized him."

"Not Vukcic, no, but you didn't prohibit letters, and he handed me one."

"Read it."

I took it from the envelope, saw that it was on engraved stationery, and wired it for sound:

New York
April 7, 1937

Dear Mr. Wolfe:

This will introduce my friend Mr. Raymond Liggett, manager and part owner of the Hotel Churchill. He wants to ask your advice or assistance, and has requested this note from me.

I hope you're enjoying yourself down there. Don't eat too much, and don't forget to come back to make life in New York pleasanter for us.

Yours

BURKE WILLIAMSON

Wolfe grunted. "You said April 7th? That's today."

"Yeah, they must have flown. Formerly a figure of speech, now listed under common carriers. Do we let them in?"

"Confound it." Wolfe let the paper down. "Courtesy is one's own affair, but decency is a debt to life. You remember that Mr. Williamson was kind enough to let us use the grounds of his estate for the ambush and robbery of Miss Anna Fiore." He sighed. "Show them in."

I went and got them, pronounced names around, and placed chairs. Wolfe greeted them, made his customary statement regarding his tendency to stay seated, and then glanced a second time at the padded one.

"Did I catch your name, sir? Malfi? Perhaps, Albert Malfi?"

The wiry one's black eyes darted at him. "That's right. I don't know how you knew the Albert."

Wolfe nodded. "Formerly Alberto. I met Mr. Berin on the train coming down here, and he told me about you. He says you are an excellent entrée man, and it is always a pleasure to meet an artist and a sound workman."

Liggett put in, "Oh, you were with Berin on the train?"

"I was." Wolfe grimaced. "We shared that ordeal. Mr. Williamson says you wish to ask me something."

"Yes. Of course you know why we came. This—Laszio. It's terrible. You were right there, weren't you? You found the body."

"I did. You wasted no time, Mr. Liggett."

"I know damn well I didn't. I usually turn in late and get up late, but this morning Malfi had me on the telephone before eight o'clock. Reporters had been after me earlier, but of course didn't get through. The city editions had the story. I knew Williamson was a friend of yours, and sent to him for that note, and hired a plane from Newark. Malfi insisted on coming along, and I'm afraid one of your jobs will be to watch him as soon as they find out who did it." Liggett showed a thin smile. "He's a Corsican, and while Laszio wasn't any relation of his, he's got pretty devoted to him. Haven't you, Malfi?"

The padded one nodded emphatically. "I have. Phillip Laszio was a mean man and a great man. He was not mean to me." He spread both palms at Wolfe. "But of course Mr. Liggett is only joking. The world thinks all Corsicans stab people. That is a wrong idea and a bad one."

"But you wanted to ask me something, Mr. Liggett?" Wolfe sounded impatient. "You said one of my jobs. I have no jobs."

"I'm hoping you will have. First, to find out who killed Laszio. Judging from the account in the papers, it looks as if it will be too tough for a West Virginia sheriff. It seems likely that whoever did it was able to use finesse for other purposes than tasting the seasonings in Sauce Printemps. I can't say I was devoted to Laszio in the sense that Malfi here was, but after all he was the chef of my hotel, and I understand he had no family except his wife, and I thought—it's an obligation. It was a damned cowardly murder, a stab in the back. He ought to be caught, and I suspect it will take you to do it. That's what I came for. Knowing your—er, peculiarities, I took the precaution of getting that note from Williamson."

"It's too bad." Wolfe sighed. "I mean too bad you came. You could have telephoned from New York."

"I asked Williamson what he thought about that, and he said if I really wanted your services I'd better come and get them."

"Indeed. I don't know why Mr. Williamson should assume difficulties. My services are on the market. Of course, in this particular instance they are unfortunately not available; that's why I say it's too bad you came."

"Why not available?"

"Because of the conditions."

"Conditions?" The irritation in Liggett's eyes became more intense. "I've made no conditions."

"Not you. Space. Geography. Should I undertake to discover Mr. Laszio's murderer, I would see it through. That might take a day, a week, with bad luck a fortnight. I intend to board a train for New York tomorrow night." Wolfe winced.

"Williamson warned me." Liggett compressed his lips. "But good Lord, man! It's your business! It's your—"

"I beg you, sir. Don't. I won't listen. If I offend by being curt, very well. Anyone has the privilege of offending who is willing to bear the odium. I will consider no engagement that might detain me in this parasitic outpost beyond to-morrow night. You said 'jobs.' Is there anything else you wish to discuss?"

"There was." Liggett looked as if he would prefer to continue the discussion with shrapnel or a machine gun. He sat and stared at Wolfe a while, then finally shrugged it off. He said, "The fact is, the main job is something quite different. The main thing I came down here for. Laszio is dead, and the way he died was terrible, and as a man I have, I hope, the proper feelings about it, but in addition to being a man I'm a business man, and the Hotel Churchill is left without a chef de cuisine. You know the Churchill's world-wide reputation, and it has to be maintained. I want to get Jerome Berin."

Wolfe's brows went up. "I don't blame you."

"Of course you don't. There are a few others as good as Berin, but they're out. Mondor wouldn't leave his Paris restaurant. Servan and Tassone are too old. I wouldn't mind having Leon Blanc back, but he is also too old. Vukcic is tied up at Rusterman's, and so on. I happen to know that Berin has received five offers from this country, two of them from New York, in the past two years, and has turned them all down. I'd like to have him. In fact, he's the only one that I consider both available and desirable. If I can't get him, Malfi can put a blue ribbon on his cap." He turned to his companion. "Is that in accord with our agreement, Albert? When you got that offer from Chicago a year ago, I told you that if you would stick, and the position of chef de cuisine at the

Churchill should become vacant, I would first try to get Berin, and if I couldn't, you could have it. Right?"

Malfi nodded. "That was the understanding."

Wolfe murmured, "This is all very interesting. But you were speaking of a job—"

"Yes. I want you to approach Berin for me. He's one of the best seven chefs in the world, but he's hard to handle. Last Saturday he deliberately spilled two plates of sausage in the middle of the carpet in my Resort Room. Williamson says you have remarkable ability as a negotiator, and you are the guest of honor here and Berin will listen to you with respect, and I believe unquestionably you can swing him. I would offer him forty thousand, but I tell you frankly I am willing to go to sixty, and your commission—"

Wolfe was showing him a palm. "Please, Mr. Liggett. It's no go. Absolutely out of the question."

"You mean you won't do it?"

"I mean I wouldn't undertake to persuade Mr. Berin to do anything whatever. I would as soon try to persuade a giraffe. I could elaborate—but I can't see that I owe you that."

"You won't even attempt it?"

"I will not. The truth is, you have come to me at the most inauspicious moment in the past twenty years, and with proposals much more likely to vex me than to interest me. I don't care a hang who your new chef will be, and while I always like to make money, that can wait until I am back in my office. There are others here better qualified to approach Mr. Berin for you than I am—Mr. Servan or Mr. Coyne, for instance, old friends of his."

"They're chefs themselves. I don't want that. You're the man to do it for me. . . ."

He was a persistent cuss, but it didn't get him anywhere. When he tried to insist Wolfe merely got curter, as he naturally would, and finally Liggett realized he was calling the wrong dog and gave it up. He popped up out of his chair, snapped at Malfi to come along, and without any ceremony showed Wolfe his back. Malfi trotted behind, and I followed them to the hall to see that the door was locked after them.

When I got back to the room, Wolfe was already behind his paper again. I felt muscle-bound and not inclined to settle down, so I said to him, "You know, Werowance, that's not a bad idea—"

A word he didn't know invariably got him. The paper went

down to the level of his nose. "What the devil is that? Did you make it up?"

"I did not. I got it from a piece in the Charleston *Journal*. Werowance is a term that was used for an Indian Chief in Virginia and Maryland. I'm going to call you Werowance instead of Boss as long as we're in this part of the country. As I was saying, Werowance, it might be a good idea to start an employment bureau for chefs and waiters, maybe later branch out into domestic help generally. You are aware, I suppose, that you have just turned down a darned good offer for a case. That Liggett has really got it in quantities. I suspect he may be half bright too; for instance, do you imagine he might have come to see you in order to let Alberto know indirectly that if he tried sticking something into Berin in order to make Berin ineligible for the Churchill job, it would have deplorable consequences? Which opens up a train of thought that might solve the unemployment question. If a job becomes vacant and you want it, first you kill all the other candidates and then—"

The paper was up again, so I knew I had made myself sufficiently obnoxious. I said, "I'm going out and wade in the brook, and maybe go to the hotel and ruin a few girls. See you later."

I got my hat, hung up the DO NOT DISTURB, and wandered out, noting that there was a greenjacket at the door of the main hall but no cop. Apparently vigilance was relaxed. I turned my nose to the hotel, just to see what there was to see, and it wasn't long before I regretted that, for if I hadn't gone to the hotel first I would have got to see the whole show that my friend Tolman was putting on, instead of arriving barely in time for the final curtain. As it was, I found various sights around the hotel entrance and lobby that served for mild diversion, including an intelligent-looking horse stepping on a fat dowager's foot so hard they had to carry her away, and it was around 3:30 when I decided to make an excursion to Pocahontas Pavilion and thank Vukcic, my host, for the good time I was having. In a secluded part of the path a guy with his necktie over his shoulder and needing a shave jumped out from behind a bush and grabbed my elbow, talking as he came: "Hey, you're Archie Goodwin, aren't you, Nero Wolfe's man? Listen, brother—"

I shook him off and told him, "Damn it, quit scaring people. I'll hold a press conference tomorrow morning in my study. I don't know a thing, and if I did and told you I'd get killed by my werowance. Do you know what a werowance is?"

He told me to go to hell and started looking for another bush.

The tableau at Pocahontas Pavilion was in two sections when I got there. The first section, not counting the pair of troopers standing outside the entrance, was in the main hall. The greenjacket who opened the door for me was looking popeyed in another direction as he pulled it open. The door to the large parlor was closed. Standing with her back against the right wall, with her arms folded tight against her and her chin up, and her dark purple eyes flashing at the guys who hemmed her in, was Constanza Berin. The hemmers were two state cops in uniform and a hefty bird in cits with a badge on his vest, and while they weren't actually touching her at the moment I entered, it looked as though they probably had been. She didn't appear to see me. A glance showed me that the door to the small parlor was open, and a voice was coming through. As I started for it one of the cops called a sharp command to me, but it seemed likely he was too occupied to interfere in person, so I ignored it and went on.

There were cops in the small parlor too, and the squint-eyed sheriff, and Tolman. Between two of the cops stood Jerome Berin, with handcuffs on his wrists. I was surprised that under the circumstances Berin wasn't breaking furniture or even skulls, but all he was doing was glaring and breathing. Tolman was telling him:

".... We appreciate that you're a foreign visitor and a stranger here, and we'll show you every consideration. In this country a man charged with murder can't get bail. Your friends will of course arrange for counsel for you. I have not only told you that anything you say may be used against you, I have advised you to say nothing until you have consulted with counsel.—Go on, boys. Take him by the back path to the sheriff's car."

But they didn't get started right then. Yells and other sounds came suddenly from the main hall, and Constanza Berin came through the door like a tornado with the cops behind. One in the parlor tried to grab her as she went by, but he might as well have tried to stop the great blizzard. I thought she was going right on over the table to get at Tolman, but she stopped there and turned with her eyes

66

blazing at the cops, and then wheeled to Tolman and yelled at him, "You fool! You pig of a fool! He's my father! Would he kill a man in the back?" She pounded the table with fists. "Let him go! Let him go, you fool!"

A cop made a pass at her arm. Berin growled and took a step, and the two held him. Tolman looked as if the one thing he could use to advantage would be a trap door. Constanza had jerked away from the cop, and Berin said something to her, low and quiet, in Italian. She walked to him, three steps, and he went to lift a hand and couldn't on account of the bracelets, and then stooped and kissed her on top of the head. She turned and stood still for ten seconds, giving Tolman a look which I couldn't see, but which probably made a trap door all the more desirable, and then turned again and walked out of the room.

Tolman couldn't speak. At least he didn't. Sheriff Pettigrew shook himself and said, "Come on, boys, I'll go along."

I shoved off without waiting for their exit. Constanza wasn't in the main hall. I halted there for an instant, thinking I might explore the large parlor in search of persons who might add to my information, and then decided that I had better first deposit what I had. So I went on out and hot-footed it back to Upshur.

Wolfe had finished with the papers and piled them neatly on the dresser, and was in the big chair, not quite big enough for him, with a book. He didn't look up as I went in, which meant that for the time being my existence was strictly my own affair. I adopted the suggestion and parked myself on the couch with a newspaper, which I opened up and looked at but didn't read. In about five minutes, after Wolfe had turned two pages, I said:

"By the way, it's a darned good thing you didn't take that job for Liggett. I mean the last one he offered. If you had, you would now be up a stump. As it stands now, you'd have a sweet time persuading Berin to be chef even for a soda fountain."

Neither he nor the book moved, but he did speak. "I presume Mr. Malfi has stabbed Mr. Berin. Good."

"No. He hasn't and he won't, because he can't get at him. Berin is wearing gyves on his way to jail. My friend Tolman has made a pinch. Justice has lit her torch."

"Pfui. If you must pester me with fairy tales, cultivate some imagination."

67

I said patiently, "Mr. Tolman has arrested Mr. Berin for the murder of Mr. Laszio and removed him to custody without bail. I saw it with these eyes."

The book went down. "Archie. If this is flummery—"

"No, sir. Straight."

"He has charged Berin?"

"Yes, sir."

"In the name of God, why? The man's a fool."

"That's what Miss Berin said. She said pig of a fool."

The book had remained suspended in the air; now it was lowered to rest on the expanse of thigh. In a few moments it was lifted again and opened for a page to get turned down, and was then deposited on a little stand beside the chair. Wolfe leaned back and shut his eyes and his fingers met at the front of his belly; and I saw his lips push out, then in again . . . then out, then in. . . . It startled me, and I wondered what all the excitement was about.

After a while he said without opening his eyes, "You understand, Archie, that I would hesitate to undertake anything which might conceivably delay our return to New York."

"It could be called hesitating. There're stronger words."

"Yes. On the other hand, I should be as great a fool as Mr. Tolman were I to ignore such an opportunity as this. It looks as if the only way to take advantage of it is to learn who killed Mr. Laszio. The question is, can we do it in thirty-one hours? Twenty-eight really, since at the dinner to-morrow evening I am to deliver my talk on American contributions to la haute cuisine. Can we do it in twenty-eight hours?"

"Sure we can." I waved a hand. "Gosh, with me to do the planning and you to handle the details—"

"Yes. Of course they may have abandoned the idea of that dinner, but I should think not, since only once in five years . . . well. The first step—"

"Excuse me." I had dropped the paper to the floor and straightened up, with a warm feeling that here was going to be a chance to get my circulation started. "Why not get in touch with Liggett and accept his offer? Since we're going to do it anyway, we might as well annex a fee along with it."

"No. If I engage with him and am not finished by to-morrow evening—no. Freedom is too precious collateral for any fee. We shall proceed. The first step is obvious. Bring Mr. Tolman here at once."

That was like him. Some day he would tell me to go get the Senate and the House of Representatives. I said, "Tolman's sore at you because you wouldn't come to the phone this morning. Also he thinks he has his man and is no longer interested. Also I don't believe—"

"Archie! You said you will do the planning. Please go for Mr. Tolman, and plan how to persuade him on the way."

I went for my hat.

6

I JOGGED smartly back along the path to Pocahontas, thinking I might catch Tolman before he got away, with my brain going faster than my feet trying to invent a swift one for him, but I was too late. The greenjacket at the door so advised me, saying that Tolman had got in his car on the driveway and headed west. I about-faced and broke into a gallop. If there had been a stop at the hotel, as seemed probable, I might head him off there. I was panting a little by the time I entered the lobby and began darting glances around through the palms and pillars and greenjackets, and customers in everything from riding togs to what resembled the last safe-guard of Gypsy Rose Lee. I was about to advance to the desk to make an inquiry when I heard a grim voice at my elbow:

"Hello, cockroach."

I wheeled and narrowed my eyes at it. "Hello, rat. Not even rat. Something I don't know the name of, because it lives underground and eats the roots of weeds."

Gershom Odell shook his head. "Not me. Wrong number. What you said about Laszio getting croaked, I had already told the night clerk just as conversation, and of course they faced me with it after it happened, and what could I do? But your shooting off your face about throwing stones—didn't you have brains enough to know you would make the damn sheriff suspicious?"

"I haven't got any brains, I'm a detective. The sheriff's busy elsewhere anyhow." I waved a hand. "Forget it. I want to see Tolman. Is he around here?"

Odell nodded. "He's in the manager's office with Ashley.

Also a few other people, including a man from New York named Liggett. Which reminds me I want to see you. You think you're so damn smart I'd like to lay you flat and sit on you, but I'll have to let that go because I want you to do me a favor."

"Let it go anyway. Sit not lest you be sat on."

"Okay. What I wanted to ask you about, I'm fed up with the sticks. It's a good job here in a way, but in other ways it's pretty crummy. To-day when Raymond Liggett landed here in a plane, the first person he asked for was Nero Wolfe, and he hoofed it right over to Upshur without going to his room or even stopping to say hello to Ashley. So I figured Wolfe must stand pretty high with him, and it occurred to me that about the best berth in this country for a house detective is the Hotel Churchill." Odell's eyes gleamed. "Boy, would that be a spot for a good honest man like me! So while Liggett's here, if you could tell Wolfe about me and he could tell Liggett and arrange for me to meet him without the bunch here getting wise in case I don't land it. . . ."

I was thinking, sure as the devil we're turning into an employment agency. I hate to disappoint people, and therefore I kidded Odell along, without actually misrepresenting the condition of Wolfe's intimacy with Raymond Liggett, and keeping one eye on the closed door which was the entrance to the manager's office. I told him that I was glad to see that he wasn't satisfied to stay in a rut and had real ambition and so forth, and it was a very nice chat, but I knocked off abruptly when I saw the closed door open and my friend Barry Tolman emerge alone. Giving Odell a friendly clap on the shoulder with enough muscle in it to give him an idea how easy I would be to sit on, I left him and followed my prey among the pillars and palms, and at a likely spot near the main entrance pounced on him.

His blue eyes looked worried and his whole face untidy. He recognized me: "Oh. What do you want? I'm in a hurry."

I said, "So am I. I'm not going to apologize about Wolfe not coming to the phone this morning, because if you know anything about Nero Wolfe you know he's eccentric and try and change him. I happened to see you going by just now, and I met you on the train Monday night and liked your face because you looked like a straight-shooter, and a little while ago I saw you pinching Berin for murder—I suppose you didn't notice me, but I was there—and I went back to the suite and told Wolfe about it, and I think you ought to know what he did when I told him. He pinched his nose."

"Well?" Tolman was frowning. "As long as he didn't pinch mine—what about it?"

"Nothing, except that if you knew Wolfe as I do . . . I have never yet seen him pinch his nose except when he was sure that some fellow being was making a complete jackass of himself. Do as you please. You're young and so you've got most of your bad mistakes ahead of you yet. I just had a friendly impulse, seeing you go by, and I *think* I can persuade Wolfe to have a talk with you if you want to come over to the suite with me right now. Anyhow, I'm willing to try it." I moved back a step. "Suit yourself, since you're in a hurry. . . ."

He kept the frown on. But I was pleased to see that he didn't waste time in fiddle-faddle. He frowned into my frank eyes a few seconds, then said abruptly, "Come on," and headed for the exit. I trotted behind glowing like a boy scout.

When we got to Upshur I had to continue the play, but I didn't feel like leaving him loose in the public hall, so I took him to the suite and put him in my room and shut the door on him. Then I went across to Wolfe's room, shutting that door too, and sat down on the couch and grinned at the fat son-of-a-gun.

"Well?" he demanded. "Couldn't you find him?"

"Of course I could find him. I've got him." I thumbed to indicate where. "I had to come in first to try to persuade you to grant him an audience. It ought to take about five minutes. It's even possible he'll sneak into the foyer to listen at the door." I raised my voice. "What about justice? What about society? What about the right of every man? . . ."

Wolfe had to listen because there was no way out. I laid it on good and thick. When I thought enough time had elapsed I closed the valve, went to my room and gave Tolman the high sign with a look of triumph, and ushered him in. He looked so preoccupied with worry that for a second I thought he was going to miss the chair when he sat down.

He plunged into it. "I understand that you think I'm pulling a boner."

Wolfe shook his head. "Not my phrase, Mr. Tolman. I can't

very well have an intelligent opinion until I know the facts that moved you. Offhand, I fear you've been precipitate."

"I don't think so." Tolman had his chin stuck out. "I talked with people in Charleston on the phone, and they agreed with me. Not that I'm passing the buck; the responsibility is mine. Incidentally, I'm supposed to be in Charleston at six o'clock for a conference, and it's sixty miles. I'm not bull-headed about it; I'll turn Berin loose like that"—he snapped his fingers—"if I'm shown cause. If you've any information I haven't got I'd have been damned thankful to get it when I phoned you this morning, and I'd be thankful now. Not to mention the duty of a citizen..."

"I have no information that would prove Mr. Berin innocent." Wolfe's tone was mild. "It was Mr. Goodwin's ebullience that brought you here. I gave you my opinion last night. It might help if I knew what you based your decision on, short of what you value as secret. You understand I have no client. I am representing no one."

"I have no secrets. But I have enough to hold Berin and indict him and I think convict him. As for opportunity, you know about that. He has threatened Laszio's life indiscriminately, in the hearing of half a dozen people. I suppose he figured that it would be calculated that a murderer would not go around advertising it in advance, but I think he overplayed it. This morning I questioned everybody again, especially Berin and Vukcic, and I counted Vukcic out. I got various pieces of information. But I admit that the most convincing fact of all came through a suggestion from you. I compared those lists with the one we found in Laszio's pocket. No one except Berin got more than two wrong."

He got papers from his pocket and selected one. "The lists of five of them, among them Vukcic, agreed exactly with the correct list. Four of them, including you, made two mistakes each, and the same ones." He returned the papers to his pocket and leaned forward at Wolfe. "Berin had just two right! Seven wrong!"

In the silence Wolfe's eyes went nearly closed. At length he murmured, "Preposterous. Nonsense."

"Precisely!" Tolman nodded with emphasis. "It is incredible that in a test on which the other nine averaged over 90% correct, Berin should score 22%. It is absolutely conclusive of one of two things: either he was so upset by a murder he had just committed or was about to commit that he couldn't distinguish the tastes, or he was so busy with the murder that he didn't have time to taste at all, and merely filled out his list haphazard. I regard it as conclusive, and I think a jury will. And I want to say that I am mighty grateful to you for the suggestion you made. I freely admit it was damned clever and it was you who thought of it."

"Thank you. Did you inform Mr. Berin of this and request an explanation?"

"Yes. He professed amazement. He couldn't explain it."

"You said 'absolutely conclusive.' That's far too strong. There are other alternatives. Berin's list may be forged."

"It's the one he himself handed to Servan, and it bears his signature. It hadn't been out of Servan's possession when he gave the lists to me. Would you suspect Servan?"

"I suspect no one. The dishes or cards might have been tampered with."

"Not the cards. Berin says they were in consecutive order when he tasted, as they were throughout. As for the dishes, who did it, and who put them back in place again after Berin left?"

After another silence Wolfe murmured again, obstinately, "It remains preposterous."

"Sure it does." Tolman leaned forward, further than before. "Look here, Wolfe. I'm a prosecuting attorney and all that, and I've got a career to make and I know what it means to have a success in a sensational case like this, but you're wrong if you think it gave me any pleasure to make a quick grab for Berin as a victim. It didn't. I . . ." He stopped. He tried it again. "I . . . well, it didn't. For certain reasons, it was the hardest thing I've ever done in my life. But let me ask you a question. I want to make it a tight question. Granted these premises as proven facts: one, that Berin made seven mistakes on the list he filled out and signed; two, that when he tasted the dishes they and the cards were in the same condition and order as when the others did; three, that nothing can be discovered to cast doubt on those facts; four, that you have taken the oath of office as prosecuting attorney. Would you have Berin arrested for murder and try to convict him?"

"I would resign."

Tolman threw up both hands. "Why?"

"Because I saw Mr. Berin's face and heard him speak less than a minute after he left the dining room last night."

"Maybe you did, but I didn't. If our positions were reversed, would you accept my word and judgment as to the evidence of Berin's face and voice?"

"No."

"Or anyone's?"

"No."

"Have you any information that will explain, or help to explain, the seven errors on Berin's list?"

"No."

"Have you any information in addition to what you have given me that would tend to prove him innocent?"

"No."

"All right." Tolman sat back. He looked at me resentfully and accusingly, which struck me as unfair, and then let his eyes go back to Wolfe. His jaw was working, in a nervous side-to-side movement, and after awhile he seemed to become suddenly aware of that and clamped it tight. Then he loosened it again: "Candidly, I was hoping you would have. From what Goodwin said, I thought maybe you did. You said if you were in my place you'd resign. But what the devil good—"

I didn't get to hear the rest of it, on account of another rupture to Wolfe's plans for an afternoon of peaceful privacy. The knock on the outer door was loud and prolonged. I went to the foyer and opened up, half expecting to see the two visitors from New York again, in view of the recent developments, but instead it was a trio of a different nature: Louis Servan, Vukcic, and Constanza Berin.

Vukcic was brusque. "We want to see Mr. Wolfe."

I told them to come in. "If you wouldn't mind waiting in here?" I indicated my room. "He's engaged at the moment with Mr. Barry Tolman."

Constanza backed up and bumped the wall of the foyer. "Oh!" Her expression would have been justified if I had told her that I had my pockets full of toads and snakes and poisonous lizards. She made a dive for the knob of the outer door. Vukcic grabbed her arm and I said: "Now, hold it. Can Mr. Wolfe help it if an attractive young fellow insists on coming to cry on his shoulder? Here, this way, all of you—"

The door to Wolfe's room opened and Tolman appeared. It was a little dim in the foyer, and it took him a second to call the roll. When he saw her, he had called it a day. He stared at her and turned a muddy white, and his mouth

74

opened three times for words which got delayed en route. It didn't seem that she got any satisfaction out of the state he was in, for apparently she didn't see him; she looked at me and said that she supposed they could see Mr. Wolfe now, and Vukcic took her elbow, and Tolman sidestepped in a daze to let them by. I stayed behind to let Tolman out, which I did after he had exchanged a couple of words with Servan.

The new influx appeared neither to cheer Wolfe nor enrage him. He received Miss Berin without enthusiasm but with a little extra courtesy, and apologized to Vukcic and Servan for having stayed away all day from the gathering at Pocahontas Pavilion. Servan assured him politely that under the unhappy circumstances no apology was required, and Vukcic sat down and ran all his fingers through his dense tangle of hair and growled something about the rotten luck for the meeting of the fifteen masters. Wolfe inquired if the scheduled activities would be abandoned, and Servan shook his head. No, Servan said, they would continue with affairs although his heart was broken. He had for years been looking forward to the time when, as doyen of Les Quinze Maîtres, he would have the great honor of entertaining them as his guests; it was to have been the climax of his career, fittingly and sweetly in his old age; and what had happened was an incredible disaster. Nevertheless, they would proceed; he would that evening, as dean and host, deliver his paper on *Les Mystères du Goût*, on the preparation of which he had spent two years; at noon the next day they would elect new members—now, alas, four—to replace those deceased; and Thursday evening they would hear Mr. Wolfe's discourse on *Contributions Américaines à la Haute Cuisine*. What a calamity, what a destruction of friendly, confraternity!

Wolfe said, "But such melancholy, Mr. Servan, is the worst possible frame of mind for digestion. Since placidity is out of the question, wouldn't active hostility be better? Hostility for the person responsible?"

Servan's brows went up. "You mean for Berin?"

"Good heavens, no. I said the person responsible. I don't think Berin did it."

"Oh!" It was a cry from Constanza. From the way she jerked up in her chair, and the look she threw at Wolfe, I was expecting her to hop over and kiss him, or at least spill ginger ale on him, but she just sat and looked.

Vukcic growled, "They seem to think they have proof.

About those seven mistakes on his list of the sauces. How the devil could that be?"

"I have no idea. Why, Marko, do you think Berin did it?"

"No. I don't think." Vukcic ran his fingers through his hair again. "It's a hell of a thing. For awhile they suspected me; they thought because I had been dancing with Dina my blood was warm. It was warm!" He sounded defiant. "You wouldn't understand that, Nero. With a woman like that. She has a fire in her that warmed me once, and it could again, no doubt of that, if it came near and I felt it and let my head go I could throw myself in it." He shrugged, and suddenly got savage. "But to stab that dog in the back—I would not have done him that honor! Pull his nose well, is all one does with that sort of fellow!

"But look here, Nero." Vukcic tossed his head around. "I brought Miss Berin and Mr. Servan around to see you. I suggested it. If we had found that you thought Berin guilty, I don't know what could have been said, but luckily you don't. It has been discussed over there among most of us, and the majority have agreed to contribute to a purse for Berin's defense—since he is here in a country strange to him—and certainly I told them that the best way to defend him is to enlist you—"

"But please," Servan broke in earnestly. "Please, Mr. Wolfe, understand that we deplore the necessity we can't avoid—you are our guest, my guest, and I know it is unforgivable that under the circumstances we should dare to ask you—"

"But the fact is," Vukcic took it up, "that they were quite generous in their contributions to the purse, after I explained your habits in the matter of fees—"

Constanza had edged to the front of her chair and put in an oar: "The eleven thousand francs I promised, it will take awhile to get them because they're in the bank in Nice—"

"Confound it!" Wolfe had to make it almost a shout. He wiggled a finger at Servan. "Apparently, sir, Marko has informed you of my rapacity. He was correct; I need lots of money and ordinarily my clients get soaked. But he could have told you that I am also an incurable romantic. To me the relationship of host and guest is sacred. The guest is a jewel resting on the cushion of hospitality. The host is king, in his parlor and his kitchen, and should not condescend to a lesser rôle. So we won't discuss—"

"Damn all the words!" Vukcic gestured impatiently. "What do you mean, Nero, you won't do anything about Berin?"

"No. I mean we won't discuss purses and fees. Certainly I shall do something about Berin, I had already decided to before you came, but I won't take money from my hosts for it. And there is no time to lose, and I want to be alone here to consider the matter. But since you are here—" His eyes moved to Constanza. "Miss Berin. You seem to be convinced that your father didn't kill Mr. Laszio. Why?"

Her eyes widened at him. "Why . . . you're convinced too. You said so. My father wouldn't."

"Never mind about me. Speaking to the law, which is what we're dealing with, what evidence have you? Any?"

"Why . . . only . . . it's absurd! Anyone—"

"I see. You haven't any. Have you any notion, or any evidence, as to who did kill Laszio?"

"No! And I don't care! Only anyone would know—"

"Please, Miss Berin. I warn you, we have a difficult task and little time for it. I suggest that on leaving here you go to your room, compose your emotions, and in your mind thoroughly recapitulate—go back over—all you have seen and heard, everything, since your arrival at Kanawha Spa. Do it thoroughly. Write down anything that appears to have the faintest significance. Remember this is a job, and the only one you can perform that offers any chance of helping your father."

He moved his eyes again. "Mr. Servan. First, the same questions as Miss Berin. Proof of Berin's innocence, or surmise or evidence of another's guilt. Have you any?"

Servan slowly shook his head.

"That's too bad. I must warn you, sir, that it will probably develop that the only way of clearing Berin is to find where the guilt belongs and fasten it there. We can't clear everybody; after all, Laszio's dead. If you know of anything that would throw suspicion elsewhere, and withhold it, you can't pretend to be helping Berin."

The dean of the masters shook his head again. "I know of nothing that would implicate anybody."

"Very well. About Berin's list of the sauces. He handed it to you himself?"

"Yes, immediately on leaving the dining room."

"It bore his signature?"

77

"Yes. I looked at each one before putting it in my pocket, to be sure they could be identified."

"How sure are you that no one had a chance to change Berin's list after he handed it to you, before you gave it to Mr. Tolman?"

"Positive. Absolutely. The lists were in my inside breast pocket every moment. Of course, I showed them to no one."

Wolfe regarded him a little, sighed, and turned to Vukcic. "You, Marko. What do you know?"

"I don't know a damned thing."

"Did you ask Mrs. Laszio to dance with you?"

"I . . . what's that got to do with it?"

Wolfe eyed him and murmured, "Now, Marko. At the moment I haven't the faintest idea how I shall discover what must be discovered, and I must be permitted any question short of insult. Did you ask Mrs. Laszio to dance, or did she ask you?"

Vukcic wrinkled his forehead and sat. Finally he growled, "I think she suggested it. I might have if she didn't."

"Did you ask her to turn on the radio?"

"No."

"Then the radio and the dancing at that particular moment were her ideas?"

"Damn it." Vukcic was scowling at his old friend. "I swear I don't see, Nero—"

"Of course you don't. Neither do I. But sometimes it's astonishing how the end of a tangled knot gets buried. It is said that two sure ways to lose a friend are to lend him money and to question the purity of a woman's gesture to him. I wouldn't lose your friendship. It is quite likely that Mrs. Laszio found the desire to dance with you irresistible.—No, Marko, please; I mean no flippancy. And now, if you don't mind . . . Miss Berin? Mr. Servan? I must consider this business."

They got up. Servan tried, delicately, to mention the purse again, but Wolfe brushed it aside. Constanza went over and took Wolfe's hand and looked at him with an expression that may or may not have been pure but certainly had appeal in it. Vukcic hadn't quite erased his scowl, but joined the others in their thanks and seemed to mean it. I went to the foyer with them to open the door.

Returning, I sat and watched Wolfe consider. He was leaning back in his favorite position, though by no means as comfortably as in his own chair at home, with his eyes closed.

He might have been asleep but for the faint movement of his lips. I did a little considering on my own hook, but I admit mine was limited. It looked to me like Berin, but I was willing to let in either Vukcic or Blanc in case they insisted. As far as I could see, everyone else was absolutely out. Of course there was still the possibility that Laszio had been absent from the dining room only temporarily, during Vukcic's session with the dishes, and had later returned and Vallenko or Rossi had mistaken him for a pincushion before or after tasting, but I couldn't see any juice in that. I had been in the large parlor the entire evening, and I tried to remember whether I had at any time noticed anyone enter the small parlor—or rather, whether I would have been able to swear that no one had. I thought I would. After over half an hour of overworking my brain, it still looked to me like Berin, and I thought it just as well Wolfe had turned down two offers of a fee, since it didn't seem very probable he was going to earn one.

I saw Wolfe stir. He opened his mouth but not his eyes.

"Archie. Those two colored men on duty in the main foyer of Pocahontas Pavilion last evening. Find out where they are."

I went to the phone in my room, deciding that the quickest way was to get hold of my friend Odell and let him do it. In less than ten minutes I was back again with the report.

"They went on at Pocahontas again at six o'clock. The same two. It is now 6:07. Their names—"

"No, thanks. I don't need the names." Wolfe pulled himself up and looked at me. "We have an enemy who has sealed himself in. He fancies himself impregnable, and he well may be—no door, no gate, no window in his walls—or hers. Possibly hers. But there is one little crack, and we'll have to see if we can pry it open." He sighed. "Amazing what a wall that is; that one crack is all I see. If that fails us..." He shrugged. Then he said bitterly, "As you know, we are dressing for dinner this evening. I would like to get to the pavilion as quickly as possible. What the tongue has promised the body must submit to."

He began operations for leaving his chair.

7

IT WAS STILL twenty minutes short of seven o'clock when we got
to Pocahontas. Wolfe had done pretty well with the black and
white, considering that Fritz Brenner was nearly a thousand
miles away, and I could have hired out as a window dummy.

Naturally I had some curiosity about Wolfe's interest in the
greenjackets, but it didn't get satisfied. In the main hall, after
we had been relieved of our hats, he motioned me on in to
the parlor, and he stayed behind. I noted that Odell's information was correct; the two colored men were the same that
had been on duty the evening before.

It was more than an hour until dinnertime, and there was
no one in the large parlor except Mamma Mondor, knitting
and sipping sherry, and Vallenko and Keith, with Lisette
Putti between them, chewing the rag on a divan. I said hello
and strolled over and tried to ask Mamma Mondor what was
the French word for knitting, but she seemed dumb at signs
and began to get excited, and it looked as it it might end in a
fight, so I shoved off.

Wolfe entered from the hall, and I saw by the look in his
eye that he hadn't lost the crack he had mentioned. He
offered greetings around, made a couple of inquiries, and was
informed that Louis Servan was in the kitchen overlooking
the preparations for dinner. Then he came up to me and in a
low tone outlined briefly an urgent errand. I thought he had a
nerve to wait until I got my glad rags on to ask me to work up
a sweat, particularly since no fee was involved, but I went for
my hat without stopping to grumble.

I cut across the lawn to get to the main path and headed for
the hotel. On the way I decided to use Odell again instead of
trying to develop new contacts, and luckily I ran across him
in the corridor by the elevators and without having to make
inquiries. He looked at me pleased and expectant.

"Did you tell Wolfe? Has he seen Liggett?"

"Nope, not yet. Give us time, can't you? Don't you worry,
old boy. Right now I need some things in a hurry. I need a
good ink pad, preferably a new one, and fifty or sixty sheets

of smooth white paper, preferably glazed, and a magnifying glass."

"Jumping Jesus." He stared at me. "Who you working for, J. Edgar Hoover?"

"No. It's all right, we're having a party. Maybe Liggett will be there. Step on it, huh?"

He told me to wait there and disappeared around the corner. In five minutes he was back, with all three items. As I took them he told me:

"I'll have to put the pad and paper on the bill. The glass is a personal loan, don't forget and skip with it."

I told him okay, thanked him, and beat it. On the way back I took the path which would carry me past Upshur, and I made a stop there and sought suite 60. I got a bottle of talcum powder from my bathroom and stuck it in my pocket, and my pen and a notebook, then found the copy of the *Journal of Criminology* I had brought along and thumbed through it to some plates illustrating new classifications of fingerprints. I cut one of the pages out of the magazine with my knife, rolled it up in the paper Odell had given me, and trotted out again and across to Pocahontas. All the time I was trying to guess at the nature of the crack Wolfe thought he was going to pry open with that array of materials.

I got no light on that point from Wolfe. He had apparently been busy, for though I hadn't been gone more than fifteen minutes I found him established in the biggest chair in the small parlor, alongside the same table behind which Tolman had been barricaded against the onslaught of Constanza Berin. Across the table from him, looking skeptical but resigned, was Sergei Vallenko.

Wolfe finished a sentence to Vallenko and then turned to me. "You have everything, Archie? Good. The pad and paper here on the table, please. I've explained to Mr. Servan that if I undertake this inquiry I shall have to ask a few questions of everyone and take fingerprint samples. He has sent Mr. Vallenko to us first. All ten prints, please."

That was a hot one. Nero Wolfe collecting fingerprints, especially after the cops had smeared all over the dining-room and it had been reopened to the public! I knew darned well it was phoney, but hadn't guessed his charade yet, so once again I had to follow his tail light without knowing the road. I got Vallenko's specimens, on two sheets, and labelled them, and Wolfe dismissed him with thanks.

I demanded, when we were alone, "What has this identification bureau—"

"Not now, Archie. Sprinkle powder on Mr. Vallenko's prints."

I stared at him. "In the name of God, why? You don't put powder—"

"It will look more professional and mysterious. Do it. Give me the page from the magazine.—Good. Satisfactory. We'll use only the upper half; cut it off and keep it in your pocket. Put the magnifying glass on the table—ah, Mme. Mondor? Asseyez-vous, s'il vous plaît."

She had her knitting along. He asked her some questions of which I never bothered him for a translation, and then turned her over to my department and I put her on record. I never felt sillier in my life than dusting that talcum powder on those fresh clear specimens. Our third customer was Lisette Putti, and she was followed by Keith, Blanc, Rossi, Mondor... Wolfe asked a few questions of all of them, but knowing his voice and manner as well as I did, it sounded to me as if his part of it was as phoney as mine. And it certainly didn't sound as if he was prying any crack open.

Then Lawrence Coyne's Chinese wife came in. She was dressed for dinner in red silk, with a sprig of mountain laurel in her black hair, and with her slim figure and little face and narrow eyes she looked like an ad for a Round the World cruise. At once I got a hint that it was her we were laying for, for Wolfe told me sharply to take my notebook, which he hadn't done for any of the others, but all he did was ask her the same line of questions and explain about the prints before I took them. However, there appeared to be more to come. As I gave her my handkerchief, already ruined, to wipe the tips of her fingers on, Wolfe settled back.

He murmured, "By the way, Mrs. Coyne, Mr. Tolman tells me that while you were outdoors last evening you saw no one but one of the attendants on one of the paths. You asked him about a bird you heard and he told you it was a whippoorwill. You had never heard a whippoorwill before?"

She had displayed no animation, and didn't now. "No, there aren't any in California."

"So I understand. I believe you went outdoors before the tasting of the sauces began, and returned to the parlor shortly after Mr. Vukcic entered the dining room. Isn't that right?"

"I went out before they began. I don't know who was in the dining room when I came back."

"I do. Mr. Vukcic." Wolfe's voice was so soft and unconcerned that I knew she was in for something. "Also, you told Mr. Tolman that you were outdoors all the time you were gone. Is that correct?"

She nodded. "Yes."

"When you left the parlor, after dinner, didn't you go to your room before you went outdoors?"

"No, it wasn't cold and I didn't need a wrap. . . ."

"All right. I'm just asking. While you were outdoors, though, perhaps you entered the left wing corridor by way of the little terrace and went to your room that way?"

"No." She sounded dull and calm. "I was outdoors all the time."

"You didn't go to your room at all?"

"No."

"Nor anywhere else?"

"Just outdoors. My husband will tell you, I like to go outdoors at night."

Wolfe grimaced. "And when you re-entered, you came straight through the main hall to the large parlor?"

"Yes, you were there. I saw you there with my husband."

"So you did. And now, Mrs. Coyne, I must admit you have me a little puzzled. Perhaps you can straighten it out. In view of what you have just told me, which agrees with your account to Mr. Tolman, what door was it that you hurt your finger in?"

She deadpanned him good. There wasn't a flicker. Maybe her eyes got a little narrower, but I couldn't see it. But she wasn't good enough to avoid stalling. After about ten seconds of the stony-facing she said, "Oh, you mean my finger." She glanced down at it and up again. "I asked my husband to kiss it."

Wolfe nodded. "I heard you. What door did you hurt it in?"

She was ready. "The big door at the entrance. You know how hard it is to push, and when it closed—"

He broke in sharply, "No, Mrs. Coyne, that won't do. The doorman and the hallman have been questioned and their statements taken. They remember your leaving and re-entering—in fact, they were questioned about it Tuesday night by Mr. Tolman. And they are both completely certain

83

that the doorman opened the door for you and closed it behind you, and there was no caught finger. Nor could it have been the door from the hall to the parlor, for I saw you come through that myself. What door was it?"

She was wearing the deadpan permanently. She said calmly, "The doorman is telling a lie because he was careless and let me get hurt."

"I don't think so."

"I know it. He is lying." Quickly and silently, she was on her feet. "I must tell my husband."

She was off, moving fast. Wolfe snapped, "Archie!" I skipped around and got in front of her, on her line to the door. She didn't try dodging, just stopped and looked up at my face. Wolfe said, "Come back and sit down. I can see that you are a person of decision, but so am I. Mr. Goodwin could hold you with one hand. You may scream and people will come, but they will go again and we'll be where we are now. Sit down, please."

She did so, and told him, "I have nothing to scream about. I merely wanted to tell my husband . . . ."

"That the doorman lied. But he didn't. However, there's no need to torment you unnecessarily.—Archie, give me the photograph of those fingerprints on the dining room door."

I thought to myself, darn you, some day you're going to push the button for my wits when they're off on vacation, and then you'll learn to let me in on things ahead of time. But of course there was only one answer to this one. I reached in my pocket for the plate of reproductions I had cut from the magazine page, and handed it to him. Then, being on at last, I pushed across the specimens I had just taken from Lio Coyne's fingers. Wolfe took the magnifying glass and began to compare. He took his time, holding the two next to each other, looking closely through the glass back and forth, with satisfied nods at the proper intervals.

Finally he said, "Three quite similar. They would probably do. But the left index finger is absolutely identical and it's exceptionally clear. Here, Archie, see what you think."

I took the prints and the glass and put on a performance. The prints from the magazine happened to be from some blunt-fingered mechanic, and I don't believe I ever saw any two sets more unlike. I did a good job of it with the comparison, even counting out loud, and handed them back to Wolfe.

"Yes, sir." I was emphatic. "They're certainly the same. Anyone could see it."

Wolfe told Mrs. Coyne gently, almost tenderly, "You see, madam. I must explain. Of course everyone knows about fingerprints, but some of the newer methods of procuring them are not widely known. Mr. Goodwin here is an expert. He went over the doors from the dining room to the terrace—among other places—and brought out prints which the local police had been unable to discover, and made photographs of them. So as you see, modern methods of searching for evidence are sometimes fertile. They have given us conclusive proof that it was the door from the terrace to the dining room in which you caught your finger Tuesday evening. I had suspected it before, but there's no need to go into that. I am not asking you to explain anything. Your explanation, naturally, will have to be given to the police, after I have turned this evidence over to them, together with an account of your false statement that it was the main entrance door in which you caught your finger. And by the way, I should warn you to expect little courtesy from the police. After all, you didn't tell Mr. Tolman the truth, and they won't like that. It would have been more sensible if you had admitted frankly, when he asked about your excursion to see the night, that you had entered the dining room from the terrace."

She was as good at the wooden-face act as anyone I could remember. You would have sworn that if her mind was working at all it was on nothing more important than where she could have lost one of her chopsticks. At last she said, "I didn't enter the dining room."

Wolfe shrugged. "Tell the police that. After your lie to Mr. Tolman, and your lies to us here which are on record in Mr. Goodwin's notebook, and your attempt to accuse the doorman—and above all, these fingerprints."

She stretched a hand out. "Give them to me. I'd like to see them."

"The police may show them to you. If they choose. Forgive me, Mrs. Coyne, but this photograph is important evidence, and I'd like to be sure of turning it over to the authorities intact."

She stirred a little, but there was no change on her face. After another silence she said, "I did go into the left wing corridor. By the little terrace. I went to my room and hurt my finger in the bathroom door. Then when Mr. Laszio was found murdered I was frightened and thought I wouldn't say I had been inside at all."

Wolfe nodded and murmured, "You might try that. Try it, by all means, if you think it's worth it. You realize, of course, that would leave your fingerprints on the dining room door to be explained. Anyhow you're in a pickle; you'll have to do the best you can." He turned abruptly to me and got snappy. "Archie, go to the booth in the foyer and phone the police at the hotel. Tell them to come at once."

I arose without excessive haste. I was prepared to stall with a little business with my notebook and pen, but it wasn't necessary. Her face showed signs of life. She blinked up at me and put out a hand at me, and then blinked at Wolfe, and extended both her cute little hands in his direction.

"Mr. Wolfe," she pleaded. "Please! I did no harm, I did nothing! Please not the police!"

"No harm, madam?" Wolfe was stern. "To the authorities investigating a murder you tell lies, and to me also, and you call that no harm? Archie, go on!"

"No!" She was on her feet. "I tell you I did nothing!"

"You entered the dining room within minutes, perhaps seconds, of the moment that Laszio was murdered. Did you kill him?"

"No! I did nothing! I didn't enter the dining room!"

"Your hand was on that door. What did you do?"

She stood with her eyes on him, and I stood with a foot poised, aching to call the cops I don't think. She ended the tableau by sitting down and telling Wolfe quietly, "I must tell you. Mustn't I?"

"Either me or the police."

"But if I tell you . . . you tell the police anyway."

"Perhaps. Perhaps not. It depends. In any event, you'll have to tell the truth sooner or later."

"I suppose so." Her hands were on the lap of her red dress with the fingers closely twined. "You see, I'm afraid. The police don't like the Chinese, and I am a Chinese woman, but that isn't it. I'm afraid of the man I saw in the dining room, because he must have killed Mr. Laszio. . . ."

Wolfe asked softly, "Who was it?"

"I don't know. But if I told about him, and he knew that I had seen him and had told . . . anyway, I am telling now. You

86

see, Mr. Wolfe, I was born in San Francisco and educated there, but I am Chinese, and we are never treated like Americans. Never. But anyway...what I told Mr. Tolman was the truth. I was outdoors all the time. I like outdoors at night. I was on the grass among the trees and shrubs, and I heard the whippoorwill, and I went across the driveway where the fountain is. Then I came back, to the side—not the left wing, the other side—and I could see dimly through the window curtains into the parlor, but I couldn't see into the dining room because the shades were drawn on the glass doors. I thought it would be amusing to watch the men tasting those dishes, which seemed very silly to me, so I went to the terrace to find a slit I could see through, but the shades were so tight there wasn't any. Then I heard a noise as if something had fallen over in the dining room. I couldn't hear just what it was like, because the sound of the radio was coming through the open window of the parlor. I stood there I don't know how long, but no other sound came, and I thought that if one of the men had got mad and threw the dishes on the floor that would be amusing, and I decided to open the door a crack and see, and I didn't think I'd be heard on account of the radio. So I opened it just a little. I didn't get it open enough even to see the table, because there was a man standing there by the corner of the screen, with his side turned to me. He had one finger pressed against his lips— you know, the way you do when you're hushing somebody. Then I saw who he was looking at. The door leading to the pantry hall was open, just a few inches, and the face of one of the Negroes was there, looking at the man by the screen. The man by the screen started to turn toward me, and I went to close the door in a hurry and my foot slipped, and I grabbed with my other hand to keep from falling, and the door shut on my finger. I thought it would be silly to get caught peeking in the dining room, so I ran back among the bushes and stood there a few minutes, and then I went to the main entrance—and you saw me enter the parlor."

Wolfe demanded, "Who was the man by the screen?"

She shook her head. "I don't know."

"Now, Mrs. Coyne. Don't start that again. You saw the man's face."

"I only saw the side of his face. Of course that was enough to tell he was a Negro."

Wolfe blinked. I blinked twice. Wolfe demanded, "A Negro? Do you mean one of the employees here?"

"Yes. In livery. Like the waiters."

"Was it one of the waiters at this pavilion?"

"No, I'm sure it wasn't. He was blacker than them and...I'm sure it wasn't. It wasn't anyone I could recognize."

"'Blacker than them and' what? What were you going to say?"

"That it wouldn't have been one of the waiters here because he came outdoors and went away. I told you I ran back among the bushes. I had only been there a few seconds when the dining room door opened and he came out and went around the path toward the rear. Of course I couldn't see very well from behind the bushes, but I supposed it was him."

"Could you see his livery?"

"Yes, a little, when he opened the door and had the light behind him. Then it was dark."

"Was he running?"

"No. Walking."

Wolfe frowned. "The one looking from the door to the pantry hall—was he in livery, or was it one of the cooks?"

"I don't know. The door was only open a crack, and I saw mostly his eyes. I couldn't recognize him either."

"Did you see Mr. Laszio?"

"No."

"No one else?"

"No. That's all I saw, just as I've told you. Everything. Then, later, when Mr. Servan told us that Mr. Laszio had been killed—then I knew what it was I had heard. I had heard Mr. Laszio fall, and I had seen the man that killed him. I knew that. I knew it must be that. But I was afraid to tell about it when they asked me questions about going outdoors...and anyway..." Her two little hands went up in a gesture to her bosom, and fell to her lap again. "Of course I was sorry when they arrested Mr. Berin, because I knew it was wrong. I was going to wait until I got back home, to San Francisco, and tell my husband about it, and if he said to I was going to write it all down and send it here."

"And in the meantime..." Wolfe shrugged. "Have you told anyone anything about it?"

"Nothing."

"Then don't." Wolfe sat up. "As a matter of fact, Mrs. Coyne, while you have acted selfishly, I confess you have acted wisely. But for the accident that you asked your husband to kiss your finger in my hearing, your secret was safe and therefore you were too. The murderer of Mr. Laszio probably knows that he was seen through that door, but not by whom, since you opened it only a few inches and outdoors was dark. Should he learn that it was you who saw him, even San Francisco might not be far enough away for you. It is in the highest degree advisable to do nothing that will permit him to learn it or cause him to suspect it. Tell no one. Should anyone show curiosity as to why you were kept so long in here while the other interviews were short, and ask you about it, tell him—or her—that you have a racial repugnance to having your fingerprints taken, and it required all my patience to overcome it. Similarly, I undertake that for the present the police will not question you, or even approach you, for that might arouse suspicion. And by the way—"

"You won't tell the police."

"I didn't say I wouldn't. You must trust my discretion. I was about to ask, has anyone questioned you particularly—except the police and me—regarding your visit to the night? Any of the guests here?"

"No."

"You're quite sure? Not even a casual question?"

"No, I don't remember . . ." Her brow was puckered above the narrow eyes. "Of course my husband—"

A tapping on the door interrupted her. Wolfe nodded at me and I went and opened it. It was Louis Servan. I let him in.

He advanced and told Wolfe apologetically, "I don't like to disturb you, but the dinner . . . it's five minutes past eight. . . ."

"Ah!" Wolfe made it to his feet in less than par. "I have been looking forward to this for six months. Thank you, Mrs. Coyne.—Archie, will you take Mrs. Coyne?—Could I have a few words with you, Mr. Servan? I'll make it as brief as possible?"

8

THE DINNER of the dean of The Fifteen Masters that evening, which by custom was given on the second day of their gathering once in every five years, was ample and elaborate as to fleshpots, but a little spotty as an occasion of festivity. The chatter during the hors d'oeuvres was nervous and jerky, and when Domenico Rossi made some loud remark in French three or four of them began to laugh and then suddenly stopped, and in the silence they all looked at one another.

To my surprise, Constanza Berin was there, but not adjoining me as on the evening before. She was on the other side, between Louis Servan, who was at the end, and a funny little duck with an uncontrolled mustache who was new to me. Leon Blanc, on my right, told me he was the French Ambassador. There were several other extra guests, among them my friend Odell's prospective employer, Raymond Liggett of the Hotel Churchill, Clay Ashley, the manager of Kanawha Spa, and Albert Malfi. Malfi's black eyes kept darting up and down the table, and on meeting the eyes of a master he delivered a flashing smile. Leon Blanc pointed a fork at him and told me, "See that fellow Malfi? He wants votes for to-morrow morning as one of Les Quinze Maîtres. Bah! He has no creation, no imagination! Berin trained him, that's all!" He waved the fork in contemptuous dismissal and then used it to scoop a mouthful of shad roe mousse.

The swamp-woman, now a swamp-widow, was absent, but everyone else—except Berin, of course—was there. Apparently Rossi hadn't been much impressed by the murder of his son-in-law; he was still ready for a scrap and full of personal and national comments. Mondor paid no attention to him. Vukcic was gloomy and ate like ten minutes for lunch. Ramsey Keith was close to pie-eyed, and about every five minutes he had a spell of giggles that might have been all right coming from his niece. During the entrée Leon Blanc told me, "That little Berin girl is a good one. You see her hold herself? Louis put her between him and the ambassador as a gesture to Berin. She justifies him; she represents her father bravely." Blanc sighed. "You heard what I told Mr. Wolfe in there when he questioned me. This was to be expected of Phillip Laszio, to let his sins catch up with him on this occasion. Infamy was in his blood. If he were alive I could kill him now—only I don't kill. I am a chef, but I couldn't be a butcher." He swallowed a mouthful of stewed rabbit and sighed again. "Look at Louis. This is a great affair for him, and this civet de lapin is in fact perfection, except for a slight excess of bouquet garni, possibly because the rabbits were young and tender flavored. Louis deserved gayety for this dinner and this salute to his cuisine, and look at us!" He went at the rabbit again.

The peak of the evening for me came with the serving of coffee and liqueurs, when Louis Servan arose to deliver his talk, which he had worked on for two years, on The Mysteries of Taste. I was warm and full inside, sipping a cognac which made me shut my eyes as it trickled into my throat—and I'm not a gourmet—so as not to leave any extra openings for the vapor to escape by, and I was prepared to be quietly entertained, maybe even instructed up to a point. Then he began: "Mesdames et messieurs, mes confrères des Quinze Maîtres: Il y a plus que cent ans un homme fameux, Brillat-Savarin le grand..." He went on from there. I was stuck. If I had known beforehand of the dean's intentions as to language I would have negotiated some sort of arrangement, but I couldn't simply get up and beat it. Anyway, the cognac bottle was two-thirds full, and the fundamental problem was to keep my eyes open, so I settled back to watch his gestures and mouth work. I guess it was a good talk. There were signs of appreciation throughout the hour and a half it lasted, nods and smiles and brows lifted, and applause here and there, and once in a while Rossi cried "Bravo!" and when Ramsey Keith got a fit of giggles Servan stopped and waited politely until Lisette Putti got him shushed. Once it got embarrassing, at least for me, when at the end of a sentence Servan was silent, and looked slowly around the table and couldn't go on, and two big tears left his eyes and rolled down his cheeks. There were murmurs, and Leon Blanc beside me blew his nose, and I cleared my throat a couple of times and reached for the cognac. When it was over they all left their places and gathered around him and shook hands, and a couple of them kissed him.

They drifted into the parlor in groups. I looked around for Constanza Berin, but apparently she had used up all her bravery for one evening, for she had disappeared. I turned to a hand on my arm and a voice:

"Pardon me, you are Mr. Goodwin? Mr. Rossi told me your name. I saw you... this afternoon with Mr. Wolfe...."

I acknowledged everything. It was Albert Malfi, the entrée man with no imagination. He made a remark or two about the dinner and Servan's speech and then went on, "I understand that Mr. Wolfe has changed his mind. He has been persuaded to investigate the...that is, the murder. I suppose that was because Mr. Berin was arrested?"

"No, I don't think so. It's just because he's a guest. A guest is a jewel resting on the cushion of hospitality."

"No doubt. Of course." The Corsican's eyes darted around and back to me. "There is something I think I should tell Mr. Wolfe."

"There he is." I nodded at where Wolfe was chinning with a trio of the masters. "Go tell him."

"But I don't like to interrupt him. He is the guest of honor of Les Quinze Maîtres." Malfi sounded awed. "I just thought I would ask you...perhaps I could see him in the morning? It may not be important. To-day we were talking with Mrs. Laszio—Mr. Liggett and I—and I was telling her about it—"

"Yeah?" I eyed him. "You a friend of Mrs. Laszio's?"

"Not a friend. A woman like her doesn't have friends, only slaves. I know her, of course. I was telling about this Zelota, and she and Mr. Liggett thought Mr. Wolfe should know. That was before Berin was arrested, when it was thought someone might have entered the dining room from the terrace—and killed Laszio. But if Mr. Wolfe is interested to clear Berin, certainly he should know." Malfi smiled at me. "You frown, Mr. Goodwin? You think if Berin is not cleared that would suit my ambition, and why am I so unselfish? I am not unselfish. It would be the greatest thing in my life if I could become chef de cuisine of the Hotel Churchill. But Jerome Berin saw my talent in the little inn at Ajaccio and took me into the world, and guided me with his genius, and I would not pay for my glory with his misfortune. Besides, I know him; he would not have killed Laszio that way, from behind. So I think I should tell Mr. Wolfe about Zelota. Mrs. Laszio and Mr. Liggett think the same. Mr. Liggett says it would do no good to tell the police, because they are satisfied with Berin."

I meditated on him. I was trying to remember where I had heard the name Zelota, and all at once it came to me. I said, "Uh-huh. You mean Zelota of Tarragona. Laszio stole something from him in 1920."

Malfi looked surprised. "You know of Zelota?"

"Oh, a little. A few things. What's he been up to? Or would you rather wait and tell Wolfe about it in the morning?"

"Not necessarily. Zelota is in New York."

"Well, he's got lots of company." I grinned. "Being in New

York is no crime. It's full of people who didn't kill Laszio. Now if he was in Kanawha Spa, that might be different."

"But maybe he is."

"He can't be in two places at once. Even a jury wouldn't believe that."

"But he might have come here. I don't know what you know about Zelota, but he hated Laszio more than—" Malfi shrugged. "He hated him bitterly. Berin often spoke to me about it. And about a month ago Zelota turned up in New York. He came and asked me for a job. I didn't give him one, because there is nothing left of him but a wreck, drink has ruined him, and because I remembered what Berin had told me about him and I thought perhaps he wanted a job at the Churchill only for a chance to get at Laszio. I heard later that Vukcic gave him a job on soup at Rusterman's, and he only lasted a week." He shrugged again. "That's all. I told Mrs. Laszio and Mr. Liggett about it, and they said I should tell Mr. Wolfe. I don't know anything more about Zelota."

"Well, much obliged. I'll tell Wolfe. Will you still be here in the morning?"

He said yes, and his eyes began to dart around again and he shoved off, apparently to electioneer. I strolled around a while, finding opportunities for a few morsels of harmless eavesdropping, and then I saw Wolfe's finger crooked at me and went to him. He announced that it was time to leave.

Which suited me. I was ready for the hay. I went to the hall and got our hats and waited with them, yawning, while Wolfe completed his good-nights. He joined me and we started out, but he stopped on the threshold and told me, "By the way, Archie. Give these men a dollar each. Appreciation for good memories."

I shelled out to the two greenjackets, from the expense roll.

In our own suite 60, over at Upshur, having switched on the lights and closed a window so the breeze wouldn't chill his delicate skin while undressing, I stood in the middle of his room and stretched and enjoyed a real yawn.

"It's a funny thing about me. If I once get to bed really late, like last night at four o'clock, I'm not really myself again until I catch up. I was afraid you were going to hang around over there and chew the rag. As it is, it's going on for midnight—"

I stopped because his actions looked suspicious. He wasn't

even unbuttoning his vest. Instead, he was getting himself arranged in the big chair in a manner which indicated that he expected to be there awhile. I demanded:

"Are you going to start your brain going at this time of night? Haven't you done enough for one evening?"

"Yes." He sounded grim. "But there is more to do. I arranged with Mr. Servan for the cooks and waiters of Pocahontas Pavilion to call on us soon as they have finished. They will be here in a quarter of an hour."

"Well for God's sake." I sat down. "Since when have we been on the night shift?"

"Since we found Mr. Laszio with a knife in him." He sounded grimmer. "We have but little time. Not enough perhaps, in view of Mrs. Coyne's story."

"And those blackbirds coming in a flock? At least a dozen."

"If by blackbirds you mean men with dark skin, yes."

"I mean Africans." I stood up again. "Listen, boss. You've lost your sense of direction, honest you have. Africans or blackbirds or whatever you like, they can't be handled this way. They don't intend to tell anything or they would have told that squint-eyed sheriff when he questioned them. Are you expecting me to use a carpetbeater on the whole bunch? The only thing is to get Tolman and the sheriff here first thing in the morning to hear Mrs. Coyne's tale, and let them go on from there."

Wolfe grunted. "They arrive at eight o'clock. They hear her story and they believe it or they don't—after all, she is Chinese. They question her at length, and even if they believe her they do not immediately release Berin, for her story doesn't explain the errors on his list. At noon they begin with the Negroes, singly. God knows what they do or how much time they take, but the chances are that Thursday midnight, when our train leaves for New York, they will not have finished with the Negroes, and they may have discovered nothing."

"They're more apt to than you are. I'm warning you, you'll see. These smokes can take it, they're used to it. Do you believe Mrs. Coyne's tale?"

"Certainly, it was obvious."

"Would you mind telling me how you knew she had hurt her finger in the dining room door?"

"I didn't. I knew she had told Tolman that she had gone directly outside, had stayed outside, and had returned directly to the parlor; and I knew that she had hurt her finger in a door. When she told me she had caught her finger in the main entrance door, which I knew to be untrue, I knew she was concealing something, and I proceeded to make use of the evidence we had prepared."

"*I* had prepared." I sat down. "Some day you'll try to bluff the trees out of their leaves. Would you mind telling me now what motive one of these smokes had for bumping off Laszio?"

"I suppose he was hired." Wolfe grimaced. "I don't like murderers, though I make my living through them. But I particularly dislike murderers who buy the death they seek. One who kills at least keeps the blood on his own hands. One who pays for killing—pfui! That is worse than repugnant, it is dishonorable. I presume the colored man was hired. Naturally, that's an annoying complication for us."

"Not so terrible." I waved a hand. "They'll be here pretty soon. I'll arrange them for you in a row. Then you'll give them a little talk on citizenship and the Ten Commandments, and explain how illegal it is to croak a guy for money even if you get paid in advance, and then you'll ask whoever stabbed Laszio to raise his hand and his hand will shoot up, and then all you'll have to do is ask who paid him and how much—"

"That will do, Archie." He sighed. "It's amazing how patiently and with what forbearance I have tolerated—but there they are. Let them in."

That was an instance when Wolfe himself jumped to an unwarranted conclusion, which was a crime he often accused me of. For when I made it through the foyer and opened the door to the hall, it wasn't Africans I found waiting there, but Dina Laszio. I stared at her a second, adjusting myself to the surprise. She put her long sleepy eyes on me and said:

"I'm sorry to disturb you so late, but—may I see Mr. Wolfe?"

I told her to wait and returned to the inner chamber.

"Not men with dark skin, but a woman. Mrs. Phillip Laszio wants to see you."

"What? Her?"

"Yes, sir. In a dark cloak and no hat."

Wolfe grimaced. "Confound that woman! Bring her in here."

9

I SAT AND WATCHED and listened and felt cynical. Wolfe rubbed his cheek with the tip of his forefinger, slowly and rhythmically, which meant he was irritated but attentive. Dina Laszio was on a chair facing him, with her cloak thrown back, her smooth neck showing above a plain black dress with no collar, her body at ease, her eyes dark in shadow.

Wolfe said, "No apology is needed, madam. Just tell me about it. I'm expecting callers and am pressed for time."

"It's about Marko," she said.

"Indeed. What about Marko?"

"You're so brusque." She smiled a little, and the smile clung to the corners of her mouth. "You should know that you can't expect a woman to be direct like that. We don't take the road, we wind around. You know that. Only I wonder how much you know about women like me."

"I couldn't say. Are you a special kind?"

She nodded. "I think I am. Yes, I know I am. Not because I want to be or try to be, but . . ." She made a little gesture. "It has made my life exciting, but not very comfortable. It will end . . . I don't know how it will end. Right now I am worried about Marko, because he thinks you suspect him of killing my husband."

Wolfe stopped rubbing his cheek. He told her, "Nonsense."

"No, it isn't. He thinks that."

"Why? Did you tell him so?"

"No. And I resent—" She stopped herself. She leaned forward, her head a little on one side, her lips not quite meeting, and looked at him. I watched her with pleasure. I suppose she was telling the truth when she said she didn't try to be a special kind of woman, but she didn't have to try. There was something in her—not only in her face, it came right out through her clothes—that gave you an instinctive impulse to start in that direction. I kept on being cynical, but it was easy to appreciate that there might be a time when cynicism wouldn't be enough.

She asked with a soft breath, "Mr. Wolfe, why do you

always jab at me? What have you got against me? Yesterday, when I told you what Phillip told me about the arsenic . . . and now when I tell you about Marko . . ."

She leaned back. "Marko told me once, long ago, that you don't like women."

Wolfe shook his head. "I can only say, nonsense again. I couldn't rise to that impudence. Not like women? They are astounding and successful animals. For reasons of convenience, I merely preserve an appearance of immunity which I developed some years ago under the pressure of necessity. I confess to a specific animus toward you. Marko Vukcic is my friend; you were his wife; and you deserted him. I don't like you."

"So long ago!" She fluttered a hand. Then she shrugged. "Anyway, I am here now in Marko's behalf."

"You mean he sent you?"

"No. But I came, for him. It is known, of course, that you have engaged to free Berin of the charge of killing my husband. How can you do that except by accusing Marko? Berin says Phillip was in the dining room, alive, when he left. Marko says Phillip was not there when he entered. So if not Berin, it must have been Marko. And then, you asked Marko to-day if he asked me to dance or suggested that I turn on the radio. There could be only one reason why you asked him that: because you suspected that he wanted the radio going so that no noise would be heard from the dining room when he . . . if anything happened in there."

"So Marko told you that I asked about the radio."

"Yes." She smiled faintly. "He thought I should know. You see, he has forgiven what you will not forgive—"

I missed the rest of that on account of a knock on the door. I went to the foyer, closing the door of Wolfe's room behind me, and opened up. The sight in the hall gave me a shock, even though I had been warned. It looked like half of Harlem. Four or five were greenjackets who a couple of hours back had been serving the dean's dinner to us, and the others, the cooks and helpers, were in their own clothes. The light brown middle-aged one in front with the bottom of one ear chopped off was the head waiter in charge at Pocahontas, and I felt friendly to him because it was he who had left the cognac bottle smack in front of me at the table. I told them to come on in and stepped aside not to get trampled, and directed them through to my room and followed them in.

"You'll have to wait in here, boys, Mr. Wolfe has a visitor. Sit on something. Sit on the bed, it's mine and it looks like I won't be using it anyway. If you go to sleep, snore a couple of good ones for me."

I left them there and went back to see how Wolfe was getting along with the woman he didn't like. Neither of them bothered with a glance at me as I sat down. She was saying:

"... but I know nothing about it beyond what I told you yesterday. Certainly I know there are other possibilities besides Berin and Marko. As you say, someone could have entered the dining room from the terrace. That's what you're thinking of, isn't it?"

"It's a possibility. But go back a little, Mrs. Laszio. Do you mean to say that Marko Vukcic told you of my asking him about the radio, and expressed the fear that I suspected him of having the radio turned on to give him an opportunity for killing your husband?"

"Well..." She hesitated. "Not exactly like that. Marko would not express a fear. But the way he told me about it—that was obviously in his mind. So I've come to you to find out if you do suspect him."

"You've come to defend him? Or to make sure that my clumsiness hasn't missed *that* inference from the timeliness of the radio?"

"Neither." She smiled at him. "You can't make me angry, Mr. Wolfe. Why, do you make other inferences? Many of them?"

Wolfe shook his head impatiently. "You can't do that, madam. Give it up. I mean your affected insouciance. I don't mind fencing when there's time for it, but it's midnight and there are men in that other room waiting to see me.—Please let me finish. Let me clear away some fog. I have admitted an animus toward you. I knew Marko Vukcic both before and after he married you. I saw the change in him. Then why was I not grateful whey you suddenly selected a new field for your activities? Because you left débris behind you. It is not decent to induce the cocaine habit in a man, but it is monstrous to do so and then suddenly withdraw his supply of the drug. Nature plainly intends that a man should nourish a woman, and a woman a man, physically and spiritually, but there is no nourishment in you for anybody; the vapor that comes from you, from your eyes, your lips, your soft skin, your contours, your movements, is not beneficent but malignant. I'll grant you everything: you were alive, with your instincts and appetites, and you saw Marko and wanted him. You enveloped him with your miasma—you made that the only air he wanted to breathe—and then by caprice, without warning, you deprived him of it and left him gasping."

She didn't bat an eyelash. "But I told you I was a special kind—"

"Permit me. I haven't finished. I am seizing an opportunity to articulate a grudge. I was wrong to say caprice, it was cold calculation. You went to Laszio, a man twice your age, because it was a step up, not emotionally but materially. Probably you had also found that Marko had too much character for you. The devil only knows why you went no higher than Laszio, in so broad a field as New York, who after all—from your standpoint—was only a salaried chef; but of course you were young, in your twenties—how old are you now?"

She smiled at him.

He shrugged. "I suppose, too, it was a matter of intelligence. You can't have much. Essentially, in fact, you are a lunatic, if a lunatic is an individual dangerously maladjusted to the natural and healthy environment of its species—since the human equipment includes, for instance, a capacity for personal affection and a willingness to strangle selfish and predatory impulse with the rope of social decency. That's why I say you're a lunatic." He sat up and wiggled a finger at her. "Now look here. I haven't time for fencing. I do not suspect Marko of killing your husband, though I admit it is possible he did it. I have considered all the plausible inferences from the coincidence of the radio, am still considering them, and have reached no conclusion. What else do you want to know?"

"All that you said. . . ." Her hand fluttered and rested again on the arm of her chair. "Did Marko tell you all that about me?"

"Marko hasn't mentioned your name for five years. What else do you want to know?"

She stirred. I saw her breast go up and down, but there was no sound of the soft sigh. "It wouldn't do any good, since I'm a lunatic. But I thought I would ask you if Malfi had told you about Zelota."

"No. What about him? Who is he?"

I horned in. "He told me." Their eyes moved to me and I

99

went on, "I hadn't had a chance to report it. Malfi told me in the parlor after dinner that Laszio stole something a long time ago from a guy named Zelota, and Zelota had sworn to kill him, and about a month ago he showed up in New York and went to Malfi to ask for a job. Malfi wouldn't give him one, but Vukcic did, at Rusterman's, and Zelota only lasted a week and then disappeared. Malfi said he told Liggett and Mrs. Laszio about it and they thought he ought to tell you."

"Thanks.—Anything else, madam?"

She sat and looked at him. Her lids were so low that I couldn't see what her eyes were like, and I doubted if he could. Then without saying anything she pulled a hot one. She got up, taking her time, leaving her cloak there on the back of the chair, and stepped over to Wolfe and put her hand on his shoulder and patted it. He moved and twisted his big neck to look up at her, but she stepped away again with a smile at the corners of her mouth, and reached for the cloak. I hopped across to hold it for her, thinking I might as well get a pat too, but apparently she didn't believe in spoiling the help. She told Wolfe good-night, neither sweet nor sour, just good-night, and started off. I went to the foyer to let her out.

I returned and grinned down at Wolfe. "Well, how do you feel? Was she marking you for slaughter? Or putting a curse on you? Or is that how she starts the miasma going?" I peered at the shoulder she had patted. "About this Zelota business, I was going to tell you when she interrupted us. You noticed that Malfi said she told him to tell you about it. It seems that Malfi and Liggett were with her during the afternoon to offer consolation."

Wolfe nodded. "But, as you see, she is inconsolable. Bring those men in."

10

IT LOOKED hopeless to me. I would have made it at least ten to one that Wolfe's unlimited conceit was going to cost us most of a night's sleep with nothing to chalk up against it. It struck me as plain silly, and I might have gone so far as to say that his tackling that array of Africans in a body showed a dangerous maladjustment to the natural and healthy environment of a detective. Picture it: Lio Coyne had caught a glimpse of a greenjacket she couldn't recognize standing by the end of the screen with his finger on his lips, and another servant's face—chiefly his eyes, and she couldn't recognize him either—peeking through a crack in the door that led to the pantry hall and on to the kitchen. That was our crop of facts. And the servants had already told the sheriff that they had seen and heard nothing. Fat chance. There might have been a slim one if they had been taken singly, but in a bunch like that, not for my money.

The chair problem was solved by letting them sit on the floor. Fourteen altogether. Wolfe, using his man-to-man tone, apologized for that. Then he wanted to know their names, and made sure that he got everyone; that used up ten minutes. I was curious to see how he would start the ball rolling, but there were other preliminaries to attend to; he asked what they would like to drink. They mumbled that they didn't want anything, but he said nonsense, we would probably be there most of the night, which seemed to startle them and caused some murmuring. It ended by my being sent to the phone to order an assortment of beer, bourbon, ginger ale, charged water, glasses, lemons, mint and ice. An expenditure like that meant that Wolfe was in dead earnest. When I rejoined the gathering he was telling a plump little runt, not a greenjacket, with a ravine in his chin:

"I'm glad of this opportunity to express my admiration, Mr. Crabtree. Mr. Servan tells me that the shad roe mousse was handled entirely by you. Any chef would have been proud of it. I noticed that Mr. Mondor asked for more. In Europe they don't have shad roe."

The runt nodded solemnly, with reserve. They were all using plenty of reserve, not to mention constraint, suspicion and reticence. Most of them weren't looking at Wolfe or at much of anything else. He sat facing them, running his eyes over them. Finally he sighed and began:

"You know, gentlemen, I have had very little experience in dealing with black men. That may strike you as a tactless remark, but it really isn't. It is certainly true that you can't deal with all men alike. It is popularly supposed that in this part of the country whites adopt a well-defined attitude in dealing with the blacks, and blacks do the same in dealing with whites. That is no doubt true up to a point, but it is subject to enormous variation, as your own experience will show you. For instance, say you wish to ask a favor here at Kanawha Spa, and you approach either Mr. Ashley, the manager, or Mr. Servan. Ashley is bourgeois, irritable, conventional, and rather pompous, Servan is gentle, generous, sentimental, and an artist—and also Latin. Your approach to Mr. Ashley would be quite different from your approach to Mr. Servan.

"But even more fundamental than the individual differences are the racial and national and tribal differences. That's what I mean when I say I've had limited experience in dealing with black men. I mean black Americans. Many years ago I handled some affairs with dark-skinned people in Egypt and Arabia and Algiers, but of course that has nothing to do with you. You gentlemen are Americans, must more completely Americans than I am, for I wasn't born here. This is your native country. It was you and your brothers, black and white, who let me come here to live, and I hope you'll let me say, without getting maudlin, that I'm grateful to you for it."

Somebody mumbled something. Wolfe disregarded it and went on: "I asked Mr. Servan to have you come over here tonight because I want to ask you some questions and find out something. That's the only thing I'm interested in: the information I want to get. I'll be frank with you; if I thought I could get it by bullying you and threatening you, I wouldn't hesitate a moment. I wouldn't use physical violence even if I could, because one of my romantic ideas is that physical violence is beneath the dignity of a man, and that whatever you get by physical aggression costs more than it is worth. But I confess that if I thought threats or tricks would serve my purpose with you, I wouldn't hesitate to use them. I'm convinced they wouldn't, having meditated on this situation, and that's why I'm in a hole. I have been told by white Americans that the only way to get anything out of black Americans is by threats, tricks, or violence. In the first place, I doubt if it's true; and even if it is true generally I'm sure it isn't in this case. I know of no threats that would be effective, I can't think up a trick that would work, and I can't use violence."

Wolfe put his hands at them palms up. "I need the information. What are we going to do?"

Someone snickered, and others glanced at him—a tall skinny one squatting against the wall, with high cheekbones, dark brown. The runt whom Wolfe had complimented on the shad roe mousse glared around like a sergeant at talking in the ranks. The one that sat stillest was the one with the flattest nose, a young one, big and muscular, a greenjacket that I had noticed at the pavilion because he never opened his mouth to reply to anything. The headwaiter with the chopped-off ear said in a low silky tone:

"You just ask us and we tell you. That's what Mr. Servan said we was to do."

Wolfe nodded at him. "I admit that seems the obvious way, Mr. Moulton. And the simplest. But I fear we would find ourselves confronted by difficulties."

"Yes, sir. What is the nature of the difficulties?"

A gruff voice boomed: "You just ask us and we tell you anything." Wolfe aimed his eyes at the source of it:

"I hope you will. Would you permit a personal remark? That is a surprising voice to come from a man named Hyacinth Brown. No one would expect it. As for the difficulties—Archie, there's the refreshment. Perhaps some of you would help Mr. Goodwin?"

That took another ten minutes, or maybe more. Four or five of them came along, under the headwaiter's direction, and we carried the supplies in and got them arranged on a table against the wall. Wolfe was provided with beer. I had forgot to include milk in the order, so I made out with a bourbon highball. The muscular kid with the flat nose, whose name was Paul Whipple, took plain ginger ale, but all the rest accepted stimulation. Getting the drinks around, and back to their places on the floor, they loosened up a little for a few observations, but fell dead silent when Wolfe put down his empty glass and started off again:

"About the difficulties, perhaps the best way is to illustrate them. You know of course that what we are concerned with is the murder of Mr. Laszio. I am aware that you have told the sheriff that you know nothing about it, but I want some details from you, and besides, you may have recollected some incident which slipped your minds at the time you talked with the sheriff. I'll begin with you, Mr. Moulton. You were in the kitchen Tuesday evening?"

"Yes, sir. All evening. There was to be the oeufs au cheval served after they got through with those sauces."

"I know. We missed that. Did you help arrange the table with the sauces?"

"Yes, sir." The headwaiter was smooth and suave. "Three of us helped Mr. Laszio. I personally took in the sauces on the serving wagon. After everything was arranged he rang for me only once, to remove the ice from the water. Except for that, I was in the kitchen all the time. All of us were."

"In the kitchen, or the pantry hall?"

"The kitchen. There was nothing to go to the pantry for. Some of the cooks were working on the oeufs au cheval, and the boys were cleaning up, and some of us were eating what was left of the duck and other things. Mr. Servan told us we could."

"Indeed. That was superlative duck."

"Yes, sir. All of these gentlemen can cook like nobody's business. They sure can cook."

"They are the world's best. They are the greatest living masters of the subtlest and kindliest of the arts." Wolfe sighed, opened beer, poured, watched it foam to the top, and then demanded abruptly, "So you saw and heard nothing of the murder?"

"No, sir."

"The last you saw of Mr. Laszio was when you went in to take the ice from the water?"

"Yes, sir."

"I understand there were two knives for slicing the squabs. One of stainless steel with a silver handle, the other a kitchen carver. Were they both on the table when you took the ice from the water?"

The greenjacket hesitated only a second. "Yes, sir, I think they were. I glanced around the table to see that everything was all right, because I felt responsible, and I would have noticed if one of the knives had been gone. I even looked at the marks on the dishes—the sauces."

"You mean the numbered cards?"

"No, sir, you wouldn't, because the numbers were small, dishes with chalk so they wouldn't get mixed up in the kitchen or while I was taking them in."

"I didn't see them."

"No, sir, you wouldn't because the numbers were small, below the rim on the far side from you. When I put the dishes by the numbered cards I turned them so the chalk numbers were at the back, facing Mr. Laszio."

"And the chalk numbers were in the proper order when you took the ice from the water?"

"Yes, sir."

"Was someone tasting the sauces when you were in there?"

"Yes, sir, Mr. Keith."

"Mr. Laszio was there alive?"

"Yes, sir, he was plenty alive. He bawled me out for putting in too much ice. He said it froze the palate."

"So it does. Not to mention the stomach. When you were in there, I don't suppose you happened to look behind either of those screens."

"No, sir. We had shoved the screens back when we cleaned up after dinner."

"And after, you didn't enter the dining room again until after Mr. Laszio's body was discovered?"

"No, sir, I didn't."

"Nor look into the dining room?"

"No, sir."

"You're sure of that?"

"Sure I'm sure. I guess I'd remember my movements."

"I suppose you would." Wolfe frowned, fingered at this glass of beer, and raised it to his mouth and gulped. The headwaiter, self-possessed, took a sip of his highball, but I noticed that his eyes didn't leave Wolfe.

Wolfe put his glass down. "Thank you, Mr. Moulton." He put his eyes on the one on Moulton's left, a medium-sized one with gray showing in his kinky hair and wrinkles on his face. "Now Mr. Grant. You're a cook?"

"Yes, sir." His tone was husky and he cleared his throat and repeated, "Yes, sir. I work on fowl and game over at the hotel, but here I'm helping Crabby. All of us best ones, Mr. Servan sent us over here, to make an *im*pression."

"Who is Crabby?"

"He means me." It was the plump runt with a ravine in his chin, the sergeant.

"Ah. Mr. Crabtree. Then you helped with the shad roe mousse."

Mr. Grant said, "Yes, sir. Crabby just su*per*vised. I done the work."

"Indeed. My respects to you. On Tuesday evening, you were in the kitchen?"

"Yes, sir. I can make it short and sweet, mister. I was in the kitchen, I didn't leave the kitchen, and in the kitchen I remained. Maybe that covers it."

"It seems to. You didn't go to the dining room or the pantry hall?"

"No, sir. I just said about remaining in the kitchen."

"So you did. No offense, Mr. Grant. I merely want to make sure." Wolfe's eyes moved on. "Mr. Whipple. I know you, of course. You are an alert and efficient waiter. You anticipated my wants at dinner. You seem young to have developed such competence. How old are you?"

The muscular kid with the flat nose looked straight at Wolfe and said, "I'm twenty-one."

Moulton, the headwater, gave him an eye and told him, "Say sir." Then turned to Wolfe: "Paul's a college boy."

"I see. What college, Mr. Whipple?"

"Howard University. Sir."

Wolfe wiggled a finger. "If you feel rebellious about the sir, dispense with it. Enforced courtesy is worse than none. You are at college for culture?"

"I'm interested in anthropology."

"Indeed. I have met Franz Boas, and have his books autographed. You were, I remember, present on Tuesday evening. You waited on me at dinner."

"Yes, sir. I helped in the dining room after dinner, cleaning up and arranging for that demonstration with the sauces."

"Your tone suggests disapproval."

"Yes, sir. If you ask me. It's frivolous and childish for mature men to waste their time and talent, and other people's time—"

"Shut up, Paul." It was Moulton.

Wolfe said, "You're young, Mr. Whipple. Besides, each of us has his special set of values, and if you expect me to respect yours you must respect mine. Also I remind you that Paul Lawrence Dunbar said 'the best thing a 'possum ever does is fill an empty belly.'"

The college boy looked at him in surprise. "Do you know Dunbar?"

"Certainly. I am not a barbarian. But to return to Tuesday evening, after you finished helping in the dining room did you go to the kitchen?"

"Yes, sir."

"And left there—"

"Not at all. Not until we got word of what had happened."

"You were in the kitchen all the time?"

"Yes, sir."

"Thank you." Wolfe's eyes moved again. "Mr. Daggett . . ."

He went on, and got more of the same. I finished my highball and tilted my chair back against the wall and closed my eyes. The voices, the questions and answers, were just noises in my ears. I didn't get the idea, and it didn't sound to me as if there was any. Of course Wolfe's declaration that he wouldn't try any tricks because he didn't know any, was the same as a giraffe saying it couldn't reach up for a bite on account of its short neck. But it seemed to me that if he thought that monotonous ring around the rosie was a good trick, the sooner he got out of the mountain air of West Virginia and back to sea level, the better. On the questions and answers went; he didn't skimp anybody and he kept getting personal; he even discovered that Hyacinth Brown's wife had gone off and left him three pickaninnies to take care of. Once in awhile I opened my eyes to see how far around he had got, and then closed them again. My wrist watch said a quarter to two when I heard, through the open window, a rooster crowing away off.

I let my chair come down when I heard my name. "Archie. Beer please."

I was a little slow on the pickup and Moulton got to his feet and beat me to it. I sat down again. Wolfe invited the others to replenish, and a lot of them did. Then, after he had emptied a glass and wiped his lips, he settled back and ran his eyes over the gang, slowly around and back, until he had them all waiting for him.

He said in a new crisp tone: "Gentlemen, I said I would illustrate the difficulty I spoke of. It now confronts us. It was suggested that I ask for the information I want. I did so. You have all heard everything that was said. I wonder how many of you know that one of you told me a direct and deliberate lie."

Perfect silence. Wolfe let it gather for five seconds and then went on:

"Doubtless you share the common knowledge that on Tuesday evening some eight or ten minutes elapsed from the moment that Mr. Berin left the dining room until the moment that Mr. Vukcic entered it, and that Mr. Berin says that when he left Mr. Laszio was there alive, and Mr. Vukcic says that when he entered Mr. Laszio was not there at all. Of course Mr. Vukcic didn't look behind the screen. During that interval of eight or ten minutes someone opened the door from the terrace to the dining room and looked in, and saw two colored men. One, in livery, was standing beside the screen with his finger to his lips; the other had opened the door, a few inches, which led to the pantry hall, and was peering through, looking directly at the man by the screen. I have no idea who the man by the screen was. The one peering through the pantry hall door was one of you who are now sitting before me. That's the one who has lied to me."

Another silence. It was broken by a loud snicker, again from the tall skinny one who was still squatting against the wall. This time he followed it with a snort: "You tell 'em, boss!" Half a dozen black heads jerked at him and Crabtree said in disgust, "Boney, you damn drunken fool!" and then apologized to Wolfe, "He's a no good clown, that young man. Yes, sir. About what you say, we're all sorry you've got to feel that one of us told you a lie. You've got hold of some bad information."

"No. I must contradict you. My information is good."

Moulton inquired in his silky musical voice, "Might I ask who looked in the door and saw all that?"

"No. I've told you what was seen, and I know it was seen." Wolfe's eyes swept the faces. "Dismiss the idea, all of you, of impeaching my information. Those of you who have no knowledge of that scene in the dining room are out of this anyway; those who know of it know also that my information comes from an eye-witness. Otherwise how would I know, for instance, that the man by the screen had his finger to his lips? No, gentlemen, the situation is simple: I know that at least one of you lied, and he knows that I know it. I wonder if there isn't a chance of ending so simple a situation in a simple manner and have it done with? Let's try. Mr. Moulton, was it you who looked through that door—the door from the dining room to the pantry hall and saw the man by the screen with his finger to his lips?"

The headwaiter with the chopped-off ear slowly shook his head. "No, sir."

"Mr. Grant, was it you?"

"No, *sir.*"

"Mr. Whipple, was it you?"

"No, sir."

He went on around, and piled up fourteen negatives out of

fourteen chances. Still batting a thousand. When he had completed that record he poured a glass of beer and sat and frowned at the foam. Nobody spoke and nobody moved. Finally, without drinking the beer, Wolfe leaned back and sighed patiently. He resumed in a murmur:

"I was afraid we would be here most of the night. I told you so. I also told you that I wasn't going to use threats, and I don't intend to. But by your unanimous denial you've turned a simple situation into a complicated one, and it has to be explained to you.

"First, let's say that you persist in the denial. In that case, the only thing I can do is inform the authorities and let them interview the person who looked into the dining room from the terrace. They will be convinced, as I am, of the correctness of the information, and they will start on you gentlemen with that knowledge in their possession. They will be certain that one of you saw the man by the screen. I don't pretend to know what they'll do to you, or how long you'll hold out, but that's what the situation will be, and I shall be out of it."

Wolfe sighed again, and surveyed the faces. "Now, whoever you are, let's say that you abandon your denial and tell me the truth, what will happen? Similarly, you will sooner or later have to deal with the local authorities, but under quite different circumstances. I am talking now to one of you—you know which one, I don't. It doesn't seem to me that any harm will be done if I tell Mr. Tolman and the sheriff that you and your colleagues came to see me at my request, and that you volunteered the information about what you saw in the dining room. There will be no reason why the person who first gave me the information should enter into it at all, if you tell the truth—though you may be sure that I am prepared to produce that person if necessary. Of course, they won't like it that you withheld so important a fact Tuesday night, but I think I can arrange beforehand that they'll be lenient about that. I shall make it a point to do so. None of the rest of you need be concerned in it at all.

"Now..." Wolfe looked around at them again "...here comes the hard part. Whoever you are, I can understand your denial and sympathize with it. You looked through the door—doubtless on account of a noise you had heard—and saw a man of your race standing by the screen, and some forty minutes later, when you learned what had happened, you knew that man had murdered Laszlo. Or at the least, strongly suspected it. You not only knew that the murderer was a black man, you probably recognized him, since he wore the Kanawha Spa livery and was therefore a fellow employee, and he directly faced you as you looked through the door. And that presents another complication. If he is a man who is close to you and has a place in your heart, I presume you'll hold to your denial in spite of anything I may say and the sheriff may do. In that event your colleagues here will share a lot of discomfort with you, but that can't be helped.

"But if he is not personally close to you, if you have refused to expose him only because he is a fellow man—or more particularly because he is of your color—I'd like to make some remarks. First the fellow man. That's nonsense. It was realized centuries ago that it is impossible for a man to protect himself against murder, because it's extremely easy to kill a man, so it was agreed that men should protect each other. But if I help protect you, you must help protect me, whether you like me or not. If you don't do your part you're out of the agreement; you're an outlaw.

"But this murderer was a black man, and you're black too. I confess that makes it ticklish. The agreements of human society embrace not only protection against murder, but thousands of other things, and it is certainly true that in America—not to mention other continents—the whites have excluded the blacks from some of the benefits of those agreements. It is said that the exclusion has sometimes even extended to murder—that in parts of this country a white man may kill a black one, if not with impunity, at least with a good chance of escaping the penalty which the agreement imposes. That's bad. It's deplorable, and I don't blame black men for resenting it. But you are confronted with a fact, not a theory, and how do you propose to change it?

"I am talking to you who saw that man by the screen. If you shield him because he is dear to you, or for any valid personal reason, I have nothing to say, because I don't like futile talk, and you'll have to fight it out with the sheriff. But if you shield him because he is your color, there is a great deal to say. You are rendering your race a serious disservice. You are helping to perpetuate and aggravate the very exclusions which you justly resent. The ideal human agreement is one in which distinctions of race and color and religion are totally disregarded; anyone helping to preserve those distinctions is postponing that ideal; and you are certainly helping to

110

preserve them. If in a question of murder you permit your action to be influenced by the complexion of the man who committed it, no matter whether you yourself are white or pink or black—"

"You're wrong!"

It was a sharp explosion from the mouth of the muscular kid with the flat nose, the college boy. Some of them jumped, I was startled, and everybody looked at him.

Wolfe said, "I think I can justify my position, Mr. Whipple. If you'll let me complete—"

"I don't mean your position. You can have your logic. I mean your facts. One of them."

Wolfe lifted his brows. "Which one?"

"The complexion of the murderer." The college boy was looking him straight in the eye. "He wasn't a black man. I saw him. He was a white man."

11

Right away I got another shock. It was another explosion— this time something crashing to the floor. It took our attention away from the college boy, until we saw it was Boney, the tall skinny one by the wall, who had been lulled to sleep by Wolfe's oration, and, partly awakened by the electricity of Whipple's announcement, had jerked himself off balance and toppled over. He started to grumble and Crabtree glared him out of it. There was a general stir.

Wolfe asked softly, "You saw the man by the screen, Mr. Whipple?"

"Yes."

"When?"

"When he was standing by the screen. It was I who opened the door and looked through."

"Indeed. And you say he was white?"

"No." Whipple's gaze was steadfast at Wolfe; he hadn't turned at the sound of Boney's crash. "I didn't say he was white, I said he was a white man. When I saw him he was black, because he had blacked himself up."

"How do you know that?"

111

"Because I saw him. Do you think I can't tell burnt cork from the real thing? I'm a black man myself. But that wasn't all. As you said, he was holding his finger against his lips, and his hand was different. It wouldn't have taken a black man to see that. He had on tight black gloves."

"Why did you go to the pantry hall and look through the door?"

"I heard a noise in the dining room. Grant wanted some paprika for the oeufs au cheval, and the can was empty, and I went to the cupboard in the hall for a fresh can. That was how I happened to hear the noise. They were making a lot of racket in the kitchen and didn't hear it in there. I was up on the ladder steps looking for the paprika, and after I found it and got down I opened the door a crack to see what the noise had been."

"Did you enter the dining room?"

"No."

Wolfe slowly wiggled a finger. "May I suggest, Mr. Whipple, that the truth is usually good, and lies are sometimes excellent, but a mixture of the two is an abomination?"

"I'm telling the truth and nothing else."

"You didn't before. Since the murderer wasn't a colored man, why not?"

"Because I've learned not to mix up in the affairs of the superior race. If it had been a colored man I would have told. Colored men have got to stop disgracing their color and leave that to white men. You see how good your logic was."

"But my dear sir. That doesn't impugn my logic, it merely shows that you agree with me. We must discuss it some time. Then you withheld this fact because you considered it white men's business and none of yours, and you knew if you divulged it you'd be making trouble for yourself."

"Plenty of trouble. You're a northerner—"

"I'm a man, or try to be. You're studying me; you're an anthropologist. You expect to be a scientist. Give me a considered answer: how sure are you that it was a white man?"

Whipple considered. In a moment he said, "Not sure at all. Burnt cork would look like that on a light brown skin or even a rather dark one, and of course anyone can wear black gloves. But I'm sure about the burnt cork or something similar, and I'm sure about the gloves, and I don't see why a colored man should be painting the lily. Therefore I took it for granted he was a white man, but of course I'm not sure."

"It seems a safe deduction. What was he doing when you saw him?"

"Standing at the end of the screen, turning around. He must have seen me by accident; he couldn't have heard me. That door is noiseless, and I only opened it two or three inches, and there was quite a lot of sound from the radio in the parlor, though the door was closed."

"He was wearing the Kanawha Spa livery?"

"Yes."

"What about his hair?"

"He had a livery cap on. I couldn't see the back of his head."

"Describe him, height, weight...."

"He was medium. I would guess five feet eight or nine, and a hundred and fifty-five or sixty. I didn't inspect him much. I saw at once that he was blacked up, and when he put his finger to his lips I thought he was one of the guests doing a stunt, probably a practical joke, and I supposed the noise I had heard was him jolting the screen or something. I let the door come shut and came away. As I did that, he was starting to turn."

"Toward the table?"

"I would say, toward the door to the terrace."

Wolfe pursed his lips. Then he opened them: "You thought it was a guest playing a joke. If you had tried to decide who it was, which guest would you have picked?"

"I don't know."

"Come, Mr. Whipple. I'm merely trying for general characteristics. Longheaded or round?"

"You asked me to name him. I couldn't name that man. I couldn't identify him. He was blacked up and his cap was pulled low. I think he had light-colored eyes. His face was neither round nor long, but medium. I only saw him one second."

"What about your feeling? Would you say that you had a feeling that you had ever seen him before?"

The college boy shook his head. "The only feeling I had was that I didn't want to interfere in a white man's joke. And afterwards, that I didn't want to interfere in a white man's murder."

The foam on Wolfe's glass of beer was all gone. Wolfe

picked it up, frowned at it, and carried it to his mouth and gulped five times, and set it down empty.

"Well." He put his eyes on Whipple again. "You must forgive me, sir, if I remind you that this story has been extracted from you against your will. I hope you haven't blacked it up—or whitewashed it. When you returned to the kitchen, did you tell anyone what you had seen?"

"No, sir."

"The unusual circumstances of a stranger in the dining room, in Kanawha Spa livery, blacked up with black gloves—you didn't think that worth mentioning?"

"No, sir."

"You damn fool, Paul." It was Crabtree, and he sounded irritated. "You think we ain't as much man as you are?" He turned to Wolfe. "This boy is awful conceited. He's got a good heart hid from people's eyesight, but his head's fixin' to bust. He's going to pack all the burden. No, sir. He came back to the kitchen and told us right off, just the same as he's told it here. We all heard it, passing it around. And for something more special about that, you might ask Moulton there."

The headwaiter with the chopped-off ear jerked around at him. "You talking, Crabby?"

The runt met his stare. "You heard me. Paul spilled it, didn't he? I didn't see anybody put you away on a shelf to save up for the Lord."

Moulton grunted. He stared at Crabtree some more seconds, then shrugged and turned to Wolfe and was again smooth and suave. "What he's referring to, I was about to tell you when Paul got through. I saw that man too."

"The man by the screen?"

"Yes, sir."

"How was that?"

"It was because I thought Paul was taking too long to find the paprika, and I went to the pantry hall after him. When I got there he was just turning away from the door, and he motioned to the dining room with his thumb and said somebody was in there. I didn't know what he meant; of course I knew Mr. Laszio was there, and I pushed the door a little to take a look. The man's back was toward me; he was walking toward the door to the terrace; so I couldn't see his face but I saw his black gloves, and of course I saw the livery he had on. I let the door come shut and asked Paul who it was, and he said he didn't know, he thought it was one of the guests blacked up. I sent Paul to the kitchen with the paprika, and opened the door another crack and looked through, but the man wasn't in sight, so I opened the door wider, thinking to ask Mr. Laszio if he wanted anything. He wasn't by the table. I went on through, and he wasn't anywhere. That looked funny, because I knew how the tasting was supposed to be done, but I can't say I was much surprised."

"Why not?"

"Well, sir . . . you'll allow me to say that these guests have acted very individual from the beginning."

"Yes, I'll allow that."

"Yes, sir. So I just supposed Mr. Laszio had gone to the parlor or somewhere."

"Did you look behind the screen?"

"No, sir. I didn't see any call for a posse."

"There was no one in the room?"

"No, sir. No one in sight."

"What did you do, return to the kitchen?"

"Yes, sir. I didn't figure—"

"You ain't shut yet." It was the plump little chef, warningly. "Mr. Wolfe here is a kindhearted man and he might as well get it and let him have it. We all remember it exactly like you told us about it."

"Oh, you do, Crabby?"

"We do you know."

Moulton shrugged and turned back to Wolfe. "What he's referring to, I was about to tell you. Before I went back to the kitchen I took a look at the table because I was responsible."

"The table with the sauces?"

"Yes, sir."

"Was one of the knives gone?"

"I don't know that. I think I would have noticed, but maybe I wouldn't, because I didn't lift the cover from the squabs, and one of them might have been under that. But I did notice something wrong. Somebody had monkeyed with the sauces. They were all changed around."

I let out a whistle before I thought. Wolfe sent me a sharp glance and then returned his eyes to Moulton and murmured, "Ah! How did you know?"

"I knew by the marks. The numbers chalked on the dishes. When I took them to the table, I put the dish with the chalk mark 1 in front of the card numbered 1, and the 2 in front of the 2, and so on. They weren't that way when I looked. They had been shifted around."

"How many of them?"

"All but two. Numbers 8 and 9 were all right, but the rest had all been moved."

"You can swear to that, Mr. Moulton?"

"I guess it looks like I'm going to have to swear to it."

"And can you?"

"I can, yes, sir."

"How would it be if at the same time you were asked to swear that, having noticed that the dishes had been moved, you replaced them in their proper positions?"

"Yes, sir. That's what I did. I suppose that's what will get me fired. It was none of my business to be correcting things, I knew it wasn't. But if Mr. Servan will listen to me, it was him I did it for. I didn't want him to lose his bet. I knew he had bet with Mr. Keith that the tasters would be eighty percent correct, and when I saw the dishes had been shifted I thought someone was framing him, so I shifted them back. Then I got out of there in a hurry."

"I don't suppose you remember just how they had been changed—where, for instance, number 1 had been moved to?"

"No, sir. I couldn't say that."

"No matter." Wolfe sighed. "I thank you, Mr. Moulton, and you, Mr. Whipple. It is late. I'm afraid we won't get much sleep, for we'll have to deal with Mr. Tolman and the sheriff as early as possible. I suppose you live on the grounds here?"

They told him yes.

"Good. I'll be sending for you. I don't think you'll lose your job, Mr. Moulton. I remember my commitment regarding beforehand arrangements with the authorities and I'll live up to it. I thank all of you gentlemen for your patience. I suppose your hats are in Mr. Goodwin's room?"

They helped me get the bottles and glasses cleared out and stacked in the foyer, and with that expert assistance it didn't take long. The college boy didn't help us because he hung back for a word with Wolfe. The hats and caps finally got distributed, and I opened the foyer door and they filed out. Hyacinth Brown had Boney by the arm, and Boney was still muttering when I shut the door.

In Wolfe's room the light of dawn was at the window, even through the thick shrubbery just outside. It was my second dawn in a row, and I was beginning to feel that I might as well join the Milkmen's Union and be done with it. My eyes felt as if someone had painted household cement on my lids and let it dry. Wolfe had his open, and was still in his chair.

I said, "Congratulations. All you need is wings to be an owl. Shall I leave a call for twelve noon? That would leave you eight hours till dinnertime, and you'd still be ahead of schedule."

He made a face. "Where have they got Mr. Berin in jail?"

"I suppose at Quinby, the county seat."

"How far away is it?"

"Oh, around twenty miles."

"Does Mr. Tolman live there?"

"I don't know. His office must be there, since he's the prosecuting attorney."

"Please find out, and get him on the phone. We want him and the sheriff here at eight o'clock. Tell him—no. When you get him, let me talk to him."

"Now?"

"Now."

I spread out my hands. "It's 4:30 a.m. Let the man—"

"Archie. Please. You tried to instruct me how to handle colored men. Will you try it with white men too?"

I went for the phone.

12

PETTIGREW, the squint-eyed sheriff, shook his head and drawled, "Thank you just the same. I got stuck in the mud and had to flounder around and I'd get that chair all dirty. I'm a pretty good stander anyhow."

My friend Barry Tolman didn't look any too neat himself, but he wasn't muddy and so he hadn't hesitated about taking a seat. It was 8:10 Thursday morning. I felt like the last nickel in a crap game, because like a darned fool I had undraped myself a little after five o'clock and got under the covers, leaving a call for 7:30, and hauling myself out again after only two hours had put me off key for good. Wolfe was having breakfast in the big chair, with a folding table pulled up to him, in a yellow dressing gown, with his face shaved and his hair combed. He possessed five yellow dressing gowns and we had brought along the light woolen one with brown lapels and a brown girdle. He had on a necktie, too.

Tolman said, "As I told you on the phone, I'm supposed to be in court at 9:30. If necessary my assistant can get a postponement, but I'd like to make it if possible. Can't you rush it?"

Wolfe was sipping at his cocoa for erosion on the bite of roll he had taken. When that was disposed of he said, "It depends a good deal on you, sir. It was impossible for me to go to Quinby, as I said, for reasons that will appear. I'll do all I can to hurry it. I haven't been to bed—"

"You said you have information—"

"I have. But the circumstances require a preamble. I take it that you arrested Mr. Berin only because you were convinced he was guilty. You don't especially fancy him as a victim. If strong doubt were cast on his guilt—"

"Certainly." Tolman was impatient. "I told you—"

"So you did. Now let's suppose something. Suppose that a lawyer has been retained to represent Mr. Berin, and I have been engaged to discover evidence in Berin's defense. Suppose further that I have discovered such evidence, of a weight that would lead inevitably to his acquittal when you put him on trial, and it is felt that it would be imprudent to disclose that evidence to you, the enemy, for the present. Suppose you demand that I produce that evidence now. It's true, isn't it, that you couldn't legally enforce that demand? That such evidence is our property until the time we see fit to make use of it—provided you don't discover it independently for yourselves?"

Tolman was frowning. "That's true, of course. But damn it, I've told you that if the evidence against Berin can be explained—"

"I know. I offer, here and now, an explanation that will clear him; but I offer it on conditions."

"What are they?"

Wolfe sipped cocoa and wiped his lips. "They're not onerous. First, that if the explanation casts strong doubt on Berin's guilt, he is to be released immediately."

"Who will decide how strong the doubt is?"

"You."

"All right, I agree. The court is sitting and it can be done in five minutes."

"Good. Second, you are to tell Mr. Berin that I discovered the evidence which set him free, I am solely responsible for it, and God only knows what would have happened to him if I hadn't done it."

Tolman, still frowning, opened his mouth, but the sheriff put in, "Now wait, Barry. Hold your horses." He squinted down at Wolfe. "If you've really got this evidence it must be around somewhere. I suppose we're pretty slow out here in West Virginia—"

"Mr. Pettigrew. Please. I'm not talking about the public credit, I'm not interested in it. Tell the newspaper men whatever you want to. But Mr. Berin is to know, unequivocally, that I did it, and Mr. Tolman is to tell him so."

Tolman asked, "Well, Sam?"

The sheriff shrugged. "I don't give a damn."

"All right," Tolman told Wolfe. "I agree to that."

"Good." Wolfe set the cocoa cup down. "Third, it is understood that I am leaving for New York at 12:40 to-night and under no circumstances—short of a suspicion that I killed Mr. Laszio myself or was an accomplice—am I to be detained."

Pettigrew said good-humoredly, "You go to hell."

"No, not hell." Wolfe sighed. "New York."

Tolman protested, "But what if this evidence makes you a material and essential witness?"

"It doesn't, you must take my word for that. I'm preparing to take yours for several things. I give you my word that within thirty minutes you'll know everything of significance that I know regarding that business in the dining room. I want it agreed that I won't be kept here beyond my train time merely because it is felt I might prove useful. Anyway, I assure you that under those circumstances I wouldn't be useful at all; I would be an insufferable nuisance. Well, sir?"

Tolman hesitated, and finally nodded. "Qualified as you put it, I agree."

If there is a way a canary bird sighs when you let it out of a cage, Wolfe sighed like that. "Now, sir. The fourth and last condition is a little vaguer than the others, but I think it can be defined. The evidence that I am going to give you was brought to me by two men. I led up to its disclosure by methods which seemed likely to be effective, and they were so. You will resent it that these gentlemen didn't give you

119

these facts when they had an opportunity, and I can't help that. I can't estop your feelings, but I can ask you to restrain them, and I have promised to do so. I want your assurance that the gentlemen will not be bullied, badgered or abused, nor be deprived of their freedom, nor in any way persecuted. This is predicated on the assumption that they are merely witnesses and have no share whatever in the guilt of the murder."

The sheriff said, "Hell, mister, we don't abuse people."

"Bullied, badgered, abused, deprived of freedom, persecuted, all excluded. Of course you'll question them as much as you please."

Tolman shook his head. "They'll be material witnesses. They might leave the state. In fact, they will. You're going to, to-night."

"You can put them under bond to remain."

"Until the trial."

Wolfe wiggled a finger. "Not Mr. Berin's trial."

"I don't mean Berin. If this evidence is as good as you say it is. But you can be damn sure there's going to *be* a trial."

"I sincerely hope so." Wolfe was breaking off a piece of roll and buttering it. "What about it, sir? Since you want to get to court. I'm not asking much; merely a decent restraint with my witnesses. Otherwise you'll have to try to dig them out for yourself, and in the meantime the longer you hold Mr. Berin the more foolish you'll look in the end."

"Very well." The blue-eyed athlete nodded. "I agree."

"To the condition as I have stated it?"

"Yes."

"Then the preamble is finished.—Archie, bring them in."

I smothered a yawn as I lifted myself up and went to my room to get them. They had been in there overlooking progress while I had dressed—Wolfe having had a telephone plugged in in his own chamber, and done his own assembling for the morning meeting, during my nap. They had reported in livery. Paul Whipple looked wide awake and defiant, and Moulton, the headwaiter, sleepy and nervous. I told them the stage was set, and let them precede me.

Wolfe told me to push chairs around, and Moulton jumped to help me. Tolman was staring. Pettigrew exclaimed, "Well I'll be damned! It's a couple of niggers! Hey, you, take that chair!" He turned to Wolfe with a grievance: "Now listen, I questioned all those boys, and by God if they—"

Wolfe snapped, "These are my witnesses. Mr. Tolman wants to get to court. I said you'd resent it, didn't I? Go ahead, but keep it to yourself." He turned to the college boy. "Mr. Whipple, I think we'll have your story first. Tell these gentlemen what you told me last night."

Pettigrew had stepped forward with a mean eye. "We don't mister niggers here in West Virginia, and we don't need anybody coming down here to tell us—"

"Shut up, Sam!" Tolman was snappy too. "We're wasting time.—Your name's Whipple? What do you do?"

"Yes, sir." The boy spoke evenly. "I'm a waiter. Mr. Servan put me on duty at Pocahontas Pavilion Tuesday noon."

"What have you got to say?"

The upshot of it was that Tolman couldn't have got to court on time, for it was after nine-thirty when he left Kanawha Spa. It took only a quarter of an hour to get all the details of the two stories, but they went on from there, or rather, back and around. Tolman did a pretty good job of questioning, but Pettigrew was too mad to be of much account. He kept making observations about how educated Whipple thought he was, and how he knew what kind of lessons it was that Whipple really needed. Tolman kept pushing the sheriff off and doing some real cross-examining, and twice or thrice I saw Wolfe, who was finishing his breakfast at leisure, give a little nod as an acknowledgment of Tolman's neat job. Whipple kept himself even-toned right through, but I could see him holding himself in when the sheriff made observations about his education and the kind of lessons he needed. Moulton started off jerky and nervous, but he smoothed off as he went along, and his only job was to stick to his facts in reply to Tolman's questions, since Pettigrew was concentrating on Whipple.

Finally Tolman's string petered out. He raised his brows at Wolfe, glanced at the sheriff, and looked back again at Moulton with a considering frown.

Pettigrew demanded, "Where did you boys leave your caps? We'll have to take you down to Quinby with us."

Wolfe was crisp right away. "Oh, no. Remember the agreement. They stay here on their jobs. I've spoken with Mr. Servan about that."

"I don't give a damn if you've spoken with Ashley himself. They go to jail till they get bond."

Wolfe's eyes moved. "Mr. Tolman?"

"Well . . . it was agreed they could be put under bond."

"But that was when you supposed that they were persons who were likely to leave your jurisdiction. These men have jobs here; why should they leave? Mr. Moulton has a wife and children. Mr. Whipple is a university man." He looked at the sheriff. "Your assumption that you know how to deal with colored men and I don't is impertinent nonsense. Tuesday night, as an officer of the law engaged in the investigation of a crime, at which you are supposed to be expert, you questioned these men and failed to learn anything. You didn't even have your suspicions aroused. Last night I had a talk with them and uncovered vital information regarding that crime. Surely you have enough intelligence to see how utterly discredited you are. Do you want your whole confounded county to know about it? Pfui!" He turned to the two greenjackets. "You men get out of here and go to your stations and get to work. You understand, of course, that Mr. Tolman will need your evidence and you will hold yourselves subject to his proper demands. If he requires bond, any lawyer can arrange it. Well, go on!"

Paul Whipple was already on his way to the door. Moulton hesitated only an instant, glancing at Tolman, and then followed. I got up and moseyed out to see that the outside door was shut behind them.

When I got back Pettigrew was in the middle of some remarks, using whatever words happened to come handy, regarding the tribal customs and personal habits of aborigines. Tolman was back on his shoulders with his hands thrust in his pockets, surveying Wolfe, and Wolfe was daintily collecting crumbs and depositing them on the fruit plate. Neither was paying any attention to the sheriff, and eventually he fizzed out.

Wolfe looked up. "Well, sir?"

Tolman nodded. "Yep, I guess you win. It looks like they're telling the truth. They can make up fancy ones when they feel like it, but this doesn't sound like their kind." His blue eyes narrowed a little. "Of course, there's something else to consider. I understand you've been appealed to, to get Berin clear, and also I've heard that you were offered a good commission to get Berin for the job that Laszio had. I learned that from Clay Ashley, who had it from his friend Liggett of the Hotel Churchill. Naturally that raises the question as to how far you yourself might go in discovering evidence that would free Berin."

"You put it delicately." The corners of Wolfe's lips went up a little. "You mean manufacturing evidence. I assure you I'm not that stupid or that desperate, to bribe strangers to tell intricate lies. Besides, I would have had to bribe not two men, but fourteen. Those stories were uncovered in this room last night, in the presence of all the cooks and waiters on duty at Pocahontas Pavilion. You may question them all. No, sir; those stories are bona fide." He upturned a palm. "But you know that; you put them to a good test. And now—since you were anxious to return to Quinby in time for your appearance in court—"

"Yeah, I know." Tolman didn't move. "This is a sweet mess now, this murder. If those niggers are telling it straight, and I guess they are, do you realize what it means? Among other things, it means that all of that bunch are out of it, except that fellow Blanc who says he was in his room. And he's a stranger here, and how the devil could he have got hold of a Kanawha Spa uniform? If you eliminate him, all you've got left is the wide world."

Wolfe murmured, "Yes, it's a pretty problem. Thank goodness it isn't mine. But as to our agreement—I've performed my part, haven't I? Have I cast strong doubt on Mr. Berin's guilt?"

The sheriff snorted. Tolman said shortly, "Yes. The fact that those sauce dishes were shifted around—certainly. But damn it, who shifted them?"

"I couldn't say. Perhaps the murderer, or possibly Mr. Laszio himself, to make a fool of Berin." Wolfe shrugged. "Quite a job for you. You will set Berin free this morning?"

"What else can I do? I can't hold him now."

"Good. Then if you don't mind . . . since you're in a hurry, and I haven't been to bed . . ."

"Yeah." Tolman stayed put. He sat with his hands still in his pockets, his legs stretched out, the toes of his shoes making little circles in the air. "A hell of a mess," he declared after a silence. "Except for Blanc, there's nowhere to begin. That nigger's description might be almost anyone. Of course, it's possible that it was a nigger that did it and used black gloves and burnt cork to throw us off, but what nigger around here could have any reason for wanting to kill Laszio?" He was silent again. Finally he abruptly sat up. "Look here. I'm not sorry you got Berin out of it, whether you made it into a mess or not. And I'll meet the conditions I agreed to, including no

123

interference with your leaving here tonight. But since you're turning over evidence, what else have you got? I admit you're good and you've made a monkey out of me on this Berin business—not to mention the sheriff here. Maybe you can come across with some more of the same. What more have you found out?"

"Nothing whatever."

"Have you any idea who it was the niggers saw in the dining room?"

"None."

"Do you think that Frenchman did it? Blanc?"

"I don't know. I doubt it."

"The Chinese woman who was outdoors—do you think she was mixed up in it?"

"No."

"Do you think the radio being turned on at that particular time had anything to do with it?"

"Certainly. It drowned the noise of Laszio's fall—and his outcry, if he made one."

"But was it turned on purposely—for that?"

"I don't know."

Tolman frowned. "When I had Berin, or thought I had, I decided that the radio was a coincidence, or a circumstance that he took advantage of. Now that's open again." He leaned forward at Wolfe. "I want you to do something for me. I don't pass for a fool, but I admit I'm a little shy on experience, and you're not only an old hand, you're recognized as one of the best there is. I'm not too proud to yell for help if I need it. It looks like the next step is a good session with Blanc, and I'd like to have you in on it. Better still, handle it yourself and let me sit and listen. Will you do that?"

"No, sir."

Tolman was taken aback. "You won't?"

"No. I won't even discuss it. Confound it, I came down here for a holiday!" Wolfe made a face. "Monday night, on the train, I got no sleep. Tuesday night it was you who kept me up until four o'clock. Last night my engagement to clear Mr. Berin prevented my going to bed at all. This evening I am supposed to deliver an important address to a group of eminent men, on their own subject. I need the refreshment of sleep, and there is my bed. As for your interview with Mr. Blanc, I remind you that you agreed to free Mr. Berin immediately upon presentation of my evidence."

He looked and sounded very final. The sheriff started to growl something, but I was called away by a knock on the door. I went to the foyer, telling myself that if it was anyone who was likely to postpone the refreshment of sleep any longer, I would lay him out with a healthy sock on the button and just leave him there.

Which might have done for Vukcic, big as he was, but I wouldn't strike a woman merely because I was sleepy, and he was accompanied by Constanza Berin. I flung the door the rest of the way and she crossed the threshold. Vukcic began a verbal request, but she wasn't bothering with amenities, she was going right ahead.

I reached for her and missed her. "Hey, wait a minute! We have company. Your friend Barry Tolman is in there."

She wheeled on me. "Who?"

"You heard me. Tolman."

She wheeled again and opened the door to Wolfe's room and breezed on through. Vukcic looked at me and shrugged, and followed her, and I went along, thinking that if I needed a broom and dustpan I could get them later.

Tolman had jumped to his feet at sight of her. For two seconds he was white, then a nice pink, and then he started for her:

"Miss Berin! Thank God—"

An icy blast hit him and stopped him in his tracks with his mouth open. It wasn't vocal; her look didn't need any accompaniment. With him frozen, she turned a different look, practically as devastating, on Nero Wolfe:

"And you said you would help us! You said you would make them free my father!" Nothing but a superworm could deserve such scorn as that. "And it was you who suggested that about his list—about the sauces! I suppose you thought no one would know—"

"My dear Miss Berin—"

"Now everybody knows! It was you who brought the evidence against him! *That* evidence! And you pretending to Mr. Servan and Mr. Vukcic and me—"

I got Wolfe's look and saw his lips moving at me, though I couldn't hear him. I stepped across and gripped her arm and turned her. "Listen, give somebody a chance—"

She was pulling, but I held on. Wolfe said sharply, "She's hysterical. Take her out of here."

125

I felt her arm relax, and turned her loose, and she moved to face Wolfe again.

She told him quietly, "I'm not hysterical."

"Of course you are. All women are. Their moments of calm are merely recuperative periods between outbursts. I want to tell you something. Will you listen?"

She stood and looked at him.

He nodded. "Thank you. I make this explanation because I don't want unfriendliness from your father. I made the suggestion that the lists be compared with the correct list, not dreaming that it would result in implicating your father—in fact, thinking that it would help to clear him. Unfortunately it happened differently, and it became necessary to undo the mischief I had unwittingly caused. The only way to do that was to discover other evidence which would establish his innocence. I have done so. Your father will be released within an hour."

Constanza stared at him, and went nearly as white as Tolman had on seeing her, and then her blood came back as his had done. She stammered, "But—but—I don't believe it. I've just been over to that place—and they wouldn't even let me see him—"

"You won't have to go again. He will rejoin you here this morning. I undertook with you and Mr. Servan and Mr. Vukcic to clear your father of this ridiculous charge, and I have done that. The evidence has been give to Mr. Tolman. Don't you understand what I'm saying?"

Apparently she was beginning to, and it was causing drastic internal adjustments. Her eyes were drawing together, diagonal creases were appearing from the corners of her nose to the corners of her mouth, her cheeks were slowly puffing up, and her chin began to move. She was going to cry, and it looked as if it might be a good one. For half a minute, evidently, she thought she was going to be able to stave it off; then all of a sudden she realized that she wasn't. She turned and ran for the door. She got it open and disappeared. That galvanized Tolman. Without stopping for farewells he jumped for the door she had left open—and he was gone too.

Vukcic and I looked at each other. Wolfe sighed.

The sheriff made a move. "Admitting you're smart," he drawled at Wolfe, "and all that, if I was Barry Tolman you wouldn't take the midnight or any other train out of here until certain details had been attended to."

Wolfe nodded and murmured, "Good day, sir."

126

He went, and banged the foyer door so hard behind him that I jumped. I sat down and observed, "My nerves are like fishing worms on hooks." Vukcic sat down too.

Wolfe looked at him and inquired, "Well, Marko? I suppose we might as well say good morning. Is that what you came for?"

"No." Vukcic ran his fingers through his hair. "It fell to me, more or less, to stand by Berin's daughter, and when she wanted to drive to Quinby—that's the town where the jail is—it was up to me to take her. Then they wouldn't let her see him. If I had known you had already found evidence to clear him . . ." He shook himself. "By the way, what's the evidence? If it isn't a secret."

"I don't know whether it's a secret or not. It doesn't belong to me any more; I've handed it over to the authorities, and I suppose they should be permitted to decide about divulging it. I can tell you one thing that's no secret: I didn't get to bed last night."

"Not at all?"

"No."

Vukcic grunted. "You don't look done up." He ran his fingers through his hair again. "Listen, Nero. I'd like to ask you something. Dina came to see you last night. Didn't she?"

"Yes."

"What did she have to say? That is, if it's proper to tell me."

"You can judge of the propriety. She told me that she is a special kind of woman and that she thought that you thought that I suspected you of killing Laszio." Wolfe grimaced. "And she patted me on the shoulder."

Vukcic said angrily, "She's a damned fool."

"I suppose so. But a very dangerous fool. Of course, a hole in the ice offers peril only to those who go skating. This is none of my business, Marko, but you brought it up."

"I know I did. What the devil made her think that I thought you suspected me of murdering Laszio?"

"Didn't you tell her so?"

"No. Did she say I did?"

Wolfe shook his head. "She wasn't on the road, she was winding around. She did say, however, that you told her of my questions about the radio and the dancing."

Vukcic nodded gloomily, and was silent. At length he shook himself. "Yes, I had a talk with her. Two talks. There's no

127

doubt about her being dangerous. She gets...you must realize that she was my wife for five years. Again yesterday I had her close to me, I had her in my arms. It isn't her tricks, I'm on to all her tricks, it's the mere fact of what she is. You wouldn't see that, Nero, or feel it, it wouldn't have any effect on you, because you've put yourself behind a barricade. As you say, a hole in the ice is dangerous only to those who go skating. But damn it, what does life consist of if you're afraid to take—"

"Marko!" Wolfe sounded peevish. "I've often told you that's your worst habit. When you argue with yourself, do it inside your head; don't pretend it's me you're persuading and shout platitudes at me. You know very well what life consists of, it consists of the humanities, and among them is a decent and intelligent control of the appetites which we share with dogs. A man doesn't wolf a carcass or howl on a hillside from dark to dawn; he eats well-cooked food, when he can get it, in judicious quantities; and he suits his ardor to his wise convenience."

Vukcic was standing up. He frowned and growled down at his old friend: "So I'm howling, am I?"

"You are and you know it."

"Well. I'm sorry. I'm damned sorry."

He turned on his heel and strode from the room.

I got up and went to the window to retrieve a curtain that had been whipped out by the draft from the opened door. In the thick shrubbery just outside a bird was singing, and I startled it. Then I went and planted myself in front of Wolfe. He had his eyes closed, and as I gazed at him his massive form went up with the leverage of a deep sigh, and down again.

I yawned and said, "Anyhow, thank the Lord they all made a quick exit. It's moving along for ten o'clock, and you need sleep, not to mention me."

He opened his eyes. "Archie. I have affection for Marko Vukcic. I hunted dragonflies with him in the mountains. Do you realize that that fool is going to let that fool make a fool of him again?"

I yawned. "Listen to you. If I did a sentence like that you'd send me from the room. You're in bad shape. I tell you, we both need sleep. Did you mean it when you told Tolman that as far as this murder is concerned you're not playing any more?"

"Certainly. Mr. Berin is cleared. We are no longer interested. We leave here to-night."

"Okay. Then for God's sake let's go to bed."

He closed his eyes and sighed again. It appeared that he wanted to sit and worry about Vukcic a while, and I couldn't help him any with that, so I turned and started out, intending not only to display the DO NOT DISTURB but also to leave positive instructions with the greenjacket in the main hall. But just as I had my hand on the knob his voice stopped me.

"Archie. You've had more sleep than I have. I was about to say, we haven't gone over that speech since we got here. I intended to rehearse it at least twice. Do you know which bag it's in? Get it, please."

If we had been in New York I would have quit the job.

13

AT TEN O'CLOCK I sat on a chair by the open window and yawned, with my eyes on the typescript, my own handiwork. We had worked through it to page 9.

Wolfe, facing me, was sitting up in bed with four cushions at his back, displaying half an acre of yellow silk pajamas. On the bedstand beside him were two empty beer bottles and an empty glass. He appeared to be frowning intently at my socks as he went on:

". . . but the indescribable flavor of the finest of Georgia hams, the quality which places them, in my opinion, definitely above the best to be found in Europe, is not due to the post mortem treatment of the flesh at all. Expert knowledge and tender care in the curing are indeed essential, but they are to be found in Czestochowa and Westphalia more frequently even than in Georgia. Poles and Westphalians have the pigs, the scholarship and the skill; what they do not have is peanuts."

He stopped to blow his nose. I shifted position. He resumed: "A pig whose diet is fifty to seventy percent peanuts grows a ham of incredibly sweet and delicate succulence which, well-cured, well-kept and well-cooked, will take precedence over any other ham the world affords. I offer this as an

129

illustration of one of the sources of the American contributions I am discussing, and as another proof that American offerings to the roll of honor of fine food are by no means confined to those items which were found here already ripe on the tree, with nothing required but the plucking. Red Indians were eating turkeys and potatoes before white men came, but they were not eating peanut-fed pigs. Those unforgettable hams are not gifts of nature; they are the product of the inventor's enterprise, the experimenter's persistence, and the connoisseur's discrimination. Similar results have been achieved by the feeding of blueberries to young chickens, beginning usually—"

"Hold it. Not chickens, poultry."

"Chickens are poultry."

"You told me to stop you."

"But not to argue with me."

"You started the argument, I didn't."

He showed me a palm. "Let's go on . . . beginning usually at the age of one week. The flavor of a four months old cockerel, trained to eat large quantities of blueberries from infancy, and cooked with mushrooms, tarragon and white wine—or, if you would add another American touch, made into a chicken and corn pudding, with onion, parsley and eggs—is not only distinctive, it is unique; and it is assuredly haute cuisine. This is even a better illustration of my thesis than the ham, for Europeans could not have fed peanuts to pigs, since they had no peanuts. But they did have chickens— chickens, Archie?"

"Poultry."

"No matter. They did have chickens and blueberries, and for centuries no one thought of having the one assimilate the other and bless us with the result. Another demonstration of the inventiveness—"

"Hey, wait! You left out a whole paragraph. 'You will say perhaps—'"

"Very well. Do you think you might sit still? You keep that chair creaking. You will say, perhaps, that all this does not belong in a discussion of cookery, but on consideration I believe you will agree that it does. Vatel had his own farm, and gave his personal attention to its husbandry. Escoffier refused fowl from a certain district, however plump and well-grown, on account of minerals in the drinking water available for them there. Brillat-Savarin paid many tributes . . ."

130

I was on my feet. Seated, I had twitches in my arms and legs and I couldn't sit still. With my eye on the script, I moved across to the table and got hold of the carafe and poured myself a glass of water and drank it. Wolfe went on, droning it out. I decided not to sit down again, and stood in the middle of the floor, flexing and unflexing the muscles of my legs to make the twitching stop.

I don't know what it was that alarmed me. I couldn't have seen anything, because my eyes were on the script, and the open window was at my left, at least a dozen feet away, at right angles to my line of vision. I don't think I heard anything. But something made me jerk my head around, and even then all I saw was a movement in the shrubbery outside the window, and I have no idea what made me throw the script. But I threw it, straight at the window. At the same moment a gun went off, good and loud. Simultaneously smoke and the smell of powder came in at the window, the script fluttered and dropped to the floor, and I heard Wolfe's voice behind me:

"Look here, Archie."

I looked and saw the blood running down the side of his face. For a second I stood dead in my tracks. I wanted to jump through the window and catch the son of a—the sharp-shooter, and give him personal treatment. And Wolfe wasn't dead, he was still sitting up. But the blood looked plenteous. I jumped to the side of the bed.

He had his lips compressed tight, but he opened them to demand, "Where is it? Is it my skull?" He shuddered. "Brains?"

"Hell no." I was looking, and was so relieved my voice cracked. "Where would brains come from? Take your hand away and hold still. Wait till I get a towel." I raced to the bathroom and back, and wrapped one towel around his neck and sopped with the other one. "I don't think it touched the cheekbone at all, it just went through skin and meat. Do you feel faint?"

"No. Bring me my shaving mirror."

"You wait till I—"

"Bring the mirror!"

"For God's sake. Hold that towel there." I hopped to the bathroom again for the mirror and handed it to him, and then went to the phone. A girl's voice said good morning sweetly.

"Yeah. Swell morning. Has this joint got a doctor? . . . No,

131

wait, I don't want to speak to him, send him over here right away, a man's been shot in Suite 60, Upshur Pavilion. . . . I said shot, and step on it, and send the doctor, and that Odell the house detective, and a state cop if there's one around loose, and a bottle of brandy. Got it? . . . Good for you, you're a wonder."

I went back to Wolfe, and whenever I want to treat myself to a laugh all I have to do is remember how he looked on that occasion. With one hand he was keeping the towel from unwinding from his neck, and with the other he was holding up the mirror, into which he was glaring with unutterable indignation and disgust. I saw he was holding his lips tight so blood wouldn't get in his mouth, and went and got some of his handkerchiefs and did some more sopping.

He moved his left shoulder up and down a little. "Some blood ran down my neck." He moved his jaw up and down, and from side to side. "I don't feel anything when I do that." He put the mirror down on the bed. "Can't you stop the confounded bleeding? Look out, don't press so hard! What's that there on the floor?"

"It's your speech. I think there's a bullet hole through it, but it's all right. You've got to get stretched out and turned over on your side. —Now damn it, don't argue—here, wait till I get rid of these cushions. . . ."

I got him horizontal, with his head raised on a couple of pillows, and went to the bathroom for a towel soaked in cold water and came back and poulticed him. He had his eyes shut. I had just got back to him with another cold towel when there was a loud knock on the door.

The doctor, a bald-headed little squirt with spectacles, had a bag in his hand and a nurse with him. As I was ushering them in somebody else came trotting down the hall, and I let him in too when I saw it was Clay Ashley, the Kanawha Spa manager. He was sputtering at me, "Who did it how did it happen where is he who is it . . ." I told him to save it up and followed the doctor and nurse inside.

The bald-headed doc was no slouch, at that. The nurse pulled up a chair for the bag and opened it, and I shoved a table over by the bed, while the doc bent over Wolfe without asking me anything. Wolfe started to turn over but was commanded to lie still.

Wolfe protested, "Confound it, I have to see your face!"

"What for? To see if I'm compos mentis? I'm all right. Hold still."

Clay Ashley's voice sounded at my elbow. "What the devil is it? You say he was shot? What happened?"

The doctor spoke without turning, with authority: "Quiet in here, until I see what we've got."

There was another loud knock on the door. I went out to it, and Ashley followed me. It was my friend Odell and a pair of state cops, and behind them the greenjacket from the main hall. Ashley told the greenjacket:

"Get out of here, and keep your mouth shut."

"I just wanted to tell you, sir, I heard a shot, and two of the guests want to know—"

"Tell them you know nothing about it. Tell them it was a backfire. Understand?"

"Yes, sir."

I took the quartette to my room. I ignored Ashley, because I had heard Wolfe say he was bourgeois, and spoke to the cops:

"Nero Wolfe was sitting up in bed, rehearsing a speech he is to deliver tonight, and I was standing four yards from the open window looking at the script to prompt him. Something outside caught my attention, I don't know whether a sound or a movement, and I looked at the window and all I consciously saw was a branch of the shrubbery moving, and I threw the script at the window. At the same time a gun went off, outside, and Wolfe called to me, and I saw his cheek was bleeding and went to him and took a look. Then I phoned the hotel, and got busy mopping blood until the doctor came, which was just before you did."

One of the cops had a notebook out. "What's your name?"

"Archie Goodwin."

He wrote it down. "Did you see anyone in the shrubbery?"

"No. If you'll permit a suggestion, it's been less than ten minutes since the shot was fired. I've told you all I know. If you let the questions wait and get busy out there, you might pick up a hot trail."

"I want to see Wolfe."

"To ask him if I shot him? Well, I didn't. I even know who did, it was the man that stabbed Laszio in Pocahontas Pavilion Tuesday night. I don't know his name, but it was that guy. Would you like to grab that murderer, you two? Get out there on the trail before it cools off."

"How do you know it was the one that killed Laszio?"

133

"Because Wolfe started digging too close to his hole and he didn't like it. There's plenty of people that would like to see Nero Wolfe dead, but not in this neighborhood."

"Is Wolfe conscious?"

"Certainly. That way, through the foyer."

"Come on, Bill."

They tramped ahead, and Ashley and I followed, with Odell behind us. In Wolfe's room the nurse had the table half covered with bandages and things, and an electric sterilizer had been plugged into an outlet. Wolfe, on his right side, had his back to us, and the doctor was bending over him with busy fingers.

"What about it, Doc?"

"Who—" The doctor's head twisted at us. "Oh, it's you fellows. Only a flesh wound in the upper cheek. I'll have to sew it."

Wolfe's voice demanded, "Who is that?"

"Quit talking. State police."

"Archie? Where are you, Archie?"

"Right here, boss." I stepped up. "The cops want to know if I shot you."

"They would. Idiots. Get them out of here. Get everybody out but you and the doctor. I'm in no condition for company."

The cop spoke up. "We want to ask you, Mr. Wolfe—"

"I have nothing to tell you, except that somebody shot at me through the window. Hasn't Mr. Goodwin told you that? Do you think *you* can catch him? Try it."

Clay Ashley said indignantly, "That's no attitude to take, Wolfe. All this damned mess comes from my permitting a gathering of people who are not of my clientele. Far from it. It seems to me—"

"I know who that is." Wolfe's head started to move, and the doctor held it firm. "That's Mr. Ashley. His clientele! Pfui! Put him out too. Put them all out. Do you hear me, Archie?"

The doctor said decisively, "That's enough. When he talks it starts bleeding."

I told the cops, "Come on, shove off. He's far enough away now so that you're in no danger." To Ashley: "You too. Give your clientele my love. Scat."

Odell had stayed over by the door and so was the first one out. Ashley and the cops were close behind. I followed them, on through the foyer, and into the public hall. There I stopped one of the cops and kept him by fastening onto a corner of his tunic, and his brother, seeing him stay, stayed with him while Ashley and Odell went on ahead. Ashley was tramping along in a fury and Odell was trotting in the rear.

"Listen," I told the cop. "You didn't like my first suggestion to get jumping, I'll try another. This individual that stabbed Laszio and took a shot at Wolfe seems to be pretty active. He might even take it into his head to try some more target practice on the same range. It's a nice April day and Wolfe wouldn't want the windows closed and the curtains drawn, and damned if I'm going to sit in there all day and watch the shrubbery. We came into your state alive, and we'd like to go out the same way at 12:40 to-night. How would it be if you stationed a guard where he could keep an eye on those windows and the shrubbery from behind? There's a nice seat not far away, by the brook."

"Much obliged." He sounded sarcastic. "Maybe you'd like to have the colonel come down from Charleston so you can give him instructions."

I waved a hand. "I'm upset. I've had no sleep and my boss got shot and darned near had his brains spilled. I'm surprised I've been as polite as I have. It *would* be nice to know that those windows are being watched. Will you do it?"

"Yes. I'll phone in a report and get a couple of men." He eyed me. "You didn't see any more than you told me. Huh?"

I told him no, and he turned and took his brother with him.

In Wolfe's room the ministrations were proceeding. I stood at the foot of the bed and watched for a few minutes, then, turning, my eye fell on the script still lying on the floor, and I picked it up and examined it. Sure enough, the bullet had gone right through it, and had torn loose one of the metal fasteners which had held the sheets together. I smoothed it out and tossed it on the bureau and resumed my post at the foot of the bed.

The doctor was a little slow but he was good and thorough. He had started the sewing, and Wolfe, who lay with his eyes closed, informed me in a murmur that he had declined the offer of a local anesthetic. His hand on the coverlet was clenched into a fist, and each time the needle went through the flesh he grunted. After a few stitches he asked, "Does my grunting hamper you?" The doctor told him no, and then the grunts got louder. When the sewing was done and the bandaging started, the doctor told me, as he worked, that the wound was superficial but would be somewhat painful and the patient should have rest and freedom from disturbance. He was dressing it so that it needn't be touched again until we got to New York. The patient insisted that he intended to deliver a speech that evening and wouldn't be persuaded out of it, and in case such excessive muscular action started a hemorrhage the doctor must be called. It was desirable for the patient to stay in bed until dinnertime.

He finished. The nurse helped him gather up paraphernalia and débris, including bloody towels. She offered to help Wolfe change the soiled pajama top for a fresh one, but he refused. I got out the expense roll, but the doctor said it would be put on the bill, and then walked around to the other side of the bed to get a front view of Wolfe's face and give him some parting admonitions.

I accompanied them as far as the main hall to tell the greenjacket there that no visitors of any description would be desired in Suite 60. Back in Wolfe's room, the patient was still lying on his right side with his eyes closed.

I went to the phone. "Hello, operator? Listen. The doctor says Mr. Wolfe must have rest and quiet. Will you please announce to the switchboard that this phone is not to ring? I don't care who—"

"Archie! Cancel that."

I told the mouthpiece, "Wait a minute.—Yes, sir?"

Wolfe hadn't moved, but he spoke again. "Cancel that order about the phone."

"But you—"

"Cancel it."

I told the operator to return to the status quo ante, and hung up, and approached the patient. "Excuse me. I wouldn't butt in on your personal affairs for anything. If you want that phone bell jangling—"

"I don't want it." He opened his eyes. "But we can't do anything if we're incommunicado. Did you say the bullet went through my speech? Let me see it, please."

His tone was such that I got the script from the bureau and handed it to him without demur. Frowning, he fingered it, and as he saw the extent of the damage the frown deepened. He handed it back. "I suppose you can decipher it. What did you throw it for?"

"Because I had it in my hand. If it hadn't deflected the bullet you might have got it for good—or it might have missed you entirely, I admit that. Depending on how good a shot he is."

"I suppose so. That man's a dolt. I had washed my hands of it. He stood an excellent chance of avoiding exposure, and now he's done for. We'll get him."

"Oh. We will."

"Certainly. I have plenty of forbearance, God knows, but I'm not a complacent target for firearms. While I was being bandaged I considered probabilities, and we have little time to act. Hand me that mirror. I suppose I'm a spectacle."

"You're pretty well decorated." I passed the mirror to him, and he studied his reflection with his lips compressed. "About getting this bird, I'm for it, but from the way you look and what the doctor said—"

"It can't be helped. Close the windows and draw the shades."

"It'll be gloomy. I told the cop to put a guard outside—"

"Do as I say, please. I don't trust guards. Besides, I would be constantly glancing at the window, and I don't want my mental processes interrupted. —No, clear to the bottom, there'll be plenty of light. That's better. The others too. —Good. Now bring me underwear, a clean shirt, the dressing gown from the closet..."

"You've got to stay in bed."

"Nonsense. There's more blood in the head lying down than sitting up. If people come here I can't very well make myself presentable, with the gibbosity of this confounded bandage, but at least I needn't give offense to decency. Get the underwear."

I collected garments while he manipulated his mass, first to a sitting position on the edge of the bed, and then onto his feet, using grunts for punctuation. He frowned in distaste at the bloody pajama top when he got it off, and I brought towels, wet and dry. As the operations progressed he instructed me as to details of the program:

"All we can do is try our luck on the possibilities until we find a fact that will allow only one interpretation. I detest alternatives, and at present that is all we have. Do you know how to black a man up with burnt cork? —Well, you can try. Get some corks—I suppose we can use matches—and get a Kanawha Spa livery, medium size, including cap. But first of all, New York on the telephone. —No, not those socks, black ones, I may not feel like changing again before dinner. We'll have to find time to finish that speech. —I presume you know the numbers of Saul Panzer and Inspector Cramer. But if we should get our fact from there, it would be undesirable to run the risk of that blackguard learning we had asked for it. We must prevent that..."

14

MY FRIEND ODELL stood beside a lobby pillar with an enormous leaf of a palm spread over his head, looking at me with a doubtful glint in his eye that I didn't deserve.

I said, "Nor am I trying to negotiate a hot date, nor am I engaged in snooping. I've told you straight, I merely want to make sure that a private phone call is private. It's not suspicion, it's just precaution. As for your having to consult the manager, what the hell kind of a house dick are you if you haven't even got the run of your own corral? You come along and stay with me, and if I start anything you don't like you can throw stones at me. Which reminds me, this Kanawha Spa seems to be pretty hard on guests. If you don't get hit with a rock you get plugged with a bullet. Huh?"

Without erasing the doubt, he made to move. "Okay. The next time I tell a man a joke it'll be the one about Pat and Mike. Come on, Rollo."

He led me through the lobby, down past the elevators, and along a ways to a narrow side corridor. It had doors with frosted glass panels, and he opened one on the right side and motioned me in. It was a small room, and all its furniture consisted of a switchboard running its entire length, perhaps fifteen feet, six maidens in a row with their backs to us, and the straight-backed chairs which the maidens inhabited. Odell went to the one at the end and conversed a moment, and then thumbed me over to the third in the line. From the back her neck looked a little scrawny, but when she turned to us she had smooth white skin and promising blue eyes. Odell said something to her, and she nodded, and I told her:

"I've just thought up a new way to make a phone call. Mr.

Wolfe in Suite 60, Upshur Pavilion, wants to put in a call to New York and I'm going to stay and watch you do it."

"Suite 60? That's the man that was shot."

"Yep."

"And it was you that told me I'm a wonder."

"Yep. In a way I came to check up. If you'll just get—"

"Excuse me." She turned and talked and listened, and monkeyed with some plugs. When she was through I said:

"Get New York, Liberty 2-3306, and put it on Suite 60."

She grinned. "Personally conducted phone calls, huh?"

"Right. I haven't had so much fun in ages."

She got busy. I became aware of activity at my elbow, and saw that Odell had got out a notebook and pencil and was writing something down. I craned the neck for a glimpse of his scrawl, and then told him pleasantly, "I like a man that knows his job the way you do. To save you the trouble of listening for the next one, it's going to be Spring 7-3100. New York Police Headquarters."

"Much obliged. What's he doing, yelling for help because he got a little scratch on the face?"

I made a fitting reply with my mind elsewhere, because I was watching operations. The board was an old style, and it was easy to tell if she was listening in. Her hands were all over the place, pushing and dropping plugs, and it was only five minutes or so before I heard her say, "Mr. Wolfe? Ready with New York. Go ahead, please." She flashed me a grin. "Who was I supposed to tell about it? Mr. Odell here?"

I grinned back. "Don't you bother your little head about it. Be good, dear child—"

"And let who will wear diamonds. I know. Have you heard the one—excuse me."

Odell stayed with me till the end. He had a long wait, for Wolfe's talk with Saul Panzer lasted a good quarter of an hour, and the second one, with Inspector Cramer—provided he got Cramer—almost as long. When it was finished and the plugs had been pulled, I thought it was only sociable to ask the maiden whether she preferred oblong diamonds or round ones, and she replied that she would much rather have a copy of the Bible because most of hers were getting worn out, she read them so much. I made a feint to pat her on the head and she ducked and Odell plucked me by the sleeve.

I left him in the lobby with thanks and an assurance that I hadn't forgotten his aspirations to the Hotel Churchill, regarding which Mr. Wolfe would sound out Mr. Liggett at the first opportunity.

A minute later I had an opportunity myself, but was too busy to take advantage of it. Going away from the main entrance in the direction of my next errand took me past the mounting block, and there was a bunch of horses around, some mounted and some not, with greenjacket grooms. I like the look of horses at a distance of ten feet or more, and I slowed down as I went by. It was there I saw Liggett, with the right clothes on which I suppose he had borrowed, dismounting from a big bay. Another reason I slowed down was because I thought I might see another guest get stepped on, but it didn't happen so. Not that I have anything against guests as guests; it's only my natural feeling about people who pay twenty bucks a day for a room to sleep in, and they always look either too damn sleek or as if they had been born with a bellyache. I know if I was a horse...

But I had errands. Wolfe had already been alone in that room for over half an hour, and although I had left strict orders with the greenjacket to admit no one to Suite 60 under any pretext, and the door was locked, I didn't care much for the setup. So I got along to Pocahontas Pavilion in quick time. I met Lisette Putti and Vallenko, with tennis rackets, near the entrance, and Mamma Mondor was on the veranda knitting. On the driveway a state cop and a plug-ugly in cits sat in a car smoking cigarettes. Inside both parlors were empty, but there was plenty going on in the kitchen—cooks and helpers, greenjackets, masters, darting around looking concentrated. Apparently another free-for-all lunch was in preparation, not to mention the dinner for that evening, which was to illustrate the subject of Wolfe's speech by consisting of dishes that had originated in America. That, of course, was to be concocted under the direction of Louis Servan, and he was there in white cap and apron, moving around feeling, looking, smelling, tasting, and instructing. I allowed myself a grin at the sight of Albert Malfi the Corsican fruit slicer, also capped and aproned, trotting at Servan's heels, before I went across to accost the dean, just missing a collision with Domenico Rossi as he bounced away from a range.

Servan's dignified old face clouded over when he saw me. "Ah, Mr. Goodwin! I've just heard of that terrible... to Mr. Wolfe. Mr. Ashley phoned from the hotel. That a guest of mine—our guest of honor—terrible! I'll call on him as soon as I can manage to leave here. It's not serious? He can be with us?"

I reassured him, and two or three others trotted up, and I accepted their sympathy for my boss and told them it would be just as well not to pay any calls for a few hours. Then I told Servan I hated to interrupt a busy man but needed a few words with him, and he went with me to the small parlor. After some conversation he called in Moulton, the headwaiter with a piece out of his ear, and gave him instructions.

When Moulton had departed Servan hesitated before he said, "I wanted to see Mr. Wolfe anyway. Mr. Ashley tells me that he got a startling story from two of my waiters. I can understand their reluctance... but I can't have... my friend Laszio murdered here in my own dining room...." He passed his hand wearily across his forehead. "This should have been such a happiness.... I'm over seventy years old, Mr. Goodwin, and this is the worst thing that has ever happened to me... and I must get back to the kitchen... Crabtree's a good man, but he's flighty and I don't trust him with all that commotion in there...."

"Forget it." I patted his arm. "I mean forget the murder. Let Nero Wolfe do the worrying, I always do. Did you elect your four new members this morning?"

"Yes. Why?"

"I was just curious about Malfi. Did he get in?"

"Malfi? In Les Quinze Maîtres? Good heavens, no!"

"Okay. I was just curious. You go on back to the kitchen and enjoy yourself. I'll give Wolfe your message about lunch."

He nodded and pattered away. I had then been gone from Upshur more than an hour, and I hotfooted it back by the shortest path.

Going in after the outdoor sunshine, Wolfe's room seemed somber, but the maid had been in and the bed was made and everything tidy. He had the big chair turned to face the windows, and sat there with his speech in his hand, frowning at the last page. I had sung out from the foyer to let him know all was well, and now approached to take a look at the bandage. It seemed in order, and there was no sign of any fresh bleeding.

I reported: "Everything's set. Servan turned the details over to Moulton. They all send their best regards and wish you were along. Servan's going to send a couple of trays of

141

lunch over to us. It's a grand day outdoors, too bad you're cooped up like this. Our client has taken advantage of it by going horseback riding."

"We have no client."

"I was referring to Mr. Liggett. I still think that since he offered to pay for a job of detective work you might as well give him that pleasure. Not to mention hiring Berin for him. Did you get Saul and Cramer?"

"Weren't you at the switchboard?"

"Yes, but I didn't know who you got."

"I got them. That alternative is being cared for." He sighed. "This thing hurts. What are they cooking for lunch?"

"Lord, I don't know. Five or six of them are messing around. Certainly it hurts, and you won't collect a damn cent for it." I sat down and rested my head against the back of the chair because I was tired of holding it up. "Not only that, it seems to have made you more contrary even than usual, it and the loss of sleep. I know you sneer at what you call routine, but I've seen you get results from it now and then, and no matter how much of a genius you are it wouldn't do any harm to find out what various people were doing at a quarter past ten this morning. For instance, if you found that Leon Blanc was in the kitchen making soup, he couldn't very well have been out there in the shrubbery shooting at you. I'm just explaining how it's done."

"Thank you."

"Thank me, and go on being contrary, huh?"

"I'm not contrary, merely intelligent. I've often told you, a search for negative evidence is a desperate last resort when no positive evidence can be found. Collecting and checking alibis is dreary and usually futile drudgery. No. Get your positive evidence, and if you find it confronted by an alibi, and if your evidence is any good, break the alibi. Anyhow, I'm not interested in the man who shot me. The man I want is the one who stabbed Laszio."

I stared. "What's this, a riddle? You yourself said it was the same one."

"Certainly. But since it was his murdering Laszio that led to his shooting me, obviously it's the murder we must prove. Unless we can prove he killed Laszio, how can we give him a motive for trying to kill me? And if you can't demonstrate a motive, what the devil does it matter where he was at a

142

quarter past ten? The only thing that will do us any good is direct evidence that he committed the murder."

"Oh, well." I waved a hand, feebly. "If that's all. Naturally you've got *that*."

"I have. It is being tested."

"I'll call. What evidence and who?"

He started to shake his head, and winced and stopped. "It is being tested. I don't pretend that the evidence is conclusive, far from it. We must await the test. It is so little conclusive that I have arranged for this performance with Mr. Blanc because we are pressed for time and no alternative can be ignored. And after all it is quite possible—though I shouldn't think he would have a gun— There's someone at the door."

The performance with Blanc was elaborate but a complete wash-out. Its only advantage was that it kept me occupied and awake until lunch time. I wasn't surprised at the result, and I don't think Wolfe was either; he was just being thorough and not neglecting anything.

The first arrivals were Moulton and Paul Whipple, and they had the props with them. I took them into Wolfe for an explanation of the project, and then deposited them in my room and shut the door on them. A few minutes later Leon Blanc came.

The chef and the gastronome had quite a chat. Blanc was of course distressed at Wolfe's injury and said so at length. Then they got on to the business. Blanc had come, he said, at Servan's request, and would answer any questions Mr. Wolfe might care to ask. That was an order for anybody, but Blanc filled it pretty well, including the pointed and insistent queries regarding the extent of his acquaintanceship with Mrs. Laszio. Blanc stuck to it that he had known her rather well when she had been Mrs. Vukcic and he had been chef de cuisine at the Churchill, but that in the past five years, since he had gone to Boston, he had seen her only two or three times, and they had never been at all intimate. Then Wolfe got onto Tuesday night and the period Blanc had spent in his room at Pocahontas Pavilion, while the others were tasting Sauce Printemps and someone was stabbing Laszio. I heard most of it from a distance because I was in the bathroom, with the door open a crack, experimenting with the burnt cork on the back of my hand. Servan had sent an alcohol burner and enough corks for a minstrel show.

Blanc balked a little when Wolfe got to the suggestion of the masquerade test, but not very strenuously, and I opened the bathroom door and invited him in. We had a picnic. With him stripped to his underwear, I first rubbed in a layer of cold cream and then started with the cork. I suppose I didn't do it like an expert, since I wasn't one, but by gosh I got him black. The ears and the edge of the hair were a problem, and he claimed I got some in his eye, but it was only because he blinked too hard. Then he put on the suit of livery, including the cap, and it wasn't a bad job at all, except that Moulton hadn't been able to dig up any black gloves, and we had to use dark brown ones.

I took him in to Wolfe for approval, and telephoned Pocahontas Pavilion and got Mrs. Coyne and told her we were ready.

In five minutes she was there. I stepped into the corridor to give her a brief explanation of the program, explaining that she wasn't to open her mouth if she wanted to help Wolfe keep her out of it, and then, admitting her to the foyer and leaving her there to pose Blanc, I went back in to pose Blanc. He had got pretty well irritated before I had finished with him in the bathroom, but now Wolfe had him all soothed down again. I stood him over beyond the foot of the bed, at what looked like the right distance, pulled his cap lower, had him put his finger to his lips, and told him to hold it. Then I went to the door to the foyer and opened it six inches.

After ten seconds I told Blanc that would do for that pose and went to the foyer and took Lio Coyne out to the corridor again.

"Well?"

She shook her head. "No. It wasn't that man."

"How do you know it wasn't?"

"His ears are too big. It wasn't him."

"Could you swear to that in a court?"

"But you . . ." Her eyes got narrow. "You said I wouldn't . . ."

"All right, you won't. But how sure are you?"

"I'm very sure. This man is more slender, too."

"Okay. Much obliged. Mr. Wolfe may want to speak to you later on."

The others said the same thing. I posed Blanc twice more, once facing the door for Paul Whipple, and the second time with his back to it for Moulton. Whipple said he would be willing to swear that the man he had seen by the screen in the dining room was not the one he had seen in Wolfe's room, and Moulton said he couldn't swear to it because he had only seen the man's back, but he thought it wasn't the same man. I sent them back to Pocahontas.

Then I had to help Blanc clean up. Getting it off was twice as hard as putting it on, and I don't know if he ever did get his ears clean again. Considering that he wasn't a murderer at all, he was pretty nice about it. What with Wolfe's blood and Blanc's burnt cork, I certainly raised cain with Kanawha Spa towels that day.

Blanc stood and told Wolfe: "I have submitted to all this because Louis Servan requested it. I know murderers are supposed to be punished. If I were one, I would expect to be. This is a frightful experience for all of us, Mr. Wolfe, frightful. I didn't kill Phillip Laszio, but if it were possible for me to bring him to life again by lifting a finger, do you know what I'd do? I would do this." He thrust both hands into his pockets as far as they would go, and kept them there.

He turned to go, but his departure was postponed a few minutes longer, by a new arrival. The change in program had of course made it necessary to tell the greenjacket in the hall that the embargo on visitors was lifted, and now came the first of a string that kept knocking at the door intermittently all afternoon.

This one was my friend Barry Tolman.

"How's Mr. Wolfe?"

"Battered and belligerent. Go on in."

He entered, opened his mouth at Wolfe, and then saw who was standing there.

"Oh. You here, Mr. Blanc?"

"Yes. At Mr. Servan's request—"

Wolfe put in, "We've been doing an experiment. I don't believe you'll need to waste time with Mr. Blanc. What about it, Archie? Did Mr. Blanc kill Laszio?"

I shook my head. "No, sir. Three outs and the side's retired."

Tolman looked at me, at Wolfe, at Blanc. "Is that so. Anyhow, I may want to see you later. You'll be at Pocahontas?"

Blanc told him yes, not very amiably, expressed a hope that Wolfe would feel better by dinnertime, and went. When I got back from escorting him to the door, Tolman had sat down and had his head cocked on one side for a look at Wolfe's bandage, and Wolfe was saying:

"Not to me, no, sir. The doctor called it superficial. But I assure you it is highly dangerous to the man who did it. And look here." He displayed the mangled script of the speech. "The bullet did that before it struck me. Mr. Goodwin saved my life by tossing my speech at the window. So he says. I am willing to grant it. Where is Mr. Berin?"

"Here. At Pocahontas with... with his daughter. I brought him myself, just now. They phoned me at Quinby about your being shot. Do you think it was the one that stabbed Laszio who did it?"

"Who else?"

"But why was he after you? You were through with it."

"He didn't know that." Wolfe stirred in his chair, winced, and added bitterly, "I'm not through with it now."

"That suits me. I don't say I'm glad you got shot... and you started on Blanc? What made you decide it wasn't him?"

Wolfe started to explain, but another interruption took me away. This time it was the lunch trays, and Louis Servan had certainly put on the dog. There were three enormous trays and three waiters, and a fourth greenjacket as an outrider for opening doors and clearing traffic. I was hungry, and the smells that came from under the covered services made me more so. The outrider, who was Moulton himself, after a bow and an announcement to Wolfe, unfolded serving stands for the trays and advanced to the table with a cloth in his hand.

Wolfe told Tolman, "Excuse me, please." With a healthy grunt he lifted himself from his chair and made his way across to the serving stands. Moulton joined him and hovered deferentially. Wolfe lifted one of the covers, bent his head and gazed, and sniffed. Then he looked at Moulton. "Piroshki?"

"Yes, sir. By Mr. Vallenko."

"Yes. I know." He lifted other covers, bent and smelled, with careful nods to himself. He straightened up again. "Artichokes barigoule?"

"I think, sir, he called them drigante. Mr. Mondor. Something like that."

"No matter. Leave it all here, please. We'll serve ourselves, if you don't mind."

"But Mr. Servan told me—"

"I prefer it that way. Leave it here on the trays."

"I'll leave a man—"

"No. Please. I'm having a conversation. Out, all of you."

They went. It appeared that if I was going to get anything

146

to eat I'd have to work for it, so I called on the muscles for another effort. As Wolfe returned to his chair I asked, "How do we do it? Boardinghouse style à la scoop shovel?"

He waited until he got deposited before he answered. Then he sighed first. "No. Telephone the hotel for a luncheon menu."

I stared at him. "Maybe you're delirious?"

"Archie." He sounded savage. "You may guess the humor I'm in. That piroshki is by Vallenko, and the artichokes are by Mondor. But how the devil do I know who was in that kitchen or what happened there? These trays were intended for us, and probably everyone knew it. For me. I am still hoping to go home to-night. Phone the hotel, and get those trays out of here so I can't smell them. Put them in your room and leave them there."

Tolman said, "But my God, man... if you really think... we can have that stuff analyzed...."

"I don't want to analyze it, I want to eat it. And I can't. I'm not going to. There probably is nothing at all wrong with it, and look at me, terrorized, intimidated by that blackguard! What good would it do to analyze it? I tell you, sir—Archie?"

It was the door again. The smell from those covered dishes had me in almost as bad a state as Wolfe, and I was hoping it might be a food inspector from the Board of Health to certify them unadulterated, but it was only the greenjacket from the hall. He had a telegram addressed to Nero Wolfe.

I went back in with it, tore the envelope open, and handed it to him.

He pulled it out and read it.

He murmured, "Indeed." At the sound of the new tone in his voice I gave him a sharp glance. He handed the telegram back to me, unfolded. "Read it to Mr. Tolman."

I did so:

NERO WOLFE KANAWHA SPA W VA
NOT MENTIONED ANY PAPER STOP CRAMER
COOPERATING STOP PROCEEDING STOP WILL
PHONE FROM DESTINATION
                                        PANZER

Wolfe said softly, "That's better. Much better. We might almost eat that piroshki now, but there's a chance... no. Phone the hotel, Archie. And Mr. Tolman, I believe there will be an opportunity for you also to cooperate...."

147

15

JEROME BERIN shook both his fists so that his chair trembled under him. "God above! Such a dirty dog! Such a—" He stopped himself abruptly and demanded, "You say it was not Blanc? Not Vukcic? Not my old friend Zelota?"

Wolfe murmured, "None of them, I think."

"Then I repeat, a dirty dog!" Berin leaned forward and tapped Wolfe on the knee. "I tell you frankly, it did not take a dog to kill Laszio. Anyone might have done that, anyone at all, merely as an incident in the disposal of garbage. En passant. True, it is bad to stab a man in the back, but when one is in a hurry the niceties must sometimes be overlooked. No, only for killing Laszio, even in that manner, I would not say a dog. But to shoot at you through a window—you, the guest of honor of Les Quinze Maîtres! Only because you had interested yourself in the cause of justice! Because you had undertaken to establish my innocence! Because you had the good sense to know that I could not possibly have made seven mistakes of those nine sauces! And let me tell you . . . will you credit it when I tell you what they gave me to eat in that place . . . in that jail in that place?"

He went on to tell, and it sounded awful. He had come, with his daughter, to express his appreciation of Wolfe's efforts in his behalf. It was nearly four o'clock, and there was sunlight in the room, for Tolman had arranged for a double guard on the windows, the other side of the shrubbery, and the shades were up and the windows open. The lunch from the hotel may not have been piroshki by Vallenko, but it had been adequate for my purposes, and Wolfe had been able to get it down in spite of the difficulty he had chewing. I had completely abandoned the idea of a little nap; there wasn't a chance. Tolman had stayed nearly until the end of lunch, and after that was finished Rossi and Mondor and Coyne had dropped in to offer commiseration for Wolfe's wound, and they had been followed by others. Even Louis Servan had made it for a few minutes, though I didn't understand how he had been able to get away from the kitchen. Also, around three o'clock, there had been a phone call from New York, which Wolfe took himself. His end of it consisted mostly of grunts, and all I knew about it when he got through was that he had been talking with Inspector Cramer. But I knew he hadn't got any bad news, for afterwards he sat and rubbed the side of his nose and looked self-satisfied.

Constanza Berin sat for twenty minutes on the edge of her chair trying to get a word in, and when her father called an intermission to get his pipe lit she finally succeeded.

"Mr. Wolfe, I ... I was terrible this morning."

He moved his eyes at her. "You were indeed, Miss Berin. I have often noticed that the more beautiful a woman is, especially a young one, the more liable she is to permit herself unreasonable fits. It's something that you acknowledge. Tell me, when you feel it coming on like that, is there nothing you can do to stop it? Have you ever tried?"

She laughed at him. "But it isn't fits. I don't have fits. I was scared and mad because they had put my father in jail for murder, and I knew he hadn't done it, and they seemed to think they had proof against him, and then I was told that it was you who had found the proof. . . . How was I going to be reasonable about that? And in a strange country I had never been in before. . . . America is an awful country."

"There are those who would disagree with you."

"I suppose so. . . . I suppose it isn't so much the country . . . maybe it's the people who live here. . . . Oh, excuse me, I don't mean you, or Mr. Goodwin . . . I'm sure you are very amiable, and of course Mr. Goodwin is, with a wife and so many children. . . ."

"Indeed." Wolfe shot me a withering glance. "How are the children, Archie? Well, I hope?"

"Fine, thanks." I waved a hand. "Doggone the little shavers, I sure do miss 'em, away from home like this. I can hardly wait to get back."

Berin took his pipe from his mouth to nod at me. "The little ones are nice. Now my daughter here . . . ." He shrugged. "She is nice, naturally, but God above, she drives me mad!" He leaned to tap Wolfe's knee with the stem of the pipe. "Speaking of getting back. Is it true what I am told, that these dogs can keep us here on and on until they permit us to go? Merely because that Laszio got a knife in his back? My daughter and I were to leave to-night, for New York, and then to Canada. I am out of jail but I am not free. Is that it?"

149

"I'm afraid that's it. Were you intending to take the midnight train to New York?"

"I was. And now they tell me no one leaves this place until they learn who killed that dog! If we wait on that for that imbecile Tolman, and that other one, that one who squints..." He replaced his pipe and puffed until he had clouds.

"But we needn't wait on them." Wolfe sighed. "Thank God. I think, sir, it would be wise to have your bags packed, and if you have reservations on that train, keep them. Fortunately you did not have to wait for Mr. Tolman to discover the truth about those sauces. If you had..."

"I might not have left at all. I know that. I might have got this." Berin used the edge of his hand for a cleaver to slice off his head. "Certainly I would still be in that jail, and within three days I would have starved. We Catalans can take death when it comes, but God above, a man that can swallow that food is not a man, he is not even a beast! I know what I owe you, and I called for blessings on you with every bite of my lunch. I discussed it with Servan. I told him how greatly I am indebted to you, and that I do no man the honor of remaining in debt to him. I told Servan I must pay you... he is our host here, and a man of delicacy. He said you would not take pay. He said it had been offered, and you had scorned it. I understand and respect your feeling, since you are our guest of honor—"

Another knock on the door made me leave Wolfe simmering in the juice of the stew he had made. I had always known that some day he would talk too much for his own good, and as I went to the foyer I was wearing a grin—I admit malicious— and reflecting on how it probably felt at the moment to be a jewel on the cushion of hospitality.

The new arrival was only Vukcic, but he served as well as another bullet through the window would have done to make a break in the conversation and take it away from vulgar things like payments for services rendered. Vukcic was in a mood. He acted embarrassed, gloomy, nervous and abstracted. A few minutes after he arrived the Berins left, and then he stood in front of Wolfe with his arms folded, frowning down, and told him that in spite of Wolfe's impertinence that morning on the subject of howling on a hillside, it was a duty of old friendship to call personally to offer sympathy and regrets for an injury suffered....

Wolfe snapped, "I was shot over six hours ago. I might have died by now."

"Oh, come, Nero. Surely not. They said it was only your cheek, and I can see for myself—"

"I lost a quart of blood.—Archie! Did you say a quart?"

I hadn't said anything, but I'm always loyal. "Yes, sir. At least that. Closer to two. Of course I couldn't stop to measure it, but it came out like a river, like Niagara Falls, like—"

"That will do. Thank you."

Vukcic still stood frowning down. His tangle of hair was tumbling for his eyes, but he didn't unfold his arms to comb it back with his fingers. He growled, "I'm sorry. It was a close call. If he had killed you . . ." A pause. "Look here, Nero. Who was it?"

"I don't know. Not with certainty—yet."

"Are you finding out?"

"Yes."

"Was it the murderer of Laszio?"

"Yes—Confound it, I like to move my head when I talk, and I can't." Wolfe put the tips of his fingers gingerly to the bandage, felt it, and let his hand drop again. "I'll tell you something, Marko. This mist that has arisen between your eyes and mine—we can't ignore it and it is futile to discuss it. All I can say is, it will shortly be dispelled."

"The devil it will. How?"

"By the course of history. By Atropos, and me as her agent. At any rate, I am counting on that. In the meantime, there is nothing we can say to each other. You are drugged again— there, I didn't mean to say that. You see we can't talk. I would offend you, and you would bore me insufferably. Au revoir, Marko."

"Good God, I don't deny I'm drugged."

"I know it. You know what you're doing, and you do it anyway. Thank you for coming."

Vukcic did then unfold his arms to comb his hair. He ran his fingers through it three times, slowly, and then without saying anything turned and walked out.

Wolfe sat a long while with his eyes closed. Then he sighed deeply and asked me to take the script of the speech for a final rehearsal.

The only interruptions that time were some phone calls, from Tolman and Clay Ashley and Louis Servan. It was six o'clock before we had another caller, and when I opened the door and saw it was Raymond Liggett of the Hotel Churchill, I put on a welcoming grin because right away I smelled a fee, and among all the other irritations I was being subjected to was my dislike of seeing Wolfe exercising his brain, blowing money on long distance calls and drinks for fourteen dark-skinned men, losing two nights' sleep, and getting shot, with maybe a permanent scar, all for nothing relating to the bank account. As a side issue, there was also the question of a job for my friend Odell. Not that I owed him anything, but in the detective business around New York you never know in which spot it may become desirable to be greeted by a friendly face. To have the house dick of the Churchill, or even one of his staff, a protégé of mine, might come in handy any time.

Sure enough, it appeared that a fee was in prospect. The first thing Liggett said, after he had got seated and expressed the proper sentiments regarding Wolfe's facial casualty, was that one of the objects of his call was to ask if Wolfe would be willing to reconsider the matter of approaching Berin about the job of chef de cuisine at the Hotel Churchill.

Wolfe murmured, "I'm surprised that you still want him—a man who has been accused of murder. The publicity?"

Liggett dismissed that with a gesture. "Why not? People don't eat publicity, they eat food. And you know what Berin's prestige is. Frankly, I'm more interested in his prestige than in his food. I have an excellent kitchen staff, from top to bottom."

"People do eat prestige then." Wolfe gently patted his tummy. "I don't believe I'd care for it."

Liggett smiled his thin smile. His gray eyes looked about as irritated as they had Wednesday morning, not less, and they couldn't more. He shrugged. "Well, they seem to like it. About Berin. I know that yesterday morning you said you wouldn't do it, but you also said you wouldn't investigate Laszio's murder, and I understand you've reconsidered that. Ashley tells me you've done something quite remarkable, I didn't gather just what."

Wolfe inclined his head an eighth of an inch. "Thank you."

"That's what Ashley said. Besides, it was what you discovered, whatever that was, that caused Berin's release. Berin knows that, and therefore you are in a particularly advantageous position to make a suggestion to him—or even a request. I explained to you yesterday why I'm especially anxious to get him. I can add to that, confidentially—"

"I don't want confidences, Mr. Liggett."

Liggett impatiently brushed that aside. "It's not much of a secret. A competitor has been after Berin for two years. Branting of the Alexander. I happen to know that Berin has an appointment with Branting in New York to-morrow afternoon. That's the main reason I rushed down here. I have to get at him before he sees Branting."

"And soon after your arrival he was taken to jail. That was unfortunate. But he's out now, and is this minute probably at Pocahontas Pavilion. He left here two hours ago. Why the deuce don't you go and see him?"

"I told you yesterday. Because I don't think I can swing him." Liggett leaned forward. "Look here. The situation as it stands now is ideal. You got him out of jail, and he's impulsive and emotional, and he's feeling grateful to you. You can do it in one talk with him. One trouble is that I don't know what Branting has offered him, or is going to offer him, but whatever it is, I'll top it. I told you yesterday that I'd like to have him for forty thousand but would go to sixty if I had to. Now the time's short and I think I might even make it seventy. You can offer him fifty at the start—"

"I haven't agreed to offer him anything."

"But I'm telling you. You can offer him fifty thousand dollars a year. That's a lot more than he's getting at San Remo, but he may have a percentage there. Anyway, New York is something else. And if you land him I'll pay you ten thousand dollars cash."

Wolfe lifted his brows. "You want him, don't you?"

"I've got to have him. My directors have discussed this— after all, Laszio was getting along in years—and I must get him. Of course I don't own the Churchill, though I have a good block of stock. You still have time to start the ball rolling before dinner. I wanted to see you earlier this afternoon, when they brought Berin back, but on account of your accident..."

"Not an accident. Chance is without intention." Wolfe touched his bandage. "This was intended—or rather, worse."

"That's true. Of course. Will you see Berin now?"

"No."

"To-night?"

"No."

Liggett jerked up. "But damn it, are you crazy? A chance to make ten thousand dollars"—he snapped his fingers—"just like that! Why not?"

"It's not my business, hiring chefs. I'm a detective. I stick to my profession."

"I'm not asking you to make a business of it. All it means probably, under the circumstances, is one good talk with him. You can tell him he will be executive chef, with complete control and no interference from the hotel administration, and nothing to report but results. Our cost distribution is handled—"

Wolfe was wiggling a finger. "Mr. Liggett. Please. This is a waste of time. I shall not approach Mr. Berin on behalf of the Hotel Churchill."

Silence. I covered a yawn. I was surprised that Liggett wasn't bouncing up with exasperation, since his tendencies seemed to run in that direction, but all he did was sit still, not a muscle moving, and look at Wolfe. Wolfe, likewise motionless, returned the gaze with half-shut eyes.

The silence lasted all of a minute. Finally Liggett said, in a level tone with no exasperation at all, "I'll give you twenty thousand cash to get Berin for me."

"It doesn't tempt me, Mr. Liggett."

"I'll . . . I'll make it thirty thousand. I can give it to you in currency to-morrow morning."

Wolfe stirred a little, without unfocusing his eyes. "No. It wouldn't be worth it to you. Mr. Berin is a master chef, but not the only one alive. See here. This childish pretense is ridiculous. You were ill-advised to come to me like this. You are probably a man of some natural sense, and with only your own interests to consult, and left to your own counsel and devices, I am sure you would never have done such a thing. You were sent here, Mr. Liggett. I know that. It was a mistake that might have been expected, considering who did it. Pfui! You might, I suppose, go back and report your failure, but if you are moved to consult further it would be vastly better to consult only yourself."

"I don't know what you're talking about. I'm making you a straight proposal."

Wolfe shrugged. "If I am incoherent, that ends communication. Report failure, then, to yourself."

"I'm not reporting failure to anyone." Liggett's eyes were hard and so was his tone. "I came to you only because it seemed practical. To save annoyance. I can do—whatever I want done—without you."

"Then by all means do it."

"But I would still like to save annoyance. I'll pay you fifty thousand dollars."

Wolfe slowly, barely perceptibly, shook his head. "You'll have to report failure, Mr. Liggett. If it is true, as the cynic said, that every man has his price, you couldn't hand me mine in currency."

The phone rang. When a man turns cold and still I like to keep my eye on him in case, so I sidled around beyond Liggett's chair without turning my back on him. The first voice I heard in the receiver sounded like the blue-eyed belle, and she said she had a New York call. Then I heard gruff tones demanding Nero Wolfe, and was informed that Inspector Cramer wanted him. I turned:

"For you, sir. Mr. Purdy."

With a grunt, he labored to lift it from the chair. He stood and looked down at our caller:

"This is a confidential affair, Mr. Liggett. And since our business is concluded . . . if you don't mind? . . ."

Liggett took it as it was given. Without a word, without either haste or hesitation, he arose and departed. I strolled behind him to the foyer, and when he was out and the door closed I turned the key.

Wolfe's conversation with Cramer lasted more than ten minutes, and this time, as I sat and listened, I got something out of it besides grunts, but not enough to make a good picture. It seemed to me that he had distrusted my powers of dissimulation as far as was necessary, so when he hung up I was all set to put in a requisition for light and lucidity, but he had barely got back in his chair when the phone rang again. This time she told me it was a call from Charleston, and after some clicking and crackling I heard a voice in my ears that was as familiar as the Ventura Skin Preserver theme song.

"Hello, Mr. Wolfe?"

"No, you little shrimp, this is the Supreme Court speaking."

"Oh, Archie! How goes it?"

"Marvelous. Having a fine rest. Hold it, here's Mr. Wolfe." I handed him the receiver. "Saul Panzer from Charleston."

That was another ten minute talk, and it afforded me a few more hints and scraps of the alternative that Wolfe had apparently settled on, though it still seemed fairly incredible in spots. When it was finished Wolfe ambled back to his seat again, leaned back with careful caution, and got his fingers joined at the dome of his rotunda.

He demanded, "What time is it?"

I glanced at my wrist. "Quarter to seven."

He grunted. "Only a little over an hour till dinner. Don't let me forget to have that speech in my pocket when we go over there. Can you remember a few things without putting them down?"

"Sure. Any quantity."

"They are all important. First I must talk with Mr. Tolman; I suppose he is at the hotel as arranged. Then I must telephone Mr. Servan; that may be difficult; I believe it is not customary to have guests the last evening. In this case the tradition must be violated. While I am telephoning you will lay out everything we shall need, pack the bags, and arrange for their delivery at the train. We may be pressed for time around midnight. Also send to the hotel for our bill, and pay it. Did I hear you say you have your pistol along?—Good. I trust it won't be needed, but carry it. And confound it, send for a barber, I can't shave myself. Then get Mr. Tolman, and start on the bags. I'll discuss the evening program while we're dressing. . . ."

16

THE TRADITION was violated, and I overheard a few grumbles about it, in the big parlor before the door to the dining room was thrown open and Louis Servan appeared on the threshold to invite us in. Chiefly, though, as they sipped sherry or vermouth in scattered groups, the grumbles were on another subject: the decree that had been issued that none of them was to leave the jurisdiction of West Virginia until permission had been given by the authorities. Domenico Rossi orated about it, making it plenty loud enough to be heard by Barry Tolman, who stood by the radio looking worried but handsome; Ramsey Keith bellowed his opinion of the outrage; while Jerome Berin said God above, it was barbarous, but they would be fools to let it interfere with digestion. Albert

156

Malfi, looking a little subdued but with darts still in his eyes, seemed to have decided that courting Mamma Mondor was a sensible first step in his campaign for election in 1942; Raymond Liggett sat on the couch conversing quietly with Marko Vukcic. My friend Tolman got it right in the neck, or rather he didn't get it at all, when Constanza Berin came in and he went up to her looking determined, and spoke. She failed to see or hear him so completely that for a second I thought he wasn't there at all, I had just imagined it.

A couple of minutes before we started for the dining room Dina Laszio entered. The noise died down. Rossi, her father, hurried over to her, and not far behind him was Vukcic; then several others went up to pay their respects to the widow. She resembled a grieving widow about as much as I resemble a whirling dervish, but of course it can't be expected that every time a woman packs for a little trip with her husband she will take weeds along in case he happens to get bumped off. And I couldn't very well disapprove of her showing up at the feast, since I knew that Nero Wolfe had requested Servan to see her personally and insist on it.

At the table I was next to Constanza again, which was tolerable. Wolfe was at Servan's right. Vukcic was on the other side of Dina Laszio, down a ways. Liggett and Malfi were directly across from me, next to each other. Berin was across from Wolfe, on Servan's left, which seemed to me quite an honor for a guy just out of jail, and next to him was Clay Ashley, not making much of a success of attempts to appear affable. The others were here and there, with the meager supply of ladies spotted at intervals. On each plate when we sat down was an engraved menu:

LES QUINZE MAITRES
Kanawha Spa, West Virginia,
Thursday, April 8th, 1937.
AMERICAN DINNER
Oysters Baked in the Shell
Terrapin Maryland   Beaten Biscuits
Pan Broiled Young Turkey
Rice Croquettes with Quince Jelly
Lima Beans in Cream   Sally Lunn
Avocado Todhunter
Pineapple Sherbet   Sponge Cake
Wisconsin Dairy Cheese   Black Coffee

As the waiters, supervised by Moulton, smoothly brought and took, Louis Servan surveyed the scene with solemn and anxious dignity. The first course should have helped to allay the anxiety, for the oysters were so plump and savory, not to mention aromatic, that it seemed likely they had been hand-fed on peanuts and blueberries. They were served with ceremony and a dash of pomp. As the waiters finished distributing the enormous tins, each holding a dozen oysters, they stood back in a line against one of the screens—the one which forty-eight hours previously had concealed the body of Phillip Laszio—and the door to the pantry hall opened to admit a brown-skinned cook in immaculate white cap and apron. He came forward a few paces, looking embarrassed enough to back right out again, but Servan stood up and beckoned to him and then turned to the table and announced to the gathering, "I wish to present to you Mr. Hyacinth Brown, the fish chef of Kanawha Spa. The baked oysters we are about to eat is his. You will judge whether it is worthy of the honor of being served to Les Quinze Maîtres. Mr. Brown wishes me to tell you that he appreciates that honor.—Isn't that so, Brown?"

"Yes, sir. You said it."

There was a ripple of applause. Brown looked more embarrassed than ever, bowed, and turned and went. The masters lifted forks and waded in, and the rest of us followed suit. There were grunts and murmurs of appreciation. Rossi called something across the length of the table. Pierre Mondor stated with quiet authority, "Superb. Extreme oven?" Servan nodded gravely, and the forks played on.

With the terrapin the performance was repeated, this time the introduction being accorded to Crabtree; and when the course was finished there was a near riot of enthusiasm and it was demanded that Crabtree reappear. Most of them got up to shake his hand, and he wasn't embarrassed at all, though he was certainly pleased. Two of them came in with the turkey. One was Grant, with wrinkled face and gray kinky hair, and the other was a tall black one that I didn't know, since he hadn't been at the party Wednesday night. I never tasted better turkey, but the other servings had been generous and my capacity limited me to one portion. Those guys eating were like a woman packing a trunk—it's not a question of capacity but of how much she has to put in. Not to mention the claret they washed it down with. They were getting

158

merrier as they went along, and even old Servan was sending happy smiles around.

Unquestionably it was first class fodder. I went slow on the wine. My head was fuzzy anyhow, and if I was going to be called on to save Wolfe's life again I might need what wits I had left.

There was nothing strained about the atmosphere, it was just a nice party with everyone well filled and the smell of good coffee and brandy in front of us, when finally, a little after ten o'clock, Wolfe arose to start his speech. He looked more like the plaintiff in a suit for damages than an after-dinner speaker, and he was certainly aware of it, but it didn't seem to bother him. We all got our chairs moved around to face him more comfortably and got settled into silence. He began in an easy informal tone:

"Mr. Servan, Ladies, Masters, Fellow Guests. I feel a little silly. Under different circumstances it might be both instructive and amusing for you, at least some of you, to listen to a discussion of American contributions to la haute cuisine, and it might be desirable to use what persuasiveness I can command to convince you that those contributions are neither negligible nor meager. But when I accepted an invitation to offer you such a discussion, which greatly pleased and flattered me, I didn't realize how unnecessary it would be at the moment scheduled for its delivery. It is delightful to talk about food, but infinitely more delightful to eat it; and we have eaten. A man once declared to me that one of the keenest pleasures in life was to close his eyes and dream of beautiful women, and when I suggested that it would be still more agreeable to open his eyes and look at them, he said not at all, for the ones he dreamed about were *all* beautiful, far more beautiful than any his eye ever encountered. Similarly it might be argued that if I am eloquent the food I talk to you about may be better than the food you have eaten; but even that specious excuse is denied me. I can describe, and pay tribute to, some superlative American dishes, but I can't surpass the oysters and terrapin and turkey which were so recently there"—he indicated the table—"and are now here." With a gentle palm he delicately patted the appropriate spot.

They applauded. Mondor cried, "Bien dit!" Servan beamed.

Properly speaking, he hadn't started the speech yet, for that wasn't in it. Now he started. For the first ten minutes or so I was uneasy. There was nothing in the world I would enjoy more than watching Nero Wolfe wallowing in discomfiture, but not in the presence of outsiders. When that happy time came, which it never had yet, I wanted it to be a special command performance for Archie Goodwin and no one else around. And I was uneasy because it seemed quite possible that the hardships on the train and loss of sleep and getting shot at might have upset him so that he would forget the darned speech, but after the first ten minutes I saw there was nothing to worry about. He was sailing along. I took another sip of brandy and relaxed.

By the time he was half through I began to worry about something else. I glanced at my wrist. It was getting late. Charleston was only sixty miles away, and Tolman had said it was a good road and could easily be made in an hour and a half. Knowing how complicated the program was, it was my opinion that there wasn't much chance of getting away that night anyhow, but it would have ruined the setup entirely if anything had happened to Saul. So my second big relief came when the greenjacket from the hall entered softly from the parlor, as he had been instructed, and gave me the high sign. I sidled out of my chair with as little disturbance as possible and tiptoed out.

There in the small parlor sat a little guy with a big nose, in need of a shave, with an old brown cap hanging on his knee. He stood up and stuck out his hand and I took it with a grin.

"Hello, darling, I never would have thought that the time would come when you would look handsome to me. Turn around, how do you look behind?"

Saul Panzer demanded, "How's Mr. Wolfe?"

"Swell. He's in there making a speech I taught him."

"You sure he's all right?"

"Why not? Oh, you mean his casualty." I waved a hand. "A mere nothing. He thinks he's a hero. I wish to God they'd shoot me next time so he'd stop bragging. Have you got anything?"

Saul nodded. "I've got everything."

"Is there anything you need to explain to Wolfe before he springs it?"

"I don't think so. I've got everything he asked for. The whole Charleston police force jumped into it."

"Yeah, I know. My friend Mr. Tolman arranged that. I've

160

got another friend named Odell that throws stones at people—remind me to tell you about it sometime. This is a jolly place. Then you wait here till you're called. I'd better go back in. Have you had anything to eat?"

He said his inside was attended to, and I left him. Back in the dining room again, I resumed my seat beside Constanza, and when Wolfe paused at the end of a paragraph, I took my handkerchief from my breast pocket, passed it across my lips, and put it back again. He gave me a fleeting glance to acknowledge the signal. he had reached the part about the introduction of filé powder to the New Orleans market by the Choctaw Indians on Bayou Lacombe, so I knew he had got to page 14. It looked as though he was putting it over in good style. Even Domenico Rossi looked absorbed, in spite of the fact that in one place Wolfe specifically stated that in the three most important centers of American contributions to fine cooking—Louisiana, South Carolina, and New England—there had been no Italian influence whatever.

He reached the end. Even though I knew his program, and knew the time was short, I had supposed he would at least pause there, and perhaps give Louis Servan a chance to make a few remarks of appreciation, but he didn't even stop long enough for them to realize that the speech was finished. He looked around—a brief glance at the rectangle of faces—and went right on:

"I hope I won't bore you if I continue, but on another subject. I count on your forbearance, for what I have to say is as much in your interest as in my own. I have finished my remarks on cooking. Now I'm going to talk to you about murder. The murder of Phillip Laszio."

There were stirs and murmurs. Lisette Putti squeaked. Louis Servan put up a hand:

"If you please. I would like to say, Mr. Wolfe does this by arrangement. It is distressing to end thus the dinner of Les Quinze Maîtres but it appears . . . unavoidable. We do not even . . . however, there is no help . . ."

Ramsey Keith, glancing at Tolman, Malfi, Liggett, Ashley, growled inhospitably, "So that's the reason these people—"

"Yes, that's the reason." Wolfe was brisk. "I beg you, all of you, don't blame me for intruding a painful subject into an occasion of festivity. The intruder was the man who killed Laszio, and thereby worked disaster on a joyous gathering, cast the gloom of suspicion over a group of eminent men, and ruined my holiday as well as yours. So not only do I have a special reason for rancor for that man"—he put the tip of a finger to his bandage—"but we all have a general one. Besides, before dinner I heard several of you complaining of the fact that you will all be detained here until the authorities release you. But you know that's a natural consequence of the misfortune that overtook you. The authorities can't be expected to let you disperse to the four corners of the earth as long as they have reason to suspect that one of you is a murderer. That's why I say I count on your forbearance. You can't leave here until the guilty man is discovered. So that's what I intend to do here and now. I'm going to expose the murderer, and demonstrate his guilt, before we leave this room."

Lisette Putti squeaked again, and then covered her mouth with her palm. There were no murmurs. A few glanced around, but most of them kept their eyes on Wolfe.

He went on, "First I think I'd better tell you what was done here—in this room—Tuesday evening, and then we can proceed to the question of who did it. There was nothing untoward until Mondor, Coyne, Keith and Servan had all been here and tasted the sauces. The instant Servan left, Laszio reached across the table and changed the position of the dishes, all but two. Doubtless he would have shifted those also if the door had not begun to open for the entrance of Berin. It was a childish and malicious trick intended to discredit Berin, and possibly Vukcic too. It may be that Laszio intended to replace the dishes when Berin left, but he didn't, because he was killed before he got a chance to.

"While Berin was in here the radio in the parlor was turned on. That was a prearranged signal for a man who was waiting for it out in the shrubbery. He was close enough to the parlor window—"

"Wait a minute!" The cry wasn't loud, nor explosive; it was quite composed. But everyone was startled into turning to Dina Laszio, who had uttered it. There was as little turmoil in her manner as in her voice, though maybe her eyes were a little longer and sleepier even than usual. They were directed at Wolfe: "Do we interrupt you when you tell lies?"

"I think not, madam—granting your premise. If each of my statements is met with a challenge we'll never get anywhere. Why don't you wait till I'm through? By that time, if I have lied, you can bankrupt me with a suit for slander."

162

"I turned on the radio. Everyone knows that. You said it was a prearranged signal. . . ."

"So I did. I beg you, let's don't turn this into a squabble. I'm discussing murder and making serious charges. Let me finish, let me expose myself, then rebut me if you can; and either I shall be discredited and disgraced, or someone here will be . . . do you hang in West Virginia, Mr. Tolman?"

Tolman, his eyes riveted on Wolfe's face, nodded.

"Then someone will die at the end of a rope.—As I was saying, the man concealed in the shrubbery out there"—he pointed to the door leading to the terrace—"was close enough to the open parlor window so that when the radio warned him he could observe the return of Berin to the parlor. Instantly he proceeded to the terrace and entered this room by that door. Laszio, here alone by the table, was surprised at the entrance of a liveried servant—for the man wore Kanawha Spa livery and had a black face. The man approached the table and made himself known, for Laszio knew him well. 'See,' the man said with a smile, 'don't you know me, I am Mr. White'—we may call him that for the present, for he was in fact a white man—'I am Mr. White, masquerading, ha ha, and we'll play a joke on these fellows. It will be quite amusing, ha ha, Laszio old chap. You go behind that screen and I'll stay here by the table . . .'

"I confess that no one except Laszio heard those words, or any others. The words actually spoken may have been quite different, but whatever they were, the upshot was that Laszio went behind the screen, and Mr. White, having procured a knife from the table, followed him there and stabbed him to the heart, from behind. It was certainly done with finesse and dispatch, since there was no struggle and no outcry loud enough to be heard in the pantry hall. Mr. White left the knife where he had put it, seeing that it had done its work, and emerged from behind the screen. As he did so a glance showed him that the door to the pantry hall—that door—was open a few inches and a man, a colored man, was peering at him through the crack. Either he had already decided what to do in case of such an emergency, or he showed great presence of mind, for he merely stood still at the end of the screen, looking straight at the eyes peering at him, and placed his finger to his lips. A simple and superb gesture. He may or may not have known—probably he didn't—that at the same moment the door leading to the terrace, behind him,

163

had also opened, and a woman was looking through at him. But his masquerade worked both ways. The colored man knew he was a fake, a white man blacked up, took him for one of the guests playing a joke, and so was not moved to inquire or interfere. The woman supposed he was a servant and let it go at that. Before he left this room Mr. White was seen by still another man—the headwaiter, Moulton here— but by the time Moulton looked through the door Mr. White was on his way out and his back was turned, so Moulton didn't see his face.—We might as well record names as we go along. The man who first peered through the door was Paul Whipple, one of our waiters here—who, by the way, is studying anthropology at Howard University. The one who saw Mr. White going out was Moulton. The woman who looked through the terrace door was Mrs. Lawrence Coyne."

Coyne jerked around to look, startled, at his wife. She put up her chin at Wolfe. "But... you promised me..."

"I promised you nothing. I'm sorry, Mrs. Coyne, but it's much better not to leave out anything I don't think—"

Coyne sputtered indignantly. "I've heard nothing—nothing—"

"Please." Wolfe put up a nand. "I assure you, sir, you and your wife have no cause for worry. Indeed, we should all be grateful to her. If she hadn't hurt her finger in the door, and asked you to kiss it in my hearing, it's quite probable that Mr. Berin would have got the noose instead of the man who earned it. But I needn't go into that.

"That's what happened here Tuesday night. I'll clear up a point now about the radio. It might be thought of, since it was turned on, as a prearranged signal, while Berin was in here tasting the sauces, that it was timed at that moment so as to throw suspicion on Berin, but not so. There was probably no intention to have suspicion aimed at any specific person, but if there was, that person was Marko Vukcic. The arrangement was that the radio should be turned on a few minutes prior to the visit of Vukcic to the dining room, no matter who was tasting the sauces at that moment. It was chance that made it Berin, and chance also that Laszio had shifted the sauces around to trick Berin. And the chance trap for Berin was actually sprung, innocently, by Moulton, who came to the table and changed the dishes back again before Vukcic entered. I haven't told you about that. But the point I am making is that the radio signal was given a few minutes prior to the scheduled entrance of Vukcic to the dining room, because Vukcic was the one man here whom Mrs. Laszio could confidently expect to detain in the parlor, delaying his visit to the dining room, and giving Mr. White the necessary time alone with Laszio to accomplish his purpose. As we all know, she insured the delay by putting herself into Vukcic's arms for dancing, and staying there."

"Lies! You know it's lies—"

"Dina! Shut up!"

It was Domenico Rossi, glaring at his daughter. Vukcic, with his jaw set, was gazing at her. Others sent glances at her and looked away again.

"But he tells lies—"

"I say shut up!" Rossi was much quieter, and more impressive, than when he was picking a scrap. "If he tells lies, let him tell all of them."

"Thank you, sir." Wolfe inclined his head half an inch. "I think now we had better decide who Mr. White is. You will notice that the fearful risks he took in this room Tuesday night were more apparent than real. Up to the moment he sank the knife into Laszio's back he was taking no risk at all; he was merely an innocent masquerader. And if afterwards he was seen—well, he *was* seen, and what if he was, since he was blacked up? The persons who saw him here Tuesday night have all seen him since, with the blacking and livery gone, and none has suspected him. He depended for safety on his certainty that he would never be suspected at all. He had several bases for that certainty, but the chief one was that on Tuesday evening he wasn't in Kanawha Spa; he was in New York."

Berin burst out, "God above! If he wasn't here—"

"I mean he wasn't supposed to be here. It is always assumed that a man is where probability places him, unless suspicion is aroused that he is somewhere else, and Mr. White figured that such a suspicion was an impossibility. But he was too confident and too careless. He permitted his own tongue to create the suspicion in a conversation with me.

"As you all know, I've had wide experience in affairs of this kind. It's my business. I told Mr. Tolman Tuesday night that I was sure Berin hadn't done it, but I withheld my best reason for that assurance, because it wasn't my case and I don't like to involve people where I have no concern. That reason was this, I was convinced that Mrs. Laszio had signaled to the murderer by turning on the radio. Other details connected with that might be attributed to chance, but it would take great credulity to believe that her hanging onto Vukcic in that dance, delaying his trip to the dining room while her husband was being killed, was also coincidence. Especially when, as I did, one saw her doing it. She made a bad mistake there. Ordinary intelligence might have caused her to reflect that I was present and that therefore more subtlety was called for.

"When Berin was arrested I did become interested, as you know, but when I had got him released I was again unconcerned with the affair. Whereupon another idiotic mistake was made, almost unbelievable. Mr. White thought I was discovering too much, and without even taking the trouble to learn that I had withdrawn, he sneaked through the shrubbery outside my window and shot me. I think I know how he approached Upshur Pavilion. My assistant, Mr. Goodwin, an hour or so later, saw him dismounting from a horse at the hotel. The bridle path runs within fifty yards of the rear of Upshur. He could easily have left the path, tied his horse, advanced through the shrubbery to my window, and after the shot got back to the horse again and off on the path without being seen. At all events, he made that mistake, and by it, instead of removing me, he encountered me. My concern revived.

"I assumed, as I say, that the murderer was in league with Mrs. Laszio. I dismissed the idea that it was solely her project and he had been hired by her, for that would have rendered the masquerade meaningless; besides, it was hard to believe that a hired murderer, a stranger to Laszio, could have entered this room, got a knife from the table, enticed Laszio behind the screen, and killed him, without an outcry or any struggle. And just as yesterday, when Berin was arrested and I undertook to find evidence to free him, I had one slender thread to start with, Mrs. Coyne's appeal to her husband to kiss her finger because she had caught it in a door, so to-day, when I undertook to catch the murderer, I had another thread just as slender. It was this. Yesterday about two o'clock Mr. Malfi and Mr. Liggett arrived at Kanawha Spa after a nonstop airplane flight from New York. They came directly to my room at Upshur Pavilion before talking with anyone but servants, and had a conversation with me. During the conversation Liggett said—I think this is verbatim: 'It seems likely that whoever did it was able to use finesse for other purposes than tasting the seasonings in Sauce Printemps.' Do you remember that, sir?"

"For God's sake." Liggett snorted. "You damn fool, are you trying to drag me into it?"

"I'm afriad I am. You may enter your action for slander along with Mrs. Laszio. Do you remember saying that?"

"No. Neither do you."

Wolfe shrugged. "It's unimportant now. It was vital in its function as my thread.—Anyway, it seemed suitable for inquiry. It seemed unlikely that such a detail as the name of the sauce we were tasting had been included in the first brief reports of the murder wired to New York. I telephoned there, to an employee of mine, and to Inspector Cramer of the police. My requests to Mr. Cramer were somewhat inclusive: for instance, I asked him to check on all passengers of airplanes, scheduled or specially chartered, from all airports, leaving New York Tuesday, which had stopped no matter where in this part of the country in time for a passenger to have arrived at Kanawha Spa by nine o'clock Tuesday evening. I made it nine o'clock because when we went to the parlor after dinner Tuesday Mrs. Laszio immediately disappeared and was not seen again for an hour; and if there was anything to my theory at all it seemed likely that that absence was for a rendezvous with her collaborator. I also asked Mr. Cramer to investigate Mrs. Laszio's life in New York—her friends and associates—now, madam. Please. You'll get a chance.—For suspicion was at that point by no means confined to Liggett. There was even one of you here not entirely clear; and I want to express publicly to Mr. Blanc my thanks for his tolerance and good nature in assisting with the experiment which eliminated him. No doubt he thought it ridiculous.

"At one o'clock this afternoon I received a telegram telling me that Sauce Printemps had not been mentioned in the account in any New York paper Tuesday morning. Since Liggett had left in the airplane before ten o'clock, had come non-stop, and had talked with no one before seeing me, how had he known it was Sauce Printemps? Probably he *had* talked with someone. He had talked with Mrs. Laszio around nine-thirty Tuesday evening, somewhere in the grounds around this building, making the arrangements which resulted in Laszio's murder."

I wasn't any too well pleased, because I couldn't see

Liggett's hands; he was across from me and the table hid them. Nor his eyes either, because they were on Wolfe. All I could see was the corner of his thin smile on the side of his mouth that was toward me, and the cord on the side of his neck as he held his jaw clamped. From where he sat he couldn't see Dina Laszio, but I could, and she had her lower lip caught by her teeth. And at that, that was the only outward sign that she wasn't quite as nonchalant as she had been when she patted Wolfe's shoulder.

Wolfe went on, "At three o'clock I had a phone call from Inspector Cramer. Among other things, he told me that Saul Panzer, my employee, had left on an airplane for Charleston in accordance with my instructions. Then—I might as well mention this—around six o'clock another silly mistake was made. To do Mr. Liggett justice, I doubt if it was his own idea; I suspect it was Mrs. Laszio who thought of it and persuaded him to try it. He came to my room and offered me fifty thousand dollars cash to ask Mr. Berin to take the job of chef de cuisine at the Hotel Churchill."

Lisette Putti squeaked again. Jerome Berin exploded, "That robbers' den! That stinking hole! Me? Rather would I fry eggs on my finger nails—"

"Just so. I declined the offer. Liggett was foolish to make it, for I am not too self-confident to welcome the encouragement of confession from the enemy, and his offer of the preposterous sum was of course confession of guilt. He will deny that; he will probably even deny he made the offer; no matter. I received other and more important encouragement: another phone call from Inspector Cramer. Time is short, and I won't bore you with all the details, but among them was the information that he had uncovered rumors of a mutual interest, going back two years, between Liggett and Mrs. Laszio. Also he had checked another point I had inquired about. Coming here on the train Monday night, Mr. Berin had told me of a visit he had made last Saturday to the Resort Room of the Hotel Churchill, where the waiters were dressed in the liveries of famous resorts, among them that of Kanawha Spa. Inspector Cramer's men had discovered that about a year ago Mr. Liggett had had a duplicate of the Kanawha Spa livery made for himself and had worn it at a fancy dress ball. No doubt it was that fact that he already owned that livery which suggested the technique he adopted for his project. So as you see, I was getting a good sketch for my picture:

iggett had known of the Sauce Printemps before he had any
ght to; he was on terms with Mrs. Laszio; and he had a
anawha Spa livery in his wardrobe. There were other items,
for instance he had left the hotel Tuesday noon, ostensibly
play golf, but had not appeared at either of the clubs
here he habitually plays; but we shall have to do some
ipping. Mr. Tolman can collect these things after Liggett is
rested. Now we'd better get on to Saul Panzer—I haven't
entioned that he telephoned me from Charleston immedi-
ely after the call from Inspector Cramer.—Will you bring
im, please, from the small parlor?"

Moulton trotted out.

Liggett said in an even tone, "The cleverest lie you've told
about my trying to bribe you. And the most dangerous lie,
ecause there's some truth in it. I did go to your room to ask
ou to approach Berin for me. And I suppose your man is
rimed to back up the lie that I offered fifty thousand—"

"Please, Mr. Liggett." Wolfe put up a palm at him. "I
ouldn't talk extempore if I were you. You'd better think it
ver carefully before you—ah, hello, Saul! It's good to see
ou."

"Yes, sir. Same to you." Saul Panzer came and stood beside
y chair. He had on his old gray suit with the pants never
ressed, and the old brown cap in his hand. After one look at
Volfe his sharp eyes darted around the rectangle of faces,
id I knew that each of those phizzes had in that moment
een registered in a portrait gallery where it would stay
rever in place.

Wolfe said, "Speak to Mr. Liggett."

"Yes, sir." Saul's eyes fastened on the target instantly. "How
you do, Mr. Liggett."

Liggett didn't turn. "Bah. It's a damned farce."

Wolfe shrugged. "We haven't much time, Saul. Confine
ourself to the essentials. Did Mr. Liggett play golf Tuesday
fternoon?"

"No, sir." Saul was husky and he cleared his throat. "On
uesday at 1:55 p.m. he boared a plane of Interstate Airways
t the Newark Airport. I was on the same plane to-day, with
ie same hostess, and showed her Liggett's picture. He left
ie plane at Charleston when it stopped there at 6:18—and
did I, to-day. About half past six he appeared at Little's
arage on Marlin Street and hired a car, a 1936 Studebaker,
aving a deposit of $200 in twenty-dollar bills. I drove the

same car here this evening; it's out in front now. I inquired at a few places on the way, but I couldn't find where he stopped on the way back to wash the black off his face—I had to hurry because you told me to get here before eleven o'clock. He showed up again at Little's Garage about a quarter after one Tuesday night and had to pay ten dollars for a fender he had dented. He walked away from the garage and on Laurel Street took a taxi, license C3428, driver Al Bissell, to the Charleston airport. There he took the night express of Interstate Airways, which landed him at Newark at 5:34 Wednesday morning. From there I don't know, but he went to New York, because he was in his apartment a few minutes before eight, when a telephone call was put through to him from Albert Malfi. At half past eight he phoned Newark to charter a plane to take him and Malfi to Kanawha Spa, and at 9:52—"

"That's enough, Saul. By then his movements were overt. You say you drove here this evening in the same car that Liggett hired Tuesday?"

"Yes, sir."

"Well. That's rubbing it in. And you had pictures of Liggett with you to show all those people—the hostess, the garage man, the taxi driver—"

"Yes, sir. He was white when he left the garage."

"No doubt he stopped for alterations on the way. It isn't as difficult as you might think; we blacked a man in my room this afternoon. Cleaning it off is harder. I don't suppose remnants of it were noticed by the man at the garage or the taxi driver?"

"No, sir. I tried that."

"Yes. You would. Of course they wouldn't examine his ears. You didn't mention luggage."

"He had a medium sized suitcase, dark tan cowhide, with brass fastenings and no straps."

"At all appearances?"

"Yes, sir. Coming and going both."

"Good. Satisfactory. I think that will do. Take that chair over by the wall."

Wolfe surveyed the faces, and though he had kept their attention with his speech on cookery, he was keeping it better now. You could have heard a pin swishing through the air before it lit. He said, "Now we're getting somewhere. You understand why I said that such details as Liggett's mention of Sauce Printemps are no longer of much importance. It is obvious that he treated so fatal a crime as murder with incredible levity, but we should remember two things: first, that he supposed that his absence from Kanawha Spa would never be questioned, and second, he was actually not sentient. He was drugged. He had drunk of the cup which Mrs. Laszio had filled for him. As far as Liggett is concerned, we seem to be done; there appears to be nothing left but for Mr. Tolman to arrest him, prepare the case, try him, and convict him. Have you any remarks on that, Mr. Liggett? I wouldn't advise any."

"I'm not saying anything." Liggett's voice was as good as ever. "Except that if Tolman swallows this and acts on it the way you've framed it, he'll be damn near as sorry as you're going to be." Liggett's chin went up a little. "I know you, Wolfe. I've heard about you. God knows why you've picked on me for this, but I'm going to know before I get through with you."

Wolfe gravely inclined his head. "Your only possible attitude. Of course. But I'm through with you, sir. I turn you over. Your biggest mistake was shooting at me when I had become merely a bystander. Look here." He reached in his pocket and pulled out the script and unfolded it. "That's where your bullet went, right through my speech, before it struck me.—Mr. Tolman, do you have women on murder juries in your state?"

"No. Men only."

"Indeed." Wolfe directed his gaze at Mrs. Laszio; he hadn't looked at her since beginning on Liggett. "That's a piece of luck for you, madam. It'll be a job to persuade twelve men to pronounce your doom." Back to Tolman: "Are you prepared to charge Liggett with the murder of Laszio?"

Tolman's voice was clear: "I am."

"Well, sir? You didn't hesitate with Mr. Berin."

Tolman got up. He had only four paces to walk. He put his hand on Liggett's shoulder and said in a loud tone, "I arrest you, Raymond Liggett. A formal charge of murder will be laid to-morrow morning." He turned and spoke sharply to Moulton: "The sheriff is out front. Tell him to come in."

Liggett twisted his head around to get Tolman's eye. "This will ruin you, young man."

Wolfe, stopping Moulton with a gesture, appealed to Tolman, "Let the sheriff wait a little. If you don't mind? I don't like him." He put his eyes at Mrs. Laszio again. "Besides, mad-

171

am, we still have you to consider. As far as Liggett is concerned, well... you see..." He moved a hand to indicate Tolman standing at Liggett's shoulder. "Now about you. You're not arrested yet. Have you got anything to say?"

The swamp-woman looked sick. I suppose she was good enough at make-up so that ordinarily only an expert would have noticed the extent of it, but it wasn't calculated to handle emergencies like this. Her face was spotty. Her lower lip didn't match the upper, on account of having been chewed on. Her shoulders were humped up and her chest pulled in. She said in a thin tone, not her rich swampy voice at all, "I didn't... only... only what I said, it's lies. Lies!"

"Do you mean what I've said about Liggett is lies? And what Saul Panzer has said? I warn you, madam, things that can be proven are not lies. You say lies. What?"

"It's all lies... about me."

"And about Liggett?"

"I... I don't know."

"Indeed. But about you. You did turn on the radio. Didn't you?"

She nodded without speaking. Wolfe snapped. "Didn't you?"

"Yes."

"And whether by accident or design, you did detain Vukcic and dance with him while your husband was being murdered?"

"Yes."

"And Tuesday evening after dinner you were absent from the gathering here nearly an hour?"

"Yes."

"And since your husband is dead... if it were not for the unfortunate circumstance that Liggett will soon be dead too, you would expect to marry him, wouldn't you?"

"I..." Her mouth twisted. "No! You can't say... no!"

"Please, Mrs. Laszio. Keep your nerve. You need it." Wolfe's tone suddenly got gentle. "I don't want to bully you. I am perfectly aware that as regards you the facts permit of two vastly different constructions. One something like this: You and Mr. Liggett wanted each other—at least he wanted you, and you wanted his name and position and wealth. But your husband was the sort of man who hangs on to his possessions, and that made it difficult. The time finally arrived when the desire was so great, and the obstacle so stubborn, that you and Liggett decided on a desperate course. It appeared that

172

the meeting of Les Quinze Maîtres offered a good opportunity for the removal of your husband, for there would be three persons present who hated him—plenty of targets for suspicion. So Liggett came to Charleston by airplane and on here by car, and met you somewhere outside, as previously arranged, at half past nine Tuesday evening. It was only then that the arrangements were perfected in detail, for Liggett could not previously have known about the wager between Servan and Keith and the test of Sauce Printemps that was being prepared to decide it. Liggett posted himself in the shrubbery. You returned to the parlor, and turned on the radio at the proper time, and delayed Vukcic by dancing with him in order to give Liggett the opportunity to enter the dining room and kill your husband. Confound it, madam, don't stare at me like that! As I say, that is one possible interpretation of your actions."

"But it's wrong. It's lies! I didn't—"

"Permit me. Don't deny too much. I confess there may be lies in it, for there's another possible construction. But understand this, and consider it well." Wolfe aimed a finger at her, and pointed his tone. "It is going to be proven that Liggett came here, and was told by someone about the test of the sauces, and that he knew precisely the moment when he could safely enter this room to kill Laszio without danger of interruption; that he *knew* that Vukcic would not enter to disturb him before the deed was done. Otherwise his proceeding as he did was senseless. That's why I say don't deny too much. If you try to maintain that you didn't meet Liggett outdoors, that you made no arrangement with him, that your turning on the radio when you did was coincidence, that your keeping Vukcic from the dining room during those fatal minutes was also coincidence—then I fear for you. Even a jury of twelve men, and even looking at you on the stand— I'm afraid they wouldn't swallow it. I believe, to put it brutally, I believe you would be convicted of murder.

"But I haven't said you're a murderer." Wolfe's tone was almost soothing. "Since the crime was committed you have unquestionably, at least by silence, tried to shield Liggett, but a woman's heart being what it is..." He shrugged. "No jury would convict you for that. And no jury would convict you at all, you wouldn't even be in jeopardy, if it could be shown that the arrangement you entered into with Liggett Tuesday evening, when you met him outdoors there, was on your part an innocent one. Merely as a hypothesis, let's say, for example, that you understood that Liggett was engaged in nothing more harmful than a practical joke. No matter what; I couldn't guess at the details even as a hypothesis, for I'm not a practical joker. But the joke required that he have a few minutes alone with Laszio before the entrance of Vukcic. That of course would explain everything—your turning on the radio, your detaining Vukcic—everything you did, without involving you in guilt. You understand, Mrs. Laszio, I'm not suggesting this as a retreat for you. I am only saying that while you can't deny what happened, you may possibly have an explanation for it that will save you. In that case, it would be quixotic to try to save Liggett too. You can't do it. And if there is such an explanation, I wouldn't wait too long... until it's too late...."

It was too much for Liggett. Slowly his head turned, irresistibly as if gripped in enormous pliers, square around, until he faced Dina Laszio. She didn't look at him. She was chewing at her lip again, and her eyes were on Wolfe, fixed and fascinated. You could almost see her chewing her brain too. That lasted a full half a minute, and then by God she smiled. It was a funny one, but it was a smile; and then I saw that her eyes had shifted to Liggett and the smile was supposed to be one of polite apology. She said in a low tone but without anything shaky in it, "I'm sorry, Ray. Oh, I'm sorry, but..."

She faltered. Liggett's eyes were boring at her.

She moved her gaze to Wolfe and said firmly, "You're right. Of course you're right and I can't help it. When I met him outdoors after dinner as we had arranged—"

"Dina! Dina, for God's sake—"

Tolman, the blue-eyed athlete, jerked Liggett back in his chair. The swamp-woman was going on:

"He had told me what he was going to do, and I believed him, I thought it was a joke. Then afterwards he told me that Phillip had attacked him, had struck at him—"

Wolfe said sharply, "You know what you're doing, madam. You're helping to send a man to his death."

"I know. I can't help it! How can I go on lying for him? He killed my husband. When I met him out there and he told me what he had planned—"

"You tricky bastard!" Liggett broke training completely. He jerked from Tolman's grasp, plunged across Mondor's legs,

174

knocked Blanc and his chair to the floor, trying to get at Wolfe. I was on my way, but by the time I got there Berin had stopped him, with both arms around him, and Liggett was kicking and yelling like a lunatic.

Dina Laszio, of course, had stopped trying to talk, with all the noise and confusion. She sat quietly looking on with her long sleepy eyes.

17

JEROME BERIN said positively, "She'll stick to it. She'll do whatever will push danger farthest from her, and that will be it."

The train was sailing like a gull across New Jersey on a sunny Friday morning, somewhere east of Philadelphia. In sixty minutes we would be tunneling under the Hudson. I was propped against the wall of the pullman bedroom again, Constanza was on the chair, and Wolfe and Berin were on the window seats with beer between them. Wolfe looked pretty seedy, since of course he wouldn't have tried to shave on the train even if there had been no bandage, but he knew that in an hour the thing would stop moving and the dawn of hope was on his face.

Berin asked, "Don't you think so?"

Wolfe shrugged. "I don't know and I don't care. The point was to nail Liggett down by establishing his presence at Kanawha Spa on Tuesday evening, and Mrs. Laszio was the only one who could do that for us. As you say, she is undoubtedly just as guilty as Liggett, maybe more, depending on your standard. I rather think Mr. Tolman will try her for murder. He took her last night as a material witness, and he may keep her that way to clinch his case against Liggett—or he may charge her as an accomplice. I doubt if it matters much. Whatever he does, he won't convict her. She's a special kind of woman, she told me so herself. Even if Liggett is bitter enough against her to confess everything in order to involve her in his doom, to persuade any dozen men that the best thing to do with that woman is to kill her would be quite a feat. I question whether Mr. Tolman is up to it."

Berin, filling his pipe, frowned at it. Wolfe upped his beer glass with one hand as he clung to the arm of the seat with the other.

Constanza smiled at me. "I try not to hear them. Talking about killing people." She shivered delicately.

I grunted. "You seem to be doing a lot of smiling. Under the circumstances."

She lifted brows above the dark purple eyes. "What circumstances?"

I just waved a hand. Berin had got his pipe lit and was talking again. "Well, it turned my stomach. Poor Rossi, did you notice him? Poor devil. When Dina Rossi was a little girl and I had her many times on this knee, and she was quiet and very sly but a nice girl. Of course, all murderers were once little children, which seems astonishing." He puffed until the little room was nicely filled with smoke. "By the way, did you know that Vukcic made this train?"

"No."

Berin nodded. "He came leaping on at the last minute, I saw him, like a lion with fleas after him. I haven't seen him around this morning, though I've been back and forth. No doubt your man told you that I stopped here at your room around eight o'clock."

Wolfe grimaced. "I wasn't dressed."

"So he told me. So I came back. I wasn't comfortable. I never am comfortable when I'm in debt, and I've got to find out what I owe you and pay it. There at Kanawha Spa you were a guest and didn't want to talk about it, but now you can. You got me out of a bad hole and maybe you even saved my life, and you did it at the request of my daughter for your professional help. That makes it a debt and I want to pay it, only I understand your fees are pretty steep. How much do you charge for a day's work?"

"How much do you?"

"What?" Berin stared. "God above. I don't work by the day. I am an artist, not a potato peeler."

"Neither am I." Wolfe wiggled a finger. "Look here, sir. Let's admit it as a postulate that I saved your life. If I did, I am willing to let it go as a gesture of amity and goodwill and take no payment for it. Will you accept that gesture?"

"No. I'm in debt to you. My daughter appealed to you. It is not to be expected that I, Jerome Berin, would accept such a favor."

176

"Well..." Wolfe sighed. "If you won't take it in friendship, you won't. In that case, the only thing I can do is render you a bill. That's simple. If any valuation at all is to be placed on the professional services I rendered it must be a high one, for the services were exceptional. So... since you insist on paying... you owe me the recipe for saucisse minuit."

"What!" Berin glared at him. "Pah! Ridiculous!"

"How ridiculous? You ask what you owe. I tell you."

Berin sputtered. "Outrageous, damn it!" He waved his pipe until sparks and ashes flew. "That recipe is priceless! And you ask it.... God above, I've refused half a million francs! And you have the impudence, the insolence—"

"If you please." Wolfe snapped. "Let's don't row about it. You put a price on your recipe. That's your privilege. I put a price on my services. That's mine. You have refused half a million francs. If you were to send me a check for half a million dollars I would tear it up—or for any sum whatever. I saved your life or I rescued you from a minor annoyance, call it what you please. You ask me what you owe me, and I tell you, you owe me that recipe, and I will accept nothing else. You pay it or you don't, suit yourself. It would be an indescribable pleasure to be able to eat saucisse minuit at my own table—at least twice a month, I should think—but it would be quite a satisfaction, of another sort, to be able to remind myself—much oftener than twice a month—that Jerome Berin owes me a debt which he refuses to pay."

"Bah!" Berin snorted. "Trickery!"

"Not at all. I attempt no coercion. I won't sue you. I'll merely regret that I employed my talents, lost a lot of sleep, and allowed myself to get shot at, without either acquiring credit for a friendly and generous act, or receiving the payment due me. I suppose I should remind you that I offered a guarantee to disclose the recipe to no one. The sausage will be prepared only in my house and served only at my table. I would like to reserve the right to serve it to guests—and of course to Mr. Goodwin, who lives with me and eats what I eat."

Berin, staring at him, muttered, "Your cook."

"He won't know it. I spend quite a little time in the kitchen myself."

Berin continued to stare, in silence. Finally he growled, "It can't be written down. It never has been."

"I won't write it down. I have a facility for memorizing."

Berin got his pipe to his mouth without looking at it, and puffed. Then he stared some more. At length he heaved a shuddering sigh and looked around at Constanza and me. He said gruffly, "I can't tell it with these people in here."

"One of them is your daughter."

"Damn it, I know my daughter when I see her. They'll have to get out."

I got up and put up my brows at Constanza. "Well?" The train lurched and Wolfe grabbed for the other arm of the seat. It would have been a shame to get wrecked then.

Constanza arose, reached down to pat her father on the head, and passed through the door as I held it open.

I supposed that was the fitting end to our holiday, since Wolfe was getting that recipe, but there was one more unexpected diversion to come. Since there was still an hour to go I invited Constanza to the club car for a drink, and she swayed and staggered behind me through three cars to that destination. There were only eight or ten customers in the club car, mostly hid behind morning papers, and plenty of seats. She specified ginger ale, which reminded me of old times, and I ordered a highball to celebrate Wolfe's collection of his fee. We had only taken a couple of sips when I became aware that a fellow passenger across the aisle had arisen, put down his paper, walked up to us, and was standing in front of Constanza, looking down at her.

He said, "You can't do this to me, you *can't*! I don't deserve it and you can't do it." He sounded urgent. "You ought to see—you ought to realize—"

Constanza said to me, chattering prettily, "I didn't suppose my father would *ever* tell that recipe to *any*one. Once in San Remo I heard him tell an Englishman, some very important person—"

The intruder moved enough inches to be standing between us, and rudely interrupted her: "Hello, Goodwin. I want to ask you—"

"Hello, Tolman." I grinned up at him. "What's the idea? You with two brand new prisoners in your jail, and here you are running around—"

"I had to get to New York. For evidence. It was too important. . . . Look here. I want to ask you if Miss Berin has any right to treat me like this. Your unbiased opinion. She won't speak to me. She won't look at me. Didn't I have to do what I did? Was there anything else I could do?"

178

"Certainly. You could have resigned. But then of course
u'd have been out of a job, and God knows when you'd
ve been able to marry. It was really a problem, I see that.
it I wouldn't worry. Only a little while ago I wondered why
iss Berin was doing so much smiling, there didn't seem to
: any special reason for it, but now I understand. She was
iiling because she knew you were on the train."

"Mr. Goodwin! That isn't true!"

"But if she won't even speak to me—"

I waved a hand. "She'll speak to you all right. You just don't
iow how to go about it. Her own method is as good a one as
ve seen recently. Watch me now, and next time you can do
yourself."

I tipped my highball glass and spilled about a jigger on her
irt where it was round over her knee.

She ejaculated and jerked. Tolman ejaculated and bent
er and reached for his handkerchief. I arose and reassured
em, "It's rite all kight, it doodn't stain." Then I went over
d picked up his morning paper and sat down where he had
:en.

ABOUT THE AUTHOR

REX STOUT, the creator of Nero Wolfe, was born in Noblesville, Indiana, in 1886, the sixth of nine children of John and Lucetta Todhunter Stout, both Quakers. Shortly after his birth, the family moved to Wakarusa, Kansas. He was educated in a country school, but, by the age of nine, was recognized throughout the state as a prodigy in arithmetic. Mr. Stout briefly attended the University of Kansas, but left to enlist in the Navy, and spent the next two years as a warrant officer on board President Theodore Roosevelt's yacht. When he left the Navy in 1908, Rex Stout began to write free-lance articles, worked as a sightseeing guide and as an itinerant bookkeeper. Later he devised and implemented a school banking system which was installed in four hundred cities and towns throughout the country. In 1927 Mr. Stout retired from the world of finance and, with the proceeds of his banking scheme, left for Paris to write serious fiction. He wrote three novels that received favorable reviews before turning to detective fiction. His first Nero Wolfe novel, *Fer-de-Lance*, appeared in 1934. It was followed by many others, among them, *Too Many Cooks, The Silent Speaker, If Death Ever Slept, The Doorbell Rang* and *Please Pass the Guilt*, which established Nero Wolfe as a leading character on a par with Erle Stanley Gardner's famous protagonist, Perry Mason. During World War II, Rex Stout waged a personal campaign against Nazism as chairman of the War Writers' Board, master of ceremonies of the radio program "Speaking of Liberty" and as a member of several national committees. After the war, he turned his attention to mobilizing public opinion against the wartime use of thermonuclear devices, was an active leader in the Authors' Guild and resumed writing his Nero Wolfe novels. All together, his Nero Wolfe novels have been translated into twenty-two languages and have sold more than forty-five million copies. Rex Stout died in 1975 at the age of eighty-eight. A month before his death, he published his forty-sixth Nero Wolfe novel, *A Family Affair*.

THE
BLOODIED IVY

Robert Goldsborough

ONE

Hale Markham's death had been big news, of course. It was even the subject of a brief conversation I had with Nero Wolfe. We were sitting in the office, he with beer and I with a Scotch-and-water, going through our copies of the *Gazette* before dinner.

"See where this guy up at Prescott U. fell into a ravine on the campus and got himself killed?" I asked, to be chatty. Wolfe only grunted, but I've never been one to let a low-grade grunt stop me. "Wasn't he the one whose book—they mention it here in the story: *Bleeding Hearts Can Kill*—got you so worked up a couple of years back?"

Wolfe lowered his paper, sighed, and glared at a spot on the wall six inches above my head. "The man was a political Neanderthal," he rumbled. "He would have been supremely happy in the court of Louis XIV. And the book to which you refer is a monumental exercise in fatuity." I sensed the subject was closed, so I grunted myself and turned to the sports pages.

I probably wouldn't have thought any more about that scrap of dialogue except now, three weeks later, a small, balding, fiftyish specimen with brown-rimmed glasses and a sportcoat that could have won a blue ribbon in a quilting contest perched on the red leather chair in the office and stubbornly repeated the statement that had persuaded me to see him in the first place.

"Hale Markham was murdered," he said. "I'm unswerving in this conviction."

Let me back up a bit. The man before me had a name: Walter Willis Cortland. He had called the day before, Monday, introducing himself as a political science professor at Prescott University and a colleague of the late Hale Markham's. He then dropped the bombshell that Markham's death had not been a mishap.

I had asked Cortland over the phone if he'd passed his contention along to the local cops. "It's no contention, Mr. Goodwin, it's a fact," he'd snapped, adding that he had indeed visited the town police in Prescott, but they hadn't seemed much interested in what he had to say. I could see why: Based on what little he told me over the phone, Cortland didn't have a scrap of evidence to prove Markham's tumble was murder, nor did he seem inclined, in his zeal for truth, to nominate a culprit. So why, you ask, had I agreed to see him? Good question. I must admit it was at least partly vanity.

When he phoned at ten-twenty that morning and I answered "Nero Wolfe's office, Archie Goodwin speaking," Cortland had cleared his throat twice, paused, and said, "Ah, yes, Mr. Archie Goodwin. You're really the one with whom I wish to converse.

I've read about your employer, Nero Wolfe, and how he devotes four hours every day, nine to eleven before lunch and four to six in the afternoon, to the sumptuous blooms on the roof of your brownstone. That's why I chose this time to call. I also know how difficult it is to galvanize Mr. Wolfe to undertake a case, but that you have a reputation for being a bit more, er . . . open-minded."

"If you're saying I'm easy, forget it," I said. "Somebody has to screen Mr. Wolfe's calls, or who knows what he'd be having to turn down himself—requests to find missing wives, missing parakeets, and even missing gerbils. And believe me when I tell you that Mr. Wolfe hates gerbils."

Cortland let loose with a tinny chuckle that probably was supposed to show he appreciated my wry brand of humor, then cleared his throat, which probably was supposed to show that now he was all business. "Oh, no, no, I didn't mean that you were . . . uh, to use your term, easy," he stumbled, trying valiantly to recover.

"No, I, uh . . ." He seemed to lose his way and cleared his throat several times before his mental processes kicked in again. "It's just that from what I've heard and read, anybody who has any, uh, hope of enticing Nero Wolfe to undertake a case has to approach you first. And that I am most willing to do. Most willing, Mr., er . . . Goodwin. I braced for another throat-clearing interlude, and sure enough, it arrived on schedule. If this was his average conversational speed, the phone company must love the guy.

"It's just that from what I've heard and read, anybody who has any hope of enticing Nero Wolfe to take a case has to approach you first. And that I am most willing to do. Most willing, Mr. Goodwin."

He treated me once again to the sound of him clearing his throat. "I will lay my jeremiad before you and you alone, and trust you to relay it accurately to Mr. Wolfe. You have a reputation, if I am not mistaken, for reporting verbatim conversations of considerable duration."

Okay, so he was working on me. I knew it—after all, he had the subtlety of a jackhammer, but maybe that was part of his charm, if you could use that term on such a guy. And I was curious as to just what "information" he had about the late Hale Markham's death. Also, the word "jeremiad" always gets my attention.

"All right," I told him, "I'll see you tomorrow. What about ten in the morning?" He said that was fine, and I gave him the address of Wolfe's brownstone on West Thirty-fifth Street near the Hudson.

The next day he rang our doorbell at precisely ten by my watch, which was one point in his favor. I've already described his appearance, which didn't surprise me at all when I saw him through the one-way glass in our front door. His looks matched his phone voice, which at least gave him another point for consistency. I let him in, shook a small but moderately firm paw, and ushered him to the red leather chair at the end of Wolfe's desk. So now you're up to speed, and we can go on.

"Okay, Mr. Cortland," I said, seated at my desk and turning to face him, "you've told me twice, on the phone and just now, that your colleague Hale Markham did not accidentally stumble down that ravine. Tell me more." I flipped open my notebook and poised a pen.

Cortland gave a tug at the knot of his blue wool tie and nudged his glasses up on his nose by pushing on one lens with his thumb, which probably explained why the glass was so smeared. "Yes. Well, perhaps I should discourse in commencement about Hale, although I'm sure you know something of him."

When I'd translated that, I nodded. "A little. I know, for instance, that he was a political conservative, to put it mildly, that he once had a newspaper column that ran all over the country, that he had written some books, and that he was more than a tad controversial."

"Succinct though superficial," Cortland said, sounding like a teacher grading his pupil. He studied the ceiling as if seeking divine guidance in choosing his next words—or else trying to reboard his train of thought. "Mr. Goodwin, Hale Markham was one of the few, uh, truly profound political thinkers in contemporary America. And like so many of the brilliant and visioned, he was constantly besieged and challenged, not just from the left, but from specious conservatives as well." He paused for breath, giving me the opportunity to cut in, but because it looked like he was on a roll I let him keep going, lest he lose his way.

"Hale was uncompromising in his philosophy, Mr. Goodwin, which is one of the myriad reasons I admired him and was a follower—a disciple, if you will. And do not discount this as mere idle palaver—I think I'm singularly qualified to speak—after all, I had known him nearly half again a score of years. Hale took a position and didn't back away. He was fiercely combative and outspoken in his convictions."

"Which were?" I asked after figuring out that half again a score is thirty.

Cortland spread his hands, palms up. "How to begin?" he said, rolling his eyes. "Among other things, that the federal government, with its welfare programs and its intrusions into other areas of the society where it has no business, has steadily—if sometimes unwittingly—been attenuating the moral fiber of the nation, and that government's size and scope must be curtailed. He had a detailed plan to reduce the government in stages over a twenty-year period. Its fundamental caveat was— "

"I get the general idea. He must have felt pretty good about Reagan."

"Oh, up to a point." Cortland fiddled some more with his tie and pushed up his glasses again with a thumb, blinking twice. "But he believed, and I concur, that the President has never truly been committed to substantially reducing the federal government's scope. The man is far more form than substance."

That was enough political philosophy to hold me. "Let's get to Markham's death," I suggested. "You say you're positive his fall down that ravine was no accident. Why?"

Cortland folded his arms and looked at the ceiling again. "Mr. Goodwin, for one thing, Hale walked a great deal." He took a deep breath as if trying to think what to say next, and he was quiet for so long that I had to stare hard at him to get his engine started again. "In recent years, walking had been his major form of exercise. Claimed it expurgated his mind. Almost every night, he followed the identical course, which he informed me was almost exactly four miles. He started from his house, just off campus, and the route took him past the Student Union and the Central Quadrangle, then around the library and through an area called the Old Oaks and then—have you ever been up to Prescott, Mr. Goodwin?"

"Once, years ago, for a football game, against Rutgers. Your boys kicked a field goal to win, right at the end. It was quite an upset."

Cortland allowed himself a sliver-thin smile, which was apparently the only kind he had, then nodded absently. "Yes . . . now that you mention it, I think I remember. Probably the only time we ever beat them. We had a . . . Rhodes Scholar in the backfield. Extraordinary chap. Name escapes me. Lives in Sri Lanka now, can't recall why." He shook his head and blinked. "Where was I? Oh, yes. Anyway, you should recall how hilly the terrain for our campus is, which isn't surprising, given that we're so close to the Hudson. Innumerable times, Prescott has been cited as the most picturesque university in the nation. There are several ravines cutting through it, and the biggest one is named Caldwell's Gash—I believe after one of the first settlers to the area. It's maybe one hundred fifty feet deep, with fairly steep sides, and the Old Oaks, a grove of trees that looks to me like it's getting perilously decrepit, is along one side of the Gash. Hale's walk always took him through the Oaks and fairly close to the edge of the Gash."

"Is there a fence?"

"A fence?" Another long pause as Cortland reexamined the ceiling. "Yes, yes, there had been—there was . . . years ago. But at some point, it must have fallen apart, and never got replaced. The paved, uh, bicycle path through the Oaks is quite a distance from the edge—maybe thirty feet—and there are warning signs posted. On his postprandial strolls, though, Hale sometimes left the path—I know, I've walked with him many a time—and took a course somewhat closer to the edge."

"So who's to say your friend didn't get a little too close just this once and go over the cliff?"

"Not Hale Markham." Cortland shook his small head vigorously, sending his glasses halfway down his nose. "This was a dedicated walker. He even wore hiking boots, for instance. And he was very surefooted—his age, which happened to be seventy-three, shouldn't deceive you. During his younger days, he'd done quite a bit of serious mountain climbing, both out west and, er, in the Alps. No, sir, Hale would not under any circumstances have slipped over the edge of the Gash."

"Was the ground wet or muddy at the time?"

"It had not rained for days."

"What about suicide?"

He bristled. "Unconceivable! Hale reveled in life too much. His health was good, remarkably good for his age. No note of any kind was discovered. I should know—I checked through his papers at home. I'm the executor of his estate."

"What about an autopsy?"

"No autopsy. The doctor who examined the body said Hale died of a broken neck, a tragic conse-quence of the fall. He estimated the time of death to have been between ten and midnight. And the medical examiner set it down as accidental death. But there really wasn't any kind of an investigation to speak of. Most distressing."

"All right," I said, "let's assume for purposes of

discussion that there is a murderer. Care to nominate any candidates?"

Cortland squirmed in the red leather chair, and twice he started to say somethng, but checked himself. He looked like he was having gas pains.

I gave him what I think of as my earnest smile. "Look, even though you're not a client—not yet, anyway—I'm treating this conversation as confidential. Now, if you have *evidence* of a murder—that's different. Then, as a law-abiding, God-fearing, licensed private investigator, I'd have to report it to the police. But my guess is you don't have evidence. Am I right?"

He nodded, but still looked like something he ate didn't sit well with him. Then he did more squirming. The guy was getting on my nerves.

"Mr. Cortland, I appreciate your not wanting to come right out and call someone a murderer without evidence, but if I can get Mr. Wolfe to see you—and I won't guarantee it—he's going to press pretty hard. You can hold out on me, but he'll demand at the very least some suppositions. Do you have any?"

Cortland made a few more twitchy movements, crossed his legs, and got more fingerprints on his lenses. "There were a number of people at Prescott who . . . weren't exactly fond of Hale," he said, avoiding my eyes. "I'd, uh, chalk a lot of it up to jealousy."

"Let's get specific. But first, was Markham married?"

"He had been, but his wife died, almost ten years ago."

"Any children?"

"None. He was devoted to Lois—that was his wife. She was one of a kind, Mr. Goodwin. I'm a bachelor, always have been, but if I'd ever been fortunate enough to meet a woman like Lois Markham, my life would have taken a Byronic richness that . . . no matter, it's in the past. As far as children are concerned, Hale told me once that it was a major disappointment to both him and Lois that they never had a family."

"What about relatives?"

"He had one brother, who has been deceased for years. His only living relative is a niece, unmarried, in California. He left her about fifty thousand dollars, plus his house. I've been trying to get her to venture here to go through Hale's effects—we can't begin to contemplate selling the place until it is cleaned out, which will be an extensive chore. Hale lived there for more than thirty years."

"Has the niece said anything about when she might come east?"

"I've talked to her on the phone several times, and she keeps procrastinating," Cortland whined. "When I spoke to her last week, she promised that she'd arrive here before Thanksgiving. We'll see."

"Okay, you mentioned jealousy earlier. Who envied Markham?"

He lifted his shoulders and let them drop. "Oh, any number of people. For one, Keith Potter." He eyed me as if expecting a reaction.

"Well, of course," I said. "Why didn't I think of him myself? Okay—I give up. Who's Keith Potter?"

Cortland looked at me as if I'd just jumped out of a spaceship nude. "Keith Potter is none other than the beloved president of Prescott." He touched his forehead with a flourish that was probably supposed to be a dazzling gesture of sarcasm.

"Why was Potter jealous of Markham?"

I got another one of those long-suffering-teacher-working-with-a-dense-student looks. "Partly because Hale was better known than Potter. In fact, Hale was arguably the most celebrated person in the university's history. And we've had *three* Nobel prize laureates through the years."

I nodded to show I was impressed. "So the president of the school resented its superstar teacher. Is that so unusual? I don't know much about the academic world, but one place or another I've gathered the impression that most colleges have a teacher or two who are often better known than the people who run the place."

"Unusual? I suppose not. But Potter—excuse me, *Doctor* Potter—is an empire builder. His not-so-secret goal is to sanctify his name by increasing the endowment to Prescott, thereby allowing him to erect more new buildings on the campus. The edifice complex, you know?" Cortland chuckled, crossed his arms over his stomach, and simpered.

"I don't mean to sound like a broken record, but that's not so unusual either, is it? Or such a bad thing for the university?"

"Maybe not," Cortland conceded, twitching. "If it's accompanied by a genuine respect for scholarship and research, uh, things that all schools aspiring to greatness should stress. But Potter desires, in effect, to upraise a monument to himself. That goal easily eclipses any desire on his part to improve the facilities purely for academic reasons."

I was itching to ask if the ends didn't justify the means, but Wolfe would be coming down from the plant rooms soon, so I pushed on. "How did Potter's obsession with buildings affect his relationship with Markham?"

Cortland sniffed. "Ah, yes, I was about to get to that, wasn't I? Potter had fastened onto Leander Bach and was working to get a bequest out of him—a considerable one. I assume you know who Bach is?" I could tell by his tone that I'd shaken his faith in my grasp of current events.

"The eccentric multimillionaire?"

"That's one way of describing the man. I prefer to think of him as left-leaning to the point of irrationality. And that was the rub: The talk all over campus was that Bach wouldn't give a cent of his millions to the school as long as Hale was on the faculty. He had the gall to call Hale a Neanderthal."

I stifled a smile, then shot a glance at my watch. "Mr. Wolfe will be down soon," I said. "And I—"

"Yes, I've been monitoring the time, as well," Cortland cut in. "And we've still got six minutes. Mr. Goodwin, as you can appreciate, my stipend as a university professor hardly qualifies me as a plutocrat. However, I've had the good fortune to inherit a substantial amount from my family. Because of that, I can comfortably afford Mr. Wolfe's fees, which I'm well aware are thought by some to border on extortionate. And I can assure you that this check," he said, reaching into the breast pocket of his crazyquilt sportcoat, "has the pecuniary financial condition, feel free to call Cyrus Griffin, president of the First Citizens Bank of Prescott. I'll supply you with the number."

"Not necessary," I said, holding up a hand and studying the check, drawn on Mr. Griffin's bank and made out to Nero Wolfe in the amount of twenty-five thousand dollars.

"That's just a good-faith retainer," Cortland said. "To show Mr. Wolfe—and you—that I'm earnest. I will be happy to match that amount on the completion of Mr. Wolfe's investigation, regardless, of its eventuation."

I tapped the check with a finger. Our bank balance could use this kind of nourishment—we hadn't pulled in a big fee in almost three months, and I was beginning to worry, even if the big panjandrum wasn't. But then, he almost never deigned to look at the checkbook. Such concerns were beneath him. Even if Wolfe refused to take Cortland on as a client, though, it would be instructive to see his reaction to somebody else who tosses around four-syllable, ten-dollar words like he does.

Maybe I could talk somebody into making a syndicated TV show out of their conversations and call it "The Battle of the Dictionary Dinosaurs." All right, so I was getting carried away, but what the hell, it *would* be fun to see these guys go at it. Besides, I'd pay admission to watch Wolfe's reaction to Cortland's mid-sentence ramblings.

"Okay, I'll hang onto this for now," I said to the little professor. "It may help me get Mr. Wolfe to see you, but I can't guarantee anything. I'll have to ask you to wait in the front room while we talk. If things go badly—and I always refuse to predict how he'll react—you may not get to see him, at least not today. But I'll try."

"I'm more than willing to remain here and plead my case with him directly." Cortland squared his narrow shoulders.

"Trust me. This is the best way to handle the situation. Now let's get you settled." I opened the soundproofed door and escorted the professor into the front room, then went down the hall to the kitchen to let Fritz know we had a guest so that he would monitor the situation. It simply wouldn't do to have people wandering through the brownstone.

That done, I returned to the office, where I just had time to get settled at my desk when the rumble of the elevator told me Wolfe was on his way down from the roof.

NERO WOLFE STEPS OUT

Every Wolfe Watcher knows that the world's largest detective wouldn't dream of leaving the brownstone on 35th street, with Fritz's three star meals, his beloved orchids and the only chair that actually suits him. But when an ultra-conservative college professor winds up dead and Archie winds up in jail, Wolfe is forced to brave the wilds of upstate New York to find a murderer.

THE BLOODIED IVY
by Robert Goldsborough
☐ 27816 $3.95

and don't miss these other Nero Wolfe mysteries by Robert Goldsborough:

☐	27024	**DEATH ON DEADLINE**	$3.95
☐	27938	**MURDER IN E MINOR**	$3.95
		"A Smashing Success"	
		—*Chicago Sun-Times*	
☐	05383	**THE LAST COINCIDENCE**	$16.95

And Bantam still offers you a whole series of Nero Wolfe mysteries by his creator, Rex Stout:

☐	27819	**FER-DE-LANCE**	$3.95
☐	27828	**DEATH TIMES THREE**	$3.95
☐	27291	**THE BLACK MOUNTAIN**	$3.95
☐	27776	**IN THE BEST FAMILIES**	$3.50
☐	27290	**TOO MANY COOKS**	$3.95
☐	27780	**THE GOLDEN SPIDERS**	$3.50
☐	25363	**PLOT IT YOURSELF**	$3.50
☐	24813	**THREE FOR THE CHAIR**	$3.50

Look for them at your bookstore or use this page to order:

Bantam Books, Dept. BD17, 414 East Golf Road, Des Plaines, IL 60016

Please send me the items I have checked above. I am enclosing $_____ (please add $2.00 to cover postage and handling). Send check or money order, no cash or C.O.D.s please.

Mr/Ms _____

Address _____

City/State _____ Zip _____

BD17-2/90

Please allow four to six weeks for delivery.
Prices and availability subject to change without notice.

Kinsey Millhone is...

"The best new private eye." —*The Detroit News*

"A tough-cookie with a soft center." —*Newsweek*

"A stand-out specimen of the new female operatives."
—*Philadelphia Inquirer*

Sue Grafton is...

The Shamus and Anthony Award winning creator of
Kinsey Millhone and quite simply one of the hottest
new mystery writers around.

Bantam is...

The proud publisher of Sue Grafton's Kinsey Millhone
mysteries:

Special Offer
Buy a Bantam Book
for only 50¢.

Now you can have Bantam's catalog filled with hundreds of titles plus take advantage of our unique and exciting bonus book offer. A special offer which gives you the opportunity to purchase a Bantam book for only 50¢. Here's how!

By ordering any five books at the regular price per order, you can also choose any other single book listed (up to a $5.95 value) for just 50¢. Some restrictions do apply, but for further details why not send for Bantam's catalog of titles today!

Just send us your name and address and we will send you a catalog!